Knot a Tie

GET KNOTTED! OMEGAVERSE

EVE NEWTON

Knot a Tie
Get Knotted! Omegaverse

By Eve Newton
Copyright © Eve Newton, 2022

Preface

Dear Reader,

There is very little to warn you about in this book, except for the British English nature of the words, spellings and idioms.

There is of course the abduction and Rayne's fear but apart from that, this is a sweetly gorgeous book, with amazing alphas, a lovely, loyal omega and a story with enough action so you aren't sitting around like a fart in wet weather waiting for the plot to get going!

Hope you enjoy!
Love Eve x

Chapter One

Rayne

Three Months Ago

"Are you absolutely sure about this, Rayne?" Doctor Fredericks asks me for the third time.

"Yes," I state with as much finality as I can muster. I'm not that great at being assertive, but I do try now and again when it suits me.

Her steely grey eyes pierce mine, searching them, looking for signs of...well, I don't really know. The possibility that I'm going to take the heat suppressants I'm after and sell them on the black market? Not likely. I want them for *me*. I am three months away from my twenty-first birthday and I'll be damned if I'm going into my first heat unmated.

Not a chance in hell.

I have enough alphas sniffing around me as it is, trying to mate with me. But none of them float my boat. That comes with the territory when you are wealthy, pretty and of course, the big one...*unmated*. Even if I manage to find a pack I like in the next three months, no way am I risking getting pregnant so soon. Not that I don't want kids. I do. But I want to know my pack first. "You know you can only use them for six months and then you need to come off them for three months, so you must time this correctly if you are adamant about this course."

"I know, and I am." I cross my arms over my chest, hopefully to show her I mean business. She is my dad's personal physician and has been for as long as I've been alive, if not longer. She is elderly, heavyset with grey hair and a constitution that usually scares the knickers off me.

Not today, Rayne. Stay your course.

"I will have to seek your father's approval, of course," she says as a test. I know it's a test. I can see it in her eyes.

"Go ahead," I say, coolly. "He knows I'm here."

The surprise in her eyes makes me want to giggle. She so wasn't expecting that, the old twat.

"Really," she says in such a derogatory tone, I nearly flinch. "Well, in that case, get on the scales."

I blink and swallow. Okay, this was the part I wasn't looking forward to. I avoid scales like the plague. I'm five foot one, fairly large breasted, with thighs that meet in the middle. To say I'm a bit curvy is definitely accurate. I'm not huge, but I'm not super skinny either. I dress to accentuate my assets with the help of a personal shopper but scales? They don't lie to you. If I was taller, I'd be happy with my body, but I'm so fucking short, it makes me cringe.

I slip my skyscraper heels off, plus the light-weight black cardigan, leaving me in my floaty black trousers and vest top. I take off the feminine gold Rolex from my left wrist and place it carefully on the desk of this grey office that matches the dour doctor to a tee. Then I remove the gold bangle from my other wrist, along with the pretty aquamarine and platinum ring that matches my eyes and that I wear on the middle finger of my right hand. I set them down and lick my lips. Doctor Fredericks is sitting back, her arms crossed, watching this with amusement.

Horrid old cow.

She probably knew I had a phobia about this.

Clearing my throat, and throwing my head back so my light brown hair bounces around my shoulders in waves, I walk the two paces to the big doctors' scales and step on. Sucking in my stomach, like that's going to help, I close my eyes, not wanting to see what it says.

She stands up and moves in next to me. "Hmm," she murmurs.

I crack an eye to see her peering down at the scales, bent over like she needs to get closer to read what it says.

Then she straightens up and goes back to her desk to type it into her computer.

Hmm.

Hmm.

Hmm?

What the fuck does 'hmm' mean?

"Everything okay?" I croak out, needing to know, but stepping off the scales quickly so I don't look down.

I hear the needle fire back to zero and wince.

"Fine," she says. "A little heavy for your height, but we can't all be supermodels, can we?" She gives me a superior glare that grates on my last nerve.

"No, we can't, as I'm sure you know yourself."

Burn, witch, burn.

She gives me a sneer and then goes back to tapping into her computer. My hands are shaking with the small confrontation. I'm a people pleaser, mostly. I like to see people smile and be happy with me. But the old bat has definitely rubbed this omega up the wrong way.

I reach for the jewellery and replace it with trembling fingers.

Slipping my shoes and cardi back on, she sets the prescription printing and whisks it off when it's done.

"Six months' supply. If you are still hell bent on suppressing your heat in half a year, don't come back until three months after. I won't help you." She holds the small, green piece of paper between us like it contains the plague.

I snatch it from her, bending down to grab my *Michael Kors* handbag. Shoving the prescription inside, I give her a curt nod and a tight-lipped smile.

"Thanks," I murmur and disappear as quickly as I can from her office before she judges me anymore. I know she's thinking I'm a raging slut who just wants to sleep around but that isn't the case. I've had a couple, okay, three or four, sexual partners so far. I'm picky. I won't fall into bed with just anyone. A pretty face doesn't cut it. I want to laugh, be treated like a princess and have them care about me. In a nutshell, I want to be loved, and I want to love back.

Stepping out into the warm Spring morning, I take in the azure, cloudless sky and the smell of the flowers in the big round flower bed outside the doctor's office. A beautiful, sweet aroma that fills my senses up and makes me smile. The perfect purple and yellow pansies are pretty, and it washes away the last of my anxiety from this appointment. Walking down the street, a spring in my step, I make my way to the pharmacy.

A few minutes later, after the lovely beta female chemist gave me an understanding expression and smile, which made me feel better about the way the doctor treated me, I click the remote key to my black Porsche 911 and slip inside. Kicking off my heels, I start the engine and drive away with my bare feet, back to the enormous country estate that I call home.

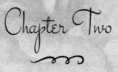

Chapter Two

James

There aren't many things that render me speechless, but on this crisp Spring day, *she* is one of them. Spotted across the courtyard, coming out of the doctor's office, I actually stop and stare. She is short with curves to die for and this beautiful wavy, light brown hair that I want to run my fingers through before I scoop it up into a ponytail to hold her in place while she sucks my cock.

"Grrr." The growl escapes me before I can stop it.

"James?"

I turn my head towards my younger brother, Spencer, to glance at him briefly before I look back at the woman across the courtyard. "What?"

"Who are you growling at?"

"Hmm?"

I start to cross over the cobblestones, keeping the delicious creature in my sights.

"Ah," Spencer says as the penny drops. "She is a fine-looking filly. I would like to bite that peachy arse."

"That's not where I want to bite her," I murmur, without even thinking.

"Whoa," Spencer says, grabbing me by the arm and drawing me to a halt. "Is that a formal declaration, brother?"

Turning towards him slowly, after I watch the perfect omega walk into the pharmacy, I search his green eyes. He is the spitting image of our father with his blonde hair and high cheekbones. I take after my raven-haired, blue-eyed mother.

"Maybe," I say, hearing the petulant tone in my voice and wincing inwardly. As his prime alpha of the powerful St. Stevens pack, I wish I'd sounded a bit more authoritative, but something about this omega has thrown me completely out of my comfort zone. Turning away from his shocked expression, I inhale deeply.

Fresh blueberry muffins.

The sheer decadence of her scent has sent a reaction straight to my dick. I groan softly, closing my eyes, feeling my cock stiffen.

"Jesus," Spencer mutters. "What the fuck?"

Eyes still closed, I grab him and shove him in front of me. "Breathe that in, Spence, and tell me you don't feel it."

I hear him draw her scent into his lungs and then let out a strangled mewl, followed up by a possessive growl.

"See?" I taunt, opening my eyes and pushing past him.

"Where did she go?" he pants, his primal side out in full force. His tongue is practically hanging out of his mouth.

"Pharmacy."

7

I march over to it and peer in the wide window of the chemist. I can see her there, handing over her prescription. I reach for the door handle when my phone rings. Under *any* other circumstances, I would ignore it, but the special ringtone tells me it's Jones.

Pulling it out of my pocket, I hover outside the pharmacy and answer it. "What is it?"

A heavy sigh comes over the line. "Sorry, Jay. You're on a wild goose chase."

A frustrated growl escapes me. "You mean *you* sent me on a wild goose chase?"

"Yeah," he admits reluctantly. "But he has definitely been spotted in the city."

"The city which we left a couple of hours ago to come to this country village because you said he was here?" I snarl.

"That's the one. Sorry, mate."

"Fucking hell," I spit out.

"It's worse," Jones ventures.

"How? How could it be worse?" I rub my hand over my face, moving further down the street, needing to pace, to move restlessly.

"He's hanging out with a loose pack called the Jets."

"A loose pack?" I need him to say that again because there is just no way. He *knows* that the Inter-pack Parliament is actively hunting the drug dealing, sex slave running, troublemaking packs of loose alphas and prosecuting them to the fullest extent of the law. "Tell me that's a joke? Or another goose chase?"

"Sorry, definitely confirmed with my own eyes. I'll send

you the image taken from a CCTV outside the Hand and Dagger pub."

"Jesus." I pull the phone away as it dings and check the image Jones just sent me. "Fucking hell!" That is definitely Richard hanging out with a bunch of thugs.

I grip the phone tighter and shake it at nothing before I visibly calm myself and breathe. "Thanks," I grit out and hang up the phone. "Richard, you utter dick!" I kick out at a tree planted in the middle of the pavement, hearing the branches shake their bright green leaves over my head.

"What is it?" Spencer asks.

"We need to go home. Now." I spin and start stalking back to the pharmacy. "Dammit!" The omega has already left.

An engine firing up catches my attention. I watch helplessly as a black Porsche blasts down the courtyard.

I click my fingers at Spencer, who is closer to the vehicle. "Reg number!" I yell at him.

He snaps his head back to the car and squints at the retreating Porsche. "O-M-3-G-A something," he huffs out.

"Great. Just great." Incensed we lost her while pratting about on the phone, I cross over to the pharmacy and open the door.

The pretty beta chemist smiles at me, giving it all that, as most women do in my presence. They know a catch when they see one. Too bad for them, I've never been interested in anyone enough to take them seriously. However, a charming smile goes a long way.

I lean on the counter, and stare at her name tag. "Sandy. How're you?"

"I'm good. How're you?" Her bright smile goes a bit sultry.

I cast my gaze up to her mouth, seeing her pout her pink lips slightly. I give her the impression that I'm thinking about them around my cock, but all I can think about is the omega. Looking up, I search her eyes. "Sandy, any chance you could tell me the name of the woman who was just in here. She dropped something outside, I want to return it."

Sandy blinks once, her disappointment crashing down over her. "I can't give out that information," she says stiffly.

"Please?" I ask, giving her my best flirty gaze, biting my lower lip in a way that I know is sexy because it's worked a thousand times in the past.

She stares at my mouth, her cheeks flushing.

Unfortunately, a thousand and one isn't today. Her professionalism falls into place, and she steps back. "No can do," she says. "If you persist in harassing me, I will call the police."

Okay, wow. Epic fail there, Jay.

I straighten up, smile still in place and hold my hands up. "Not here to cause trouble, just want to return something."

"You can leave it here, if she comes back."

"My brother has it outside," I say and back out of the pharmacy, well and truly cock-blocked.

Spencer is staring at me, trying his hardest not to laugh. "Fucking fail, Jay. Ouch."

Stopping in front of him, I flick him on the forehead. "Shut the fuck up, bellend."

He glares at me and rubs his forehead. "Oww."

"Come on. We'd better get back to London. Ring Jones

and ask him to do everything in his investigative power to find me that omega. I'm not letting her go as easily as this."

"You've really fallen, haven't you?"

"Haven't you?"

His glance down the road where her car roared off, is all the confirmation I need. Two votes out of four, but mine weighs heavier. Blueberry-muffins is going to be our omega, and I don't care how I make that happen. She has bewitched me, and I thought I was immune to such charms. That alone makes me *need* to know her.

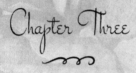

Chapter Three

Rayne

Getting out of the car in the huge, red bricked driveway of the country house that is my home, I lean over to grab my shoes and slip them on my feet. Snatching up my bag stuffed full of the heat suppressants from the passenger seat, I slam the door shut. I skip up the four stone steps that lead to the big red front doors of the house. Pushing one open, I call out, "Daddy, I'm back."

He appears out of his office, which is the first door on the right. "Hi, Ray-ray. Did you get sorted?"

I close the front door and cross over the entrance hall, the thick, plush Windsor patterned carpet, soft under my heels. "I did. She is a real battle-axe. Did she ring you after I left?"

My dad chuckles and nods his head. "She did."

"Witch," I mutter under my breath. "Why did you make me go there? Don't you pay her a lot of money every month for her to come here?"

Daddy tuts at me. "If I had shown you preferential treatment, she wouldn't respect you."

"She doesn't anyway. She thinks I'm a raging slut."

"Rayne," he warns me. "You know I don't like that word."

"Yeah, well, me either, but that is how she made me feel." I sulk and cross my arms over my chest.

"Look, Ray-ray, we know here why you're doing this, and we support your decision. That's all that matters."

I grin, my mood forgotten and go to him, slipping into his embrace. He gives me a tight squeeze and then holds me out at arm's length. "There's someone here to see you."

My face falls into a frown. "Oh?"

"He's in the informal sitting room." The tone tells me all I need to know.

"Daddyyyyy," I whine, dropping my arm so that my bag swings and hits my leg. "Who are you trying to set me up with?"

"Why, no one, dear," he says with a smug smile and then hastily disappears back into his office, shutting the door promptly in my face.

"Mean!" I call out and hear him chuckle.

I smile, and with an eyeroll, I lift my bag back onto my bent arm and head towards the informal sitting room on the left-hand side of the staircase, opposite the formal sitting room, or as I like to call it, the mausoleum.

I catch his musky scent the second I walk into the room. "Andy," I say, spotting him looking out of the window at the far side of the room.

"Ray-ray," he says, turning around to smile at me. "How's things?"

I cross over to him, meeting him half-way and give him two air kisses before stepping back. He's cute, in a cute puppy kind of way, posh and nerdy. We've banged a few times, but seriously, it's to scratch an itch. He doesn't do it for me. Yes, I may have only had four sexual partners since I had my first shag two years ago, but that doesn't mean I haven't enjoyed them along the way. Andy here took my v-card and held it dear to him. Still does. He sniffs around every so often, looking for me to join his pack of posh, nerdy, puppy dog alphas but nope. I want posh and hot, sexy and growly, older than me, preferably so I feel taken care of in ways that young Scrappy Doo here couldn't possibly do.

"Fine," I reply. "You?"

"Better now."

Ugh.

Also, I want someone with better chat than that. Even an 'I'm shit, but if you suck my cock, it will make it all better,' would be hotter than that.

"What are you doing here?" I ask, getting to the point. I want to hurry this along, go upstairs and stab myself in the stomach with my first suppressant and get that show on the road.

"I was in the neighbourhood; thought I'd drop in and see how you were."

I nod slowly. "Well, I'm a bit busy right now. Can I ring you later and we'll hang out?"

His face falls.

He recognises a brush off when he hears one.

He has no choice but to comply, or have my father

throw him out. "Of course," he says, giving me that stiff-upper lip he is renowned for. "I look forward to it."

With a soft smile, he heads out and I breathe out in relief.

"Time to get stabby."

I make my way up the wide staircase, trailing my hand over the light, highly glossed wood to the first floor. Passing the portrait of my mum and dad on their wedding day, I smile. They look so happy, *are* still happy. I envy them, but only in a happy way. I know I will find my pack eventually. I've known since I first learned about love and relationships that I wanted to be mated to a pack, not just one. My family is fine with my decision. They just want me to be happy. I'm so lucky to have them support me.

Entering my pretty, pale pink bedroom, I close the door and head into the ensuite. Pulling the box of tiny disposable injections out of my bag, along with the small yellow sharps bin, I arrange the injection on the countertop and pull up my clothes to expose my stomach. Picking it up, I remove the sterile cap with my teeth and then jab myself in the bit of flesh I've squeezed together.

"Oww," I mutter around the lid.

I drop the needle in the sharps bin and then the lid, placing it on top of the small wall cabinet out of the way.

Dropping my top back into place, I smile and kick off my shoes, ready to relax the rest of today before I go about haranguing my dad to let me help with his business. He's a top barrister for the Inter-pack Parliament. It's always been something that has fascinated me, but dad is old-skool. As much as I love him, his whole omegas should be barefoot and pregnant in the kitchen ideals are outdated as fuck. It's any wonder he supports my decision to delay my heat, but I intend to bring him into the twenty-first century if it kills me.

Chapter Four

Spencer

It's been three months since Richard was caught creating mayhem with the Jets, but we still haven't found him. It is also three long-arsed months since James and I spotted that omega. Jones did a thorough search on all black 911s with that partial licence plate, but none came back registered to anyone even remotely close in area or owner. He's still digging, but the longer it takes, the grumpier James gets. He is not a patient man, and these two situations have him at the end of his rope.

Three years older than me, he often acts like he's my dad. I'm thirty-two, a grown-arsed alpha in one of the most prestigious packs in England, and yet one look from him can chastise me more than our actual dad can.

Right now, I'm being bellowed at by him in his fancy office on the ground floor of the big mansion where our pack resides in Chelsea. I tuned him out a while ago because I'm still not sure what I've done wrong. I'm not taking it personally. Someone is in need of a good rut with a hot omega to knot inside of, but that is not happening. Two of us, namely him and me, have decided to suffer in our search for Blueberry-muffins. Even going back to the village, multiple times, hasn't born any...berries. This omega is protected by state-of-the-art security, which just intrigues us all the more. Jones is good, but he isn't *that* good. So, we have ended up omega-less and with two pissed off alphas, who a) didn't get to see Blueberry-muffins and b) are ready to mate an omega.

Luckily, James and I are holding firm. It's BM or no one.

"Are you even listening to me?"

I blink and focus on James. "Huh?"

"Spence!" he roars. "Have I been talking to myself for the last twenty minutes."

"Yep," I say and stand up out of the uncomfortable chair on the other side of his big walnut desk. "I don't even know why you're yelling at me."

"Because you're here and..." He glares at me and then huffs. "I'm frustrated."

"No shit, Sherlock. Look, I'm in the same boat as you, but we decided to try to find Blueberry-muffins. If you need to go and knot an omega, go." I make a shooing motion with my hands to make my point.

"Will you?" It's almost pleading.

I shake my head.

"Then I won't either," he growls, getting his back up. Mind you, his back is that far up already, he might as well go and live in Notre Dame.

"How about we take a road trip?" I say soothingly,

knowing how to calm the beast that is simmering under James' less-than-cool exterior. "One last visit, make a concerted effort and if we get nowhere, we sit down and talk about letting her go?"

I have zero intention of letting her go, but James needs *something* before he tears me a new one for breathing in his direction. My own beast is about ready to burst out, and no one wants that. Least of all him. Least of all *me*.

He nods slowly, his thinking face on. "Has it really come to this?" he sighs.

"'Fraid so."

"Bollocks."

"Yep."

"You don't really mean that, do you?" he asks, slumping into his big, comfy-looking, black leather desk chair.

No. "Yes."

"One last road trip. We stay overnight and we don't stop hunting."

"Deal."

He raises his chin at me in acknowledgment, and off I go to pack an overnight bag. Crossing the white, marble-tiled hallway and up the thick, white carpeted stairs, I make my way to my bedroom. It's airy and light with a wooden floor and huge four-poster, king size bed in the middle of the room. Stripping off, I flex my shoulders, relieved to be free from the burden of clothes. Naked is much more free-ing. Pulling a bag out from inside the wardrobe, I go around the room, throwing a few things in that I might need overnight and then pause. A shiver goes down my spine. I tense up and look over my shoulder, but of course, no one is there.

"What the fuck was that?"

An omen?

A sign?

Destiny knocking?

Who can guess?

All I know is, it was creepy as fuck and encourages me to hurry up. Reluctantly, I put my clothes back on, a white t-shirt and black combat pants, black boots and a black cashmere coat. Picking up my bag, I head down the stairs and run into the very irritated William on my way down.

"Where are you going?" the giant, dark-haired alpha snaps at me, giving my overnight bag the stink eye with his spooky black eyes.

"One last visit to see if we can find the omega. If we fail, then we vote as a pack to find a mate as soon as possible."

He grunts, an alpha of few words. He hunches his shoulders. "Were you going to invite me?"

"You'd have to ask James." No way am I being the one to tell the ferocious alpha that he can't come on the road trip. I like my head attached to my shoulders.

"Invite you where?" Cameron asks, appearing out of nowhere. "Can I come?"

I groan. The baby of the pack at only twenty-eight, he is like a joyful, light blonde-haired puppy. It's irritating as fuck on days like today where I just want to focus and get on with shit.

Luckily, I'm saved by the bell...or bellow, in this case.

"Spence, move your arse!" James yells up the stairs.

"Coming!" I call back and with a fake apologetic look, I duck around Will and take the stairs two at a time.

"What about us?" Will snarls. "You're just leaving us?"

"You don't even know what she looks like. You won't be of any use to us searching for her," James has the balls to say.

"We can help sniff her out," Cameron pants, following me down the stairs.

I exchange a look with James. The two of us are focused and prepared for the gruelling, possibly heart-breaking attempt at trying to find her.

"Fine," James huffs out, probably just so we can stop deliberating and move out. "But you come right now, or not at all."

Cameron nods enthusiastically. William less so, but he plods down the stairs with just the clothes on his back.

I sigh.

This is going to be fun times.

And if you didn't catch the sarcasm there, then we can't be friends.

"Shotgun," Cameron calls out as James slides into the driver's seat of the black Range Rover.

"Fuck you and the horse you rode in on," I growl, grabbing him by his preppy shirt, and yanking him out of the car. I sling my bag into the footwell and get in, slamming the door in Cam's face.

"You're a dick," he jibes, but it's like being yapped at by a small dog.

I feel a bit bad and turn to give him a real apologetic look. He's a good man. "Sorry, get car sick in the back," I inform him truthfully.

"Oh, yeah," he says with a nod. "You're not a dick."

"Thanks," I murmur with a small smile. The car jostles

when William folds his enormous frame into the back seat of the car and slams the door.

"Let's go and find our omega one way or the other," I mutter into the uneasy silence.

No more words are spoken as we head out of London on the fifty-mile drive to the village of Lakesview, hoping and praying that BM lands in our lap, somehow or other.

Chapter Five

Rayne

"I don't want you driving all that way," Mum complains in my direction as I pack my bag excitedly for my trip to London to see my cousin.

"I'll be fine. Don't worry so much."

"You'll ring me as soon as you get there?"

"I'll text you." I give her a pointed look. Phone calls make me nervous. Why call when I can email or text, is my philosophy.

She nods. "Okay. I need to go and take that video call. Be safe." She leans over to give me a kiss.

I watch her leave, giving her a little wave. She runs her own clothing company and is a busy woman, but she is happy and fulfilled.

I wish I was.

I can't wait to be a mate, but I know I can be a good omega as well as having something in my life away from the pack. In fact, it will probably make me an even better omega.

Hastily, I shove the rest of my stuff into my bag and then chuck my phone in my handbag. I already said bye to my dad earlier, so picking up the two bags, I make my way downstairs and out to my new car. I decided I didn't like the 911, so about three months ago, the day after I saw Doctor Battle-axe, Daddy got rid of it and purchased this sleek black Mercedes SLK. I adore it.

Slinging my bags in, my stomach tensing up slightly at the thought of being away from home for a while, I start up the car. It roars to life, and I edge out of the driveway, trying to calm my nerves. As soon as I drive through the gates, I start to relax and head towards the motorway. I have about half an hour until I reach the slip road, so I flick the radio on and enjoy the music.

Driving out of the village and through the winding country roads, I finally reach the, what passes for, a main road about twenty minutes later. Indicating to turn left, I wait for the big black Audi A8 to go past. I ease out and around the first bend and put my foot down. I shoot forward with a smile, not even seeing the obstruction in the middle of the road until it's too late.

"Shit!" I cry out and swerve, but it's too late.

Gripping the steering wheel as the car jostles, I drive over the plank of wood with a soft, "Eek!"

The motion causes me to yank the steering wheel to the left and I hit the curb, mounting it before I thunk back down and onto the road.

"Shit!" I gasp and slow down to an almost crawl, the sweat beading on my forehead. "Why the fuck is there a fucking plank of wood in the fucking road!" I expostulate, my nerves getting the better of me. Luckily, this road is deserted, and no one was behind me, nor a pedestrian on the narrow pavement.

Motoring forward, I turn another bend and then hear the pfft-pfft-pfft.

"No! No! No!" I wail as the smooth drive becomes bumpy and I fear the worst.

A punctured tyre.

"Whyyyyyy?" I cry out and flick my hazard lights on before pulling up onto the curb outside of an abandoned old mill. Glancing in the side mirror to check for traffic, I crack the door open and slip out. Shutting it, I glare down at the flat tyre and huff out a breath.

"Great. Just great. Fucking plank wanker."

Now, I like to think of myself as fairly capable. I can cook, clean, sew; I'm fairly handy with a screwdriver and arts and crafts are my jam, but changing a tyre or anything beyond checking the oil and water on a car is a big, fat nope.

Stomping onto the pavement, I yank the passenger door open and root around in my handbag for my phone as well as the breakdown service information.

Chewing my lip, knowing I *have* to make a phone call, I inhale deeply and then exhale slowly, calming the anxiety at having to speak to some stranger through the airwaves.

Hoisting my handbag onto my shoulder, I dial and listen to it ring. I go through the whole automated spiel before the muzak comes on and I wait. Tapping my foot impatiently, I hear another car coming and cringe. This road is pretty narrow and I'm taking up half the road. I frown when I see a black Audi A8 sail past me, again, but then brush it off. It's a pretty popular car, especially around here where luxury saloons are the thing.

I jump when the man on the other side of the phone line answers my call.

"Hello!" I shout louder than necessary. "I've got a flat tyre. I need someone to come out and change it for me." I close my eyes and shake my head. I sound like a helpless arsehole.

"No problem," he says. "Which tyre is it?"

"The front one."

A small, awkward pause.

"Offside or near?"

"Huh?"

He sighs. "Passenger side or driver's?" His slow, condescending tone immediately fires up my anger. Fucking prick.

"Driver's side," I grit out.

"So offside."

"If you say so."

I can practically *feel* the smugness radiating down through the phone line.

"Do you have a spare?" he asks, tapping into his little computer.

Closing my eyes, I wince. "Uhm..." I rack my brains. Daddy did say something about a spare tyre...what was it again? I wasn't paying attention, thinking if I ever got a flat, the fucking RAC would sort it out. Why aren't they doing that?

"Go to your boot and lift up the bottom like a lid," he says slowly, in *that* tone again.

Gritting my teeth, I do as he says, noticing as I open the boot, a black Audi A8 driving past me going the other way.

"Weird," I murmur.

"Pardon?"

"No, nothing...uhm...hang on..." I focus and find the latch that lifts the base of the boot up. "Yes!" I shout in jubilation and then feel like a left tit that popped out on the red carpet. "It's in here," I add, in a deeper, more serious tone.

"Grand," he says, stifling his laughter. "Let me just check your licence plate again."

Slamming the boot shut, I come face to face with my new vanity plate. "H-0-T-0-M-3-G-A." I shield my eyes with my free hand as he repeats it back to me, the laughter actually coming through now. Why, oh why, didn't I stick with Omega228?

Oh, yeah, because Dad decided me driving around with my birthday on the license plate was a stupid idea.

"Can you give me a road name and landmark," he snickers.

"Trebuchet Way, near the old mill," I snap.

"Half an hour to an hour."

"Thanks," I say and hang up.

I turn to step back onto the pavement when I hear a car pull up behind me. Turning, I see it's a black A8.

My heart hammers in my chest. I grip my phone; glad I've worn jeans and trainers to drive down to London. If I have to run, I can run.

I'm glad when I see a different car coming down the road. They overtake us and keep on going. I growl softly, wishing they'd stopped. Something about this A8 is making me seriously nervous.

The back door opens, and a man steps out. He is good-looking, but in a rough and ready kind of way. Dark-haired and unshaven for a day or two. As he approaches, I catch his scent and know he is an alpha. He smells like cedarwood. I back up, trying to get to the passenger door so I can slip in and lock the doors.

"You need some help?" he asks, his voice deep and a little bit scary.

"No, I'm good. The RAC will be here any minute." Okay, that's a lie and we both know it. No way would they be here in five minutes' time, and I'm guessing they know *exactly* when I broke down...in fact, I'm starting to think they caused it.

I scramble to open the car door, but he lunges forward and grabs my arm, dragging me towards him.

I shriek, but he slaps his hand over my mouth. I struggle to get away from him, fighting like a hellcat scratching and clawing at him, but he doesn't let go. His grip gets tighter. My bag half falls from my shoulder, tipping out some of the contents onto the pavement.

"Unmated," he says, drawing in a deep breath. "Just as expected."

He starts to walk back to the A8, dragging me kicking and screaming along with him.

"Let me go, you fucking arsehole!" I bellow, but what's the point? He's not going to let me go and there is no one around to hear me and help me. I kick him, but all that does is make him pick me up in his tree trunk arms and carry me squirming to his car. The next thing I know, I'm being shoved into the back of the A8, growly alpha is squashing in next to me and we are shooting off down the road as my abductor says smugly to his three alpha friends, "As advertised, one unmated omega."

"Fuck, oh, fuck!" I scream, but I have no one to hear me and nowhere to go.

I am stuck in the back of this car with four alphas who want to do fuck knows what to me.

This is bad. This is very, very bad.

Chapter Six

James

"It wasn't a Porsche," I insist, not wanting to believe Spencer is telling the truth.

"Turn this fucking car around and go back, I'm telling you, that was her," Spencer growls at me, his hand threatening to strangle me. He probably would try if I wasn't driving, thus killing all of us.

"You'd better be right," I snarl and search for a place to turn around.

As it happens, there aren't any. We are on the so-called main road in this part of the country, but it's narrow and deserted. I'm just going to have to risk it.

I swerve and mount the curb. "Watch that back end," I grit out to William in the back.

Executing a turn in the road, which takes more than three points, we narrowly avoid a black Audi shooting past us the other way.

"Jesus!" I exclaim. "Slow the fuck down, arsehole."

"No, wait!" Spencer says, fucking me off wholly and undeniably. "That's the car that pulled up behind her."

"And?"

He looks over his shoulder, chewing his lip. "I don't know."

I roll my eyes and when we arrive back at the Merc, there is no one there. Pulling up in front of it, I get out and examine the slashed tyre.

"That plank of wood in the road." I click my fingers to Spencer and gesticulate further away.

He runs off to get it and returns with it in his hand. "Nails."

"Deliberate?"

"I'm guessing. They took her."

"Fuck!" I roar and kick the deflated tyre, causing it to release more air. "Why? What do they want with her?"

"Let's go and find out," Spencer says, chucking the wood onto the pavement and climbing back in the car impatiently.

"This is..."

I don't even bother finishing the sentence, because it's pointless. There are no words to describe how ridiculous this is. Pausing to glare at the car door, I try it and it opens. I lean in and inhale deeply.

Blueberry muffins.

Straightening up, I slam the door and stalk back to the car, revving the engine and skidding around, now not caring if I hit an oncoming car or send us into the wall of the old mill in the process.

"Was I right?" Spencer asks, after I gun it down the road in pursuit of the Audi.

"Yep."

"Fuck. Fuck. Fuck."

"Pretty, brown hair," Cameron pipes up from the back.

"You saw her?"

I see him nod in the rearview mirror. "I approve."

"So glad you do," I mutter. "Will?"

He grunts, but it's less aggressive than usual. I'll take it as a 'yes'.

"So you see why we've put you through the wringer with the last rut?"

"Pretty, pretty girl," Cam sings, bouncing up and down. "Where is she? Let's find her and take her home."

"Well, that's the plan," I point out unnecessarily. "Spence?"

He is sitting forward in his seat, eyes darting all over, even though there is only one way and that's forward. "They've got a head start. Put your foot down, will you?"

I'm already doing fifty, but slam my foot down, gripping the steering wheel as we fly around the tight bends on this unfamiliar road.

"There!" Spencer exclaims as we hit a junction which leads onto an actual main road, with cars whizzing up and down it, heading to and from the motorway.

"Nope, not it," William says. "Wrong reg number."

"What?" Spencer says, turning in his seat.

"The one that drove past us was newer, a 71 plate. That one is a 20."

"How the fuck do you know that?" Spence bellows, panic in his voice.

I cast a glance at him, as I pull up behind the A8 at the red light. "Are you sure, Will?"

"Positive."

"Fuck!" I slam my hand on the steering wheel. "We've lost her."

"No!" Spencer says and shoves the car door open.

"Spence," I growl, knowing the light is going to change any second.

We watch as he raps on the window and starts shouting at the driver.

"Fucking hell. He's going to get himself arrested in a minute. But where the fuck did this knobber come from? The only car in front of us was the other Audi."

"We passed a couple of side roads," William informs me.

Ah, okay. That makes sense. And I did not see them, so focused was I on not careening off the road. "Buuuut, could *they* have gone down one of the side roads?"

"Possibly."

"Fuck."

Spencer, yelling obscenities to the poor hapless driver in front of us, gets back in and slams the door shut, absolutely fuming. There is no doubt in my mind that his whole, 'we talk about letting her go' speech was the biggest pile of horse manure that he's ever shovelled in my direction. And there's been a few mountains of it over the years.

"Not them," he grits out.

"You don't fucking say."

He fixes me with that angry glare that makes me fully aware that he is about to do something...Spencer-ish. We don't like to talk about it in real terms, but he has a temper that far exceeds my own and seeing as he isn't the prime alpha of this pack, he gets to let his loose more often than I can.

"So, which way?" Cameron asks, so not reading the room.

The light turns green, and I have to make a decision. North or South.

I head South, back towards London.

"I'll ring Jones and ask him to track the reg number," William says after a pause.

I heave a sigh as Spencer turns to him and hisses. "You have the entire number?"

"Yes."

"Why are you only telling us this now?"

"I was waiting to see if you got yourself into some shit by acting like a knobbing lunatic," Will growls. "Someone has to watch your back when you fly off the wall."

Spencer scrabbles over the back of the seat to reach the enormous alpha, bumping into me and sending the car swerving dangerously all over the road.

"Fucking hell, man," I snap, my temper breaking under the strain and outright aggression wafting around the enclosed quarters. "Will, just do it and Spencer, sit your fucking arse back down before I pull over and kick it back to London. Got it?"

As much as he wants to, he can't ignore a direct order from his prime. He glowers at me, but keeps his trap shut and sits down, arms crossed, sulking that he didn't get to kill anyone today.

There's still time yet.

If we find that Audi, we find our omega and not a single obstruction will stop us from claiming her.

Even if she has been mated already.

Chapter Seven

Rayne

"You can't do this! You can't just snatch me off the side of the road! You've...you've...*omeganapped* me, you twats!" I scream, louder and louder in the hopes that it will sink in.

It doesn't.

I wave my phone about and that's when the panic stops, and I groan at how stupid I am. "I'm calling 999!" I shriek and unlock my phone, only to have it whipped out of my hand by the tree-man who grabbed me.

"Give that back!" I claw at him, struggling with an alpha three times as strong as me, if not more. He places his hand on my forehead and gently shoves me away from him, closer to the alpha on my right.

"Fuck you! Fuck you!" I snarl, kicking out.

"Love," the right-side alpha says in a voice that's like honey and melted chocolate.

I pause and simmering, I turn my head, hand still attached to my forehead, and glare at him. "What?"

"We aren't going to hurt you. We just need you to win, that's all."

I take in his handsome face and quite beautiful blue eyes. His black hair is slightly shaggy and unkempt, but wow, he is too delicious. Shame he's a felon.

"Win what?" I clip out. I catch a whiff of pine cones coming from his direction.

"A scavenger hunt," he informs me. "A few packs are playing, the one to get the last item wins."

"Item? How fucking dare you!"

He grins at me and holds his phone up. "You are the last item: an unmated omega." He touches the screen with his index finger, checking off the last box on the list. I watch as he presses submit and then pin his eyes with mine.

"This is sick! Sick!"

I'm hoping the more I shriek, the more fed up with it they'll get and let me go. Fat chance though.

The one in the passenger seat growls and turns around. His dark eyes are dead, and I gulp when he snaps, "Shut the fuck up."

"Humph," I mutter and cross my arms. "Do you know who my father is? Do you? You are all in so much shit, but if you let me go, I won't say a word, and you can all go on your merry way."

He blinks. "Who is your father?" He doesn't seem that interested, but there again, it's hard to tell with his deadpan features and tone.

I lean forward and hiss in his face. "Jeremy Halstead. Heard of him? Chief Justice of the IPP, so fuck you, arsehole."

"Jesus, you've got a mouth on you, don't you, love?" Pinecones snickers.

"Yeah, we should wash it out with soap," Dead-eyes says, and hunches his shoulders. He smells like burnt toast and it makes me shudder.

"Fuck. You." I give him the middle finger, just so he knows that I'm not done with him yet.

His hand zips out and grabs my finger, bending it back.

"Ow, ow, owwww," I rasp, twisting my arm in an effort to stop him from breaking my finger.

"Shut the fuck up," he growls at me again and roughly lets me go.

He turns to face forward again, and I swallow, bunching my hands into fists and trying not to cry. Now that the initial shock has worn off, deep panic is setting in.

"Don't worry, Blueberry-muffins," Pinecones whispers to me. "As soon as you are verified, we'll let you go."

"Did you set me up with that plank?" I ask, tears pooling in my eyes even though I'm digging my sharp nails into my palms to try to stop it.

His sheepish expression says it all. "Sorry," he murmurs. "No omega was going to come with us willingly." His face turns grim.

"So you just took me? My cousin is expecting me soon and my parents will be wondering why I haven't rung them." They don't know that I said I'd text. They could easily text on my behalf and my parents would be none the wiser.

"Please let me go," I plead with him. He seems the most reasonable out of the four. Although, I couldn't say for sure because the driver hasn't spoken a word yet, nor even looked at me.

As we drive down the slip road and onto the motorway, I look back over my shoulder and remember my bag. I clutch it in front of me as a useless sort of shield and let out a soft sob.

Pinecones takes my hand and holds it gently. With every fibre of my being, I want to snatch it back, or bite it, but I don't. It feels nice...comforting.

It annoys me on a level that I can't even express but do nothing about because all of my bravado has vanished.

"I promise you; we will let you go soon," he mutters.

If I didn't know better, I'd think he felt bad.

I draw my hand back, knowing I'm being played. He is the worst kind of dangerous. Seemingly all sweet and what-not, but as soon as he's lured you in, bam! It's too late and your heart is cut out. Maybe literally in this case.

It makes my own heart pound against my ribs. Sweat forms under my armpits and on my palms. I need to get myself together and get myself out of this, somehow or another.

You can do this, Rayne.

You have completely got this.

We pass a sign on the motorway, and I make a note. And another note at the next one.

Minutes pass in silence.

A horrible uneasy silence which I'm desperate to break. But that's just my awkwardness at its best. I glare out of the front windscreen from my place in the middle of the back-seat. The sky has gone darker, and speckles of rain start to fall. The driver switches the windscreen wipers on, and I watch them swish back and forth, back and forth.

"What's your name?" Pinecones asks me quietly, startling me.

"Rayne," I whimper, squeezing my bag tighter.

"Hi, Rayne," he murmurs, his eyes never leaving mine. "I'm Richard."

Chapter Eight

Richard

My gaze is riveted to hers. Rayne. It's the prettiest name for the prettiest omega. Her blue-grey eyes are brimming with tears she is trying desperately not to shed, and it makes me feel like a pile of shit for hurting her.

I wasn't too keen on this hunt to begin with but went along with it because I had no choice. I kept my mouth shut and my head down. It's my preferred method of dealing with things.

"Rrrrrichard," she practically purrs at me, which not only bewilders me beyond comprehension, but sets the alpha inside me alight with the burning flames of desire.

The driver swerves, sensing the tension going up a few notches.

Rayne slides over the small gap between us and presses against me. She is quick to scoot back, but not too close to Bryan on her other side.

Mick turns around from the front, a salacious grin on his face.

She bites her lip and clutches her bag even closer to her as if that's going to stop anyone from attacking her. She needn't worry though. I will kill anyone who touches her now. I have fallen like Wile. E. Coyote chasing the Roadrunner off a cliff.

Suddenly. Shockingly. Scarily.

I don't 'do' relationships, or feelings, or love, or any of that shit. I just don't want to. Not that I'm not capable, but no one has ever even come close to bringing that out in me. I use omegas to get me through the rut, but that's about the limit, and even that disgusts me. I hate touching anyone in a sexual way, and to have them touch me back like that, turns my stomach to the point where I have to physically stop myself from throwing up.

"Hands off," I growl at Bryan, tearing my gaze from Rayne to give him a death stare. "That's not what she is here for."

Rayne's slight whimper ignites my possessive side. A side that I never even knew I had before this moment.

"You don't need to worry about Mick," I snarl, cutting my gaze across to the leader of this loose pack. Prime just isn't the right word for it. "You aren't his type."

She blinks when I look back at her. I stifle my chuckle when I see that she's insulted by that. I don't blame her. She is clearly wealthy, definitely gorgeous and unmated. She's everybody's type.

Except Mick's.

He likes his woman soft and subordinate, scared and pitiful.

Rayne is none of those things, despite her current despondency. She will come out fighting again, I have no doubt and I look forward to seeing it.

Mick sneers at her, but turns around again.

I hear her breathe out in relief.

I want to tell her she has nothing to worry about, that I'll protect her, that I'm stronger than all of these alphas put together. They don't know it. No one knows it. No one knows that I'm a prime alpha hiding out from my family pack because I just don't want what they were trying to force on me. I just want to be me. I don't want to lead, or show diplomacy and restraint, or any of the other things that prime alphas should do.

"Where are we going?" she asks after another minute of silence.

"London," I reply.

"I was headed there. I'm meeting my cousin. I'm supposed to check in with my parents, by phone call," she says emphatically, turning to give Bryan the side eye.

"You can ring them when we get where we're going," I inform her.

"Can I make you a deal?" she asks, her former strength resurfacing.

"What is it?" Mick growls, turning around again.

She tears her gaze from mine and fixes him with a glare that I would not like to be on the receiving end of. "I will be your prize. I will parade around in front of the other players in this game, hell, they can even give me a good whiff to *verify* me, if they must. But then, you drive me back to my car and we part ways, never to see each other again. I won't utter a word to my father, as long as I make it back to my

Mercedes in one piece without a scratch *or a bite* on me. Deal?"

I'm flabbergasted. She has balls of steel. No one demands anything of Mick. It's the other way around.

"Deal," Mick says, his eyes sliding to the side to indicate he is lying.

She huffs out, knowing it as well as I do.

She scoots in closer to me, an almost smug smile aimed in my direction. "Deal?" she asks me, sending the car into a state of disarray.

She knows.

She can sense it.

She has singled me out as the strongest of the pack.

Not good.

That is not good for anyone.

Least of all me.

Chapter Nine

Rayne

I'm not sure why he is hiding his true nature under the guise of a docile, do-as-Burnt-toast says, but this Richard is *definitely* not the weakest link. Searching his eyes, I evaluate him. He lets me see it all. A warning, if you will, of not to single him out as the leader of this sorry-arse loose pack of shitty alphas. He doesn't belong here, so *why* is he here? He is better than them. If he didn't let me see it on his face, I'd have known anyway by his attitude. Out of a primal instinct, which is coming solely from the omega inside me and not the woman, I shuffle a bit closer to him. I know that he will protect me. I don't know how I know; I just know.

Again, it's instinct.

He smiles warily down at me, and I return it with a tight one of my own. Feeling some of my sass come back, I lean forward and rap sharply on Burnt-toast's shoulder.

"I said *deal*?"

He turns to look at me again. I resist the urge to shy away from his cold glare. "So did I."

"I don't believe you mean it," I bite back.

"Well, tough titties for you." He faces forward again after his gaze drops to my ample chest briefly.

Okay, that was a bit rude. Mind you, on a scale of snatching me off the street and shoving me into the back of this car, it's more a one than anything else. But still. Manners, people.

Richard leans over and whispers in my ear. "I'll make sure you get back to your car in one piece."

I give him a weak smile, hoping he means it.

He sits back and then barks at the alpha on the other side of me, "Let her ring her parents and cousin."

Tree-man glares at me. "Fine, but you tell them everything is great and make it believable."

I nod as he pulls my phone out and holds it up to my face to unlock it. Grimacing at him, I watch helplessly while he invades my privacy and accesses my contacts. "Who is your cousin?" he snaps.

"Morgan," I reply, my lower lip trembling slightly. What am I going to tell her? Delayed? She might ring my parents. Not coming? She'll ask why not. We've both been looking forward to reconnecting, it will raise more red flags.

Tree-man opens up the messages. "No, a phone call," I insist.

"You can speak to your parents, but I'm not giving you twice the opportunity to screw us over. Text. What do you want to say?"

Uhm. Fuck. The pressure is getting to me. Sweat beads on my forehead. "Uhm," I stammer when he gives me an impatient, menacing glare. "Hey cuz. Sorry about this. Still coming, but slightly delayed. Met a hot alpha in the services, and well dot dot dot, then add the winky face emoji." I groan inwardly as Burnt-toast snickers. Yeah, I sound like a big slag but tough. It'll keep her off my back for a day or so.

I feel Richard's fingers squeeze mine again.

Tree-man, with a smirk on his face, presses send and then roots around for my parent's number. He dials and my mouth goes dry. My mum is going to know there's a problem because I'm ringing, not texting.

Think, Rayne. Think fast.

"Rayne?" Mum's voice comes over the line in concern. "Everything okay?"

In a flash, Burnt-toast's hand snaps out and grips my loose hair, tightening just enough in warning to make me wince.

"Yep, I'm here now. Thought I'd ring as you prefer."

"Oh, good," she says distractedly and my heart falls into my stomach. "Have fun and say hi for us."

"Will do. I'll check in again in a few hours," I rush out, needing to get that in so these arseholes know they have to keep me alive for long enough to do that at least.

"Okay, love. Bye."

"Bye," I whisper and then I'm cut off from the safety of the call and back to reality and the scary situation I've been thrust into.

Tree-man pockets my phone again, but Richard's fingers tighten on mine. This time, I squeeze back. Whatever his place is here, it's not aligned with the others. I need to get him firmly on my side, even if that side is my unmated omega, pretty, shaven pussy.

Use what you've got, Rayne. Do whatever it takes to get out of this alive and quickly.

Looking up through lowered lashes, I give Richard a demure, yet alluring smile. He pulls me closer to him and I raise my gaze, staring into his baby-blues filled with lust and possession.

The rain stops and in true English weather fashion, the clouds clear rapidly to reveal the blue sky and bright sunshine. It's almost as if the weather is changing with my mood. I've hooked him. Now all I need to do is reel him in until he feels enough for me to let me go unharmed.

No pressure. None at all.

Moments later, we're circumventing London on the M25 and within fifteen minutes, we're pulling off towards Southall.

Resisting the urge to go full-on nympho on Richard in order to move my plan along, but knowing it will only make him suspicious, I take in all the sights, sounds and smells of the west London suburb before we eventually reach our destination.

Pulling a moue of distaste at the rundown old house we've pulled up outside, I make sure that Richard has a firm hold of me when he opens the door. I'm not leaving his side, come hell or high water. Well, until he does what I want him to, and I ditch him to flee back home, of course.

"I won't let anything happen to you," he murmurs, lacing our fingers together. "I promise."

"I'll be holding you to that," I mutter back, shivering in the chill breeze on the crooked pavement of this dingy part of the neighbourhood.

He draws me closer to him, protectively and reassuringly.

If this is all an act to get *me* on *his* side, he should be nominated for an Oscar. Mind you, my own performance isn't lacking. I wonder briefly if things were different, and we'd met at a time when he wasn't a party to my abduction, how I'd feel about him. Right now, he is my safety net and my ticket out of here.

Nothing else matters when he leads me up to the front door with the faded, peeling green paint, of the two-storey terraced house. He ushers me inside with my heart hammering in my chest and sweat sheening every part of my body, ahead of the rest of my omeganappers.

Chapter Ten

William

It has been forty-five minutes since I rang Jones with the number plate of the A8. We are already nearly back home, but he hasn't rung back yet. I'm concerned. Marginally. I don't know this omega, so I have no feelings for her, but she is pretty from what I saw. However, James and Spencer definitely have a thing for her, and Cameron would chase the skirt on a sheep if it suited his mood at the time. Right now, he is being a major pain in the arse.

"Fuck off, will you?" I growl, placing my hand on his face and shoving him gently away from me. He is too close. I dislike anyone in my personal space. I take up a lot of it. I'm not a small man. At six-five and built like a brick shithouse, like my father and grandfathers before me, I try to be as unassuming as possible. I don't speak much, I try not to cause waves, but I feel strongly about staying away from people. My discomfort comes across as aggression, but it's not really. Most of the time. I can lose it as much as an alpha, but mostly, I'm just trying to keep the focus off me and literally, anywhere else.

I didn't have a pretty homelife, so at thirty-five, I'm grateful to be away from them and with these arseholes, even if it means being a guard dog to Spence. He has a temper that defies all logic and the rest of the pack look to me to have his back when he does something outrageously unwarranted. I think it's because I'm the only one that can lift the slighter man off his feet, and sling him over my shoulder to physically remove him from situations he definitely causes. Everyone can see he's a wildcard and they do their best to avoid confrontation with him. Sadly, he gets off on the conflict and seeks it out wherever and whenever possible. And if it's not there, he creates it.

"Check your phone again," Cam harangues me for the hundredth time. "We need to find that pretty omega."

"We will," James snaps at him.

I'm thankful for the support. James knows a little bit about what I'm like and tries to respect that. Except in the case of wrangling Spencer.

Glaring out of the window, hunching my shoulders to try to diminish the amount of room I'm taking up, my heart thumps when my phone rings. Outwardly, I don't show any sign of being startled, I just grunt and answer the phone.

"What?"

"Hello to you, too," Jones drawls down the line.

"Did you find the car?"

"Yeah, you're not gonna like it. Put me on speaker."

Silently, I do as he asks.

"James, you there?"

"Yeah."

"Okay, that car, bad news, pal. It belongs to the leader of the Jets, Mick Savoy."

I hear James groan and watch him exchange a glance with Spencer.

What aren't they telling me?

Flicking my glare to Cam, I see him looking a bit out of the loop as well, but that's not hard. To say he is all pretty face and no brains, wouldn't be doing him a disservice.

"Dammit," James growls. "Any chance of an address?"

"Weirdly, yeah, one in Southall, but whether it's real or not, I guess that's up to you to go and find out."

"Thanks," he mutters and then I hang up the phone.

"Jets?" I inquire gruffly, knowing something else is going on here.

"Mm-hm," James murmurs, all of a sudden totally focused on overtaking a lorry and muttering about arsehole lorry drivers who overtake other arsehole lorry drivers on the motorway and taking up two lanes.

One of my pet peeves is being ignored. I don't like talking so being forced to repeat myself is a crime against my nature. And it puts me in a really bad mood.

I lean forward, through the gap in the seats and grip Spence's shirt, dragging him towards me.

"Hey!"

"What about the Jets?"

"Nothing."

"Don't," I growl. "I will throw you out of this car, and you know I will. I abhor lies and you avoiding this subject is an insult."

51

"James," he complains when I tighten my fist in his shirt.

"Let him go, Will. I told him to keep it quiet. We're trying to find someone. He is apparently running with the Jets. They'd gone underground after kicking up a stink in the East End a few months ago, but clearly, they are back and abducting omegas off the side of the road. *Our* omega, specifically."

Grunting, I let Spence go. He huffs and puffs as I sit back. "Who?"

"Just someone. We were hoping to find him before we had a pack meeting about it. Can you trust me and leave it at that?"

I meet his gaze in the rear view mirror.

I *do* trust him. He is one of three people I trust. The other two are also in this car. But I don't like lies, and secrets are the same.

"Please don't make me go into this now," James says, his tone telling me all I need to know. It's deeply personal, painful even, and he will talk about it when he's ready.

I get that.

More than anyone, I get that.

Giving him a grim nod, I break eye contact and turn to glare out of the window instead, hoping that whatever, *whoever*, it is, it doesn't upset the balance of our pack.

"So, are we going to find this omega now?" Cam asks, breaking the silence, having seemingly ignored the betrayal of the two brothers.

"Yes," James replies. "We fucking well are. No one takes what's ours. *No one.*"

Ours.

Ours.

Our omega.

The more I say it in my head, the more I like it. I hope that she is everything James and Spence want her to be, but if she has just been abducted by the Jets, she is going to be even more mistrustful of our intentions. That is something we can hopefully reassure her of, if her scent is what I hope it will be and that these two idiots in the front haven't just built up in their minds because they haven't been able to find her. I won't allow myself to take this too seriously until then.

Only then.

Chapter Eleven

Rayne

I'm shoved, not so gently, into a front room, with Tree-man right behind me.

"No, I'll stay with her. You guard the outside," Richard says to him firmly, leaving no room for doubt that he will back up his words with his fists, if he has to.

It shouldn't, it really, really, shouldn't, but it makes me feel a bit fuzzy inside.

Richard slams the door shut and I look around. Threadbare carpet, which was once not that expensive anyway. White, peeling wallpaper walls. About the size of my bathroom at home, but I'm not so entitled that I can't understand it's a good-sized room for this house. There is no furniture in it, which makes it impossible to sit down, unless it's on the floor.

I grip the handle of my bag, which is slung over my

shoulder and glare at the alpha who has gone over to stare out of the window covered with a dirty white voile.

Several minutes pass in a silence which I don't know how to break. I chew my lip awkwardly and wonder what Richard is staring at. I start to move over, but stop dead when he speaks.

"I'm very confused about this."

"About what?" I prompt when he doesn't say anything else.

"You."

"Oh?" The word comes out as a small squeak, and I clear my throat.

More silence.

"There's this thing with me," he says quietly, contemplatively. "It's one of several reasons why I left my family pack, but a big one."

"You don't have to tell me…"

"I want to. I want to explain, because I can see you know what I am, and I want you to know." His bewildered tone leaves me slightly breathless.

"I feel things, a lot of things, mostly disgust at myself, but one thing that I have never managed to feel is a sexual attraction to any creature, male or female. It repulses me when people touch me and when I have to touch them, it makes my skin crawl."

"Uhm…" I wipe my hand on my joggers trying to get rid of the imprint of his hand in mine. I feel insulted and slightly sick that he found touching me so gross, even though another part of me knows it's not *me*, per se.

"I have to participate in the rut. If I don't, it's bad.

Really bad. Have you had a heat yet, Rayne?" he asks this wildly personal question, turning to look at me over his shoulder with a curious look on his face.

I shake my head dumbly.

He nods and looks back out of the window.

"It's difficult to explain, but the need to knot overpowers my need to stay away from people. I hate it. I wish it wasn't the case, but it is, so I do it."

"I think you've explained that fine," I murmur as silence descends again.

"Hmm. You have confused me, Rayne. You have made me feel something that I didn't think was there."

"What's that then?" I can't seem to keep my mouth shut. My heart is beating quickly, and while this conversation is distracting me a little bit from my predicament, I'm still in deep shit here and I wish he would crack on, so I could try to figure out my next move.

"Desire. Sexual attraction. It's strange and sudden and I'm not sure what to do about it."

"You fancy me?"

He turns his whole body around to face me, hands behind his back. His blue eyes are dancing with amusement, thankfully. This conversation is a bit heavy for someone I've just met and who abducted me, for fuck's sake.

"Yeah, I fancy you. I have never fancied anyone before. I know what I feel, even though it's new to me and I think I know why?"

"Why?"

"Do you fancy me?" His schoolboy question throws me off my game slightly.

Not that I had much to begin with, what with being omeganapped and held against my will in a dingy house with mean alphas. "You're cute. You know, for a felon."

"Felon!" he lets out a loud guffaw. "Well, yeah, can't argue with that. I must apologise about all of this. I'm so sorry, Rayne. I have been wandering around in a very dark tunnel for a very long time. You are the light at the end of that. Do you feel what I'm feeling?" His sudden demand startles me.

"What are you feeling?" I ask, licking my lips nervously.

He takes two giant strides and is in front of me, looking down at me from his considerable height, his eyes searching mine.

Reaching out, he strokes the back of my cheek with this hand. "This."

A spark of electricity that is hard to deny, skitters across my skin, warming my blood so that my cheeks go hot.

"I feel it."

He removes his hand with a slow nod. "It makes me want to protect you, cherish you, make you mine."

I don't say anything. I mean, what can I say?

Yes, is out of the question.

No, is a bit hasty.

Maybe?

He has a lot of grovelling to do first before I give him anything.

"I see," he says. "I understand."

He turns back to the window and stalks over grimly.

"First things first," he states, his voice returning to business. "You are in danger here, Rayne. Mick has no intention of letting you go."

"Well, I figured that," I mutter, glad we've changed the subject to the more important one at hand.

"No, you don't understand."

"Then explain it to me."

He sighs. "Mick is ambitious. He isn't a prime alpha, he wishes he was, but the only way to emulate that is by being the leader of a loose pack. But it's not enough for him. He wants more. He is going to use you to build a super-pack. A large group of loose alphas that will fall under his rule, as it were."

"What?" I snap. "What do you mean?"

My warm blood is now running icy-cold. I don't like the sound of this one bit.

"You are a prize, Rayne. A trophy even. This wasn't about a scavenger hunt, so much as a plain old hunt. Bryan found your name a few weeks ago through an idiot prime alpha who still belongs in nappies. Got drunk and spilled the details on who you are, who your father is, that he took your virginity, the whole sordid tale."

His tone has gone scathing, but I don't think he's getting at me.

"Andy," I growl. "That little prick." I clench my fist tightly. I'll fucking kill him. Also, they know exactly who I am? That means... "So if he spilled the details, why did they go after me and not my dad?"

It needs asking.

Richard snickers. "He passed out before he could tell them your *exact* location. He knew you were going away this weekend and told them the best place to abduct you. He didn't rat out your dad or your address, because they didn't ask before he fell unconscious. Besides, the end goal was always to get to *you* not your dad directly. He's too high profile. You were an easier target and are serious leverage, Rayne."

Okay, that makes sense, I guess. But fucking Andy! How dare he take the information I gave him and use it against me? Prick.

"So you asking me my name, was what? A ploy to get me on your side?"

"No. Yes, I already knew who you were, yes, we set you up to get you on the side of the road on your own, but the second you entered the car, and your scent filled my senses, things changed. *I* changed. I wanted you to tell me your name because you wanted to."

"How am I expected to believe you are a good guy when you went along with all of this?" I ask, wanting to yell at him and beat him with my tiny fists.

"You aren't. I hope you can forgive me and learn to trust me, but I did you wrong, Rayne and I regret it. The dark tunnel is no excuse."

Grimacing at him, I turn my back, but then quickly spin around again, needing to keep my gaze on him.

My whole plan has gone down the toilet and I have to rethink. Figure out how the hell I'm going to get out of this.

"So basically, I've been completely stitched up," I hiss.

"Yes. I need to figure out how to get you out of this. So far, I have come up with two options. One, I have already dismissed out of respect for you, but the other, as demeaning as it is, it's the only way."

"What's that then?" I ask warily, backing away from him out of instinct.

When he turns towards me again, his face is grim. "I need to bite you, to keep you safe."

I slap my hand to my neck as my mouth drops open. "Oh, hell no!" I bellow.

His face distorts into a pained expression, and he makes a shushing gesture with his hand. "I don't mean like that," he says, but wistfully as if he wishes he *did* mean it like that. It makes it very clear what his other option was.

I hold my hand up, and back further away from him. "Don't even think about it."

"If I mark you as belonging to me, even unmated, it will offer you some protection," he says, desperation seeping into his tone.

"Belonging," I repeat slowly, realisation dawning on me. "You want to claim me as a possession." I. Am. Livid. "How dare you even suggest that to me!"

"It's a means to an end, Rayne. It doesn't mean anything." His gaze goes slightly wild. He is *imploring* me to let him bite me. What the actual fuck?

"If you have another idea, I'm all ears."

"Smuggle me out of here?" It's lame. We are surrounded by alphas who have no intention of letting me go anywhere, it seems.

He growls and spins back to the window. "Rayne," he warns. "You are out of time, love. The packs are converging."

I race to the window and stare out at many alphas heading our way. They all look as vicious and horrid as this

Mick character. "Tell me again what they want from me," I whisper in panic.

"To mate you, bringing the packs together under Mick's rule, using you for your money and status. They will rape you repeatedly and there will be nothing you can do except survive as best you can."

"Jesus." Tears prick my eyes at the horror he has painted out vividly. I can't. I just can't. I had already talked myself into doing whatever it takes to get out of this. What's one little bite?

Hastily I remove my watch and gold bangle and slip them inside my bag. My ring follows. I don't want them stripping me of my jewellery. Each piece holds sentimental value. Although, my bag isn't exactly the safest place, at least they aren't visible. With a shaking hand and fear and doubt fogging up my senses, I breathe in his scent deeply and focus on that *connection* I know I feel with him, despite the shit he has helped cause for me. He grips my fingers and pulls me closer to him, turning me into his chest. His desire, that he claims is so new to him, makes the air in here cloistered and fragrant, clouding my senses. With our gazes locked, he brings my wrist up to his mouth. He kisses the sensitive skin lightly, a soft growl escaping his lips. I resist the urge to purr and pounce on him, reminding myself what he's done, of the danger I'm in. When his teeth sink into my flesh, I cry out softly, feeling slick dampen my knickers. He closes his eyes and bites harder, marking me, possessing me, *owning* me.

I'm lost to his bite as I know he is as well. His pulse is pounding in his throat, visible to my gaze when I drop it to stare at the exposed skin of his neck.

My breathing becomes heavier, sweat forms on my forehead, my shaking hands are ice-cold, almost numb.

When he releases me, I swallow and then the door bursts open.

Mick strides in and snaps his fingers to Tree-man. "Get her and bring her outside."

Chapter Twelve

Rayne

"Eep!" I squeal when Tree-man grabs my arm and hauls me out of the room.

I clutch my handbag, wondering how it's even still with me after this harrowing adventure.

"Hey!" Richard barks out, following us. "Let her go."

Mick slaps a hand to his chest to stop him. "I see what's going on here," he growls, deeply. "But you'll get your turn to fuck her during the mating."

I shudder at his vile, crass words. The thought of being mated to him, Tree-man, Driver-guy and any other creep that wants a go, swirls my breakfast around in my stomach, threatening to shove it upwards and all over Mick's tatty white trainers.

Looking back over my shoulder, I see Richard slap Mick's hand away, showing his superior strength and possibly outing himself in the process.

"Rayne!" Richard calls out, following us down the short hallway and into the kitchen. I don't have time to take in its sparse delights as I'm shoved unceremoniously out of the grungy white UPVC back door and into a flagged yard. There are weeds growing through the cracks, and a sad looking washing line hanging limply between the rusted old Sky Satellite dish and a small, lone tree in the corner of the neighbour's yard.

How I manage to take all of this in, while in fear for my life and faced with what must be twenty-five alphas crowded into the crappy, fenced off yard, is beyond me. Maybe it's to try and deflect from the absolute crap I've found myself in. I press my cold lips together to stop the whimper that wants to break free. I will not show them I'm scared. I will not break.

The stench of scents from so many nasty alphas makes me feel even more nauseous and it becomes a battle of my will, not to throw up everywhere as I'm dragged along to the back of the yard, shown off as the prized omega that will tie these alphas to Mick.

I'm not a tie. I'm not a tie.

I repeat this mantra out of a lack of anything else to think about.

Casting my desperate gaze to Richard, who is forcefully shoving his way through the crowd, I feel all of their eyes on me. It makes my skin prickle and want to crawl off my body. Clutching at my bag again, wishing I had any form of weapon in there to hold these alphas at bay, the tears that I'd been trying to hold back, pool my eyes. Richard is just one alpha in a sea of many. There is no way he can protect me, no matter how strong he is.

I'm done for.

I look around, panic folding itself around me like a heavy, smothering cloak. The neighbouring houses are all quiet, there's no kids playing outside or dogs barking. I'm all alone and about to find out what true horror really is.

I swallow loudly, keeping the mewl of fear, trapped in my throat. My head is spinning. Mick grabs me from Tree-man, glaring at my wrist. He draws it to his nose and sniffs. A feral growl escapes his throat, chilling me to my very core. "That won't save you, princess," he snarls. "You have no idea how much I want you." He gives my face a salacious lick, making me shudder with revulsion.

He turns to the crowd and starts to speak, his fingers digging into my arm, bruising me. I can't really hear what he's saying. The blood is roaring in my ears as I wonder how far I'd get if I made a run for it and over the back wall. I'm not that athletic, but I bet adrenaline would get me up and over it. Surely, it's better than just standing here. Surely, I have to try?

Before my bottle vanishes, I yank my arm from Mick's grip, surprising him into letting me go. I launch myself at the back wall, my bag thumping next to my side. I don't even make it before he grips my hair tightly, pulling back too hard. I yelp.

"Fucking cunt," he growls and backhands me across the face.

Gasping, I bring my hand up to my cheek, dizzy, but not going down yet. I coil the strong leather handle of my bag around my hand and swing out wildly with it, smacking Mick in the head with it.

It barely registers with him, though. He lets go of my hair, only to wrap his hand around my throat.

"Rayne!"

Richard's voice seems like it's coming from a few miles away.

I kick out at Mick, aiming for his balls.

With luck on my side, I connect with the soft tissue, and he grunts, releasing me from his hold as he doubles over. I whack him over the head with my bag, feeling a sense of triumph when he goes down. So I whack him again. And again.

"Rayne!" Richard's desperate call cuts through my victory as I'm dragged away from Mick by an alpha that wasn't in the car earlier.

"You aren't going anywhere, sweetheart," he breathes on me, his foetid breath making me retch. He reaches out and squeezes my left boob, which ignites my self-preservation into an inferno of burning survival instinct.

No way. No fucking way will any of these disgusting perverts lay their hands on me.

I kick out again, aiming for knees, balls, anything that will hurt enough for him to let me go.

Sadly, he is prepared and I'm getting tired. He knows it, and sneers at me as Richard, finally free of the horde of alphas who'd blocked his way to me, punches him in the side of the head so hard, his eyes roll back, and he drops like a rock.

"Eep!" I squeal again and jump back as someone lands on Richard's back, trying to throttle him from behind.

I lash out with my trusty bag, determined to give a five-star review on Yelp for this extraordinary accessory that is currently keeping me free, keeping me from being enslaved.

"Ooof!" Richard exclaims when I catch him on the side of the head.

"Sorry!" I cry out, sheepishly. "Sorry!"

"Run!" he chokes out. "Fucking run."

All of the aggression has fired up the loose alphas with bad tempers and they have turned on one another.

"I'm not leaving you!" I shout back, slamming my bag into the correct alpha now and stunning him momentarily. But it's enough to get him off Richard's back.

Unfortunately, the alphas now know he's trying to help me escape.

About seven of them swarm him, sending him down as they kick and punch him.

"Richard!" I scream, the scent of blood hitting my nose.

"Go!" he spits out. "Rayne!"

"No!"

My hesitation to leave him is my downfall. I'm grabbed by two alphas, one on each arm and held tightly as I struggle. Why didn't I run? What the fuck is wrong with me?

"Hold her still!" Mick bellows, approaching me menacingly. "Let's show this cunt, she can't mess with us."

My breath leaves me as my arms are yanked out further, hurting me, terrifying me with Mick looming over me, a dark expression etched into his features.

"No!" I scream, bucking wildly. "No!"

The next thing I see is like a vision out of a movie. Richard has gotten to his feet and is literally throwing alphas off him, his need to get to me amping up the prime alpha he has buried deep down. His loud, ferocious growl makes the hairs on the back of my neck stand on end. He smashes Mick in the face, sending him sprawling over the yard before he reaches down and snatches me out of the grip of the two lesser alphas, pulling my shoulders practically out of joint and making me moan in agony. He flings me over his shoulder, my bag hitting him in the arse, when a commotion over by the back door stops his advance towards the house.

"Fuck!" he roars as a noise that sounds like a firework, goes off right near my ear.

Richard stumbles, going down to his knees, dropping me on the floor.

I scramble, ignoring the searing pain in my shoulders. "Richard!" I scream when I see the red blood welling up on the side of his shirt.

"Take her," he mutters. "Take her and keep her safe for me, brother."

"Richard!" I scream when another alpha man handles me, his blonde hair smelling strongly of product.

"James!" he bellows.

"Just go," Richard says. "Get her out of here."

"We aren't leaving you, you utter prick," Blondie says as another shot is fired, followed by a loud crunch and howl of epic agony that makes my own seem like a pinch.

We are surrounded by angry, bloody alphas; ten, twenty, more.

"Richard!" I scream, struggling as they flock over him, keeping him down, his loud grunts of pain slicing through me.

"Go!" he finds the energy to thunder. "Spencer, go!

Please just keep her safe, please don't let anything happen to her..."

"Fuck," Spencer mutters and turns to head back to the house.

"No!" I shout out. "Don't leave him!" I wiggle and squirm, but the alpha is strong and marches through the house with me, two other alphas joining him. All I can see are their shoes because I'm exhausted and slumped over Spencer like a sack of spuds, my bag hitting him in the back of the knees as he leaves through the front door.

"This is not a fight we can win," Spencer mutters. "He asked us to take this one to safety."

"Is it her?"

"Yeah."

"Are they mated?" The croak in his voice intrigues me.

"He's bitten her, but they aren't mated, I don't think."

I stay quiet. I don't know what to say. Richard trusts them, so I can trust them. Can't I? I'm honestly too tired, mentally, physically, and emotionally to care right now. This has been a day from hell, so when Spencer gently lowers me into the backseat of a car and slides in next to me, I fall into an exhausted heap. I register the one who asked if we were mated saying, "I'm going back in. I'll meet you at home."

"James," Spencer says as the other two alphas get in the front. "You will lose."

"I'm not leaving him. Do as he asked and get her to safety."

The door slams shut, and we drive off into the bright, sunny, late afternoon, my bag clutched to me as all thoughts and feelings drain away, leaving me with nothing.

Chapter Thirteen

Cameron

"Wait," I say, as William sets off like a bat out of hell. "They're going to follow, and we can't leave James. Let me out."

The good thing about William is he doesn't talk much. So he slams on the brakes, lets me out of the car and then shoots off again without a word. Spencer didn't even get a look in, it all happened that fast. I watch the car go for a moment, savouring the sight of the beautiful omega in the back seat. She is scared and has zoned out. It will take some doing to get her back. But that is another reason why I stepped out of the vehicle. The fewer intimidating alphas around her, the safer she will feel. I spin quickly as the car vanishes out of sight, already with one on its tail. I know William is capable of losing them, but I would like to stop as many as I can to make it easier for him.

Jogging back to the rundown house, I come up against

a rough-looking alpha nearly twice my size, trying to get into his car. Whatever this loose pack wants with the omega, they are desperate to track her down.

But I won't let that happen. I reach him, and being fairly small and unassuming next to him, he ignores me to his peril. I smash his face into the car door before he knows I'm even there and then dart off while he slumps to the ground in a daze. I chuckle to myself. I grew up with my fists swinging. You have to when you attend an all-boys boarding academy and getting into fisticuffs with the upperclassmen was a daily occurrence. If you didn't learn quickly how to protect your nose and your nuts, you were written off as a wimp and picked on even more. Being smaller than the average alpha, with a good-looking face and rather attached to my nuts, I learned super-fast how to defend myself and even enjoyed it on occasion. But I downplay my ability to fight. It draws too much attention to me, and then people start inquiring about you and what else you are capable of if they find out you're good at something. It's why I act like I'm all pretty face and no brains. It lowers people's expectations when they think you're a himbo. Not that I'm the smartest tool in the shed, but I'm not as dumb as I make out either. Even to the pack. It's just easier to fly under the radar.

Before I've even made it a few yards, a fight tumbles out of the front door with four or five alphas involved, having turned on themselves when the fights started, it seems. I stand on my tiptoes to try and get a look around them to see if I can see James, but he has already disappeared into the house. I duck around the cluster of alphas, getting a sneaky jab in to another one who appears to be on his way to his car, with his keys in his hand. I get him under the ribs and shoot off before he knows who hit him. He blames the group punching the shit out of each other and joins in, the omega chase temporarily forgotten.

"James," I hiss, when I see him at the far end of the hallway.

"Cam," he says quietly, spotting me when he turns. "What are you doing here?"

"Not leaving you in here by yourself."

"I'm good."

I shrug. He will never admit to needing my help, but that's okay. It's who he is, so I give him the out. "Also, I wanted to get out of the car, so the omega didn't feel so overwhelmed."

He nods slowly. "Good thinking. Come on. The police will be here soon." He gestures me forward.

"So who are we here for?" I didn't get a good look, nor any inkling of who is in here that James and Spencer know.

"There," James says, evading the question, but racing forward to an alpha on the ground, bleeding and with his face smashed in.

Another alpha is standing over him, gripping his shirt while he punches the downed alpha repeatedly in the face and another kicks him in the ribs.

His head is lolling back, and he is unconscious.

"Fuckers," James hisses and grabs the puncher by the back of his jumper.

I take the kicker and giving him a dose of his own medicine, I stamp my foot on the back of his ankle, making him yelp and hop away. I give him a boot up the arse that sends him sprawling into a dazed alpha, wandering around with his hand to his head.

Jesus. This is an absolute cluster-fuck.

James drags the puncher away while he scrabbles to regain his footing after such an abrupt departure from the ground. Surprised at the strength of the prime alpha, he cowers but James is in no mood to suffer fools. He smashes him in the face, and he drops like a rock, out for the count.

"Help me," James mutters, bending down as we hear the sirens in the distance. He tries to lift the unconscious alpha up from one side.

Without a word, I immediately grab the other side and haul up the shot and battered alpha, wrestling his arm over my shoulder, so we can drag him out of the yard and back into the house. He is the worse for wear. His nose is bust, his lips are split and bleeding, his eyes are swollen shut.

"What are we going to do with him?" I don't ask the obvious question of who he is. If James wanted me to know, he'd have said already. I will wait and he can inform me when he's ready. I assume that will be when we are back at home and he can tell William as well, so he doesn't have to repeat himself.

"He's badly injured. We need to get him to a hospital."

"He's been shot," I point out, having heard the shot fired and seen him go down earlier. "Won't the hospital contact the authorities?"

"Dammit," James mutters. He gives me a frown and I shut my mouth, going back to pretty and uninformed.

I don't need to tell him it's an election year. He knows all of this and is processing. His first instinct to protect over sense, goes some way to letting me know who this alpha is.

He's family.

With an inward sigh, I speak up. "I know a guy," I murmur. "An old school buddy. We can go there."

James gives me a grateful look and silently we dodge around the infighting alphas, hoping that not too many took off after the omega. I wish I knew her name. She is gorgeous and that scent...

I push it all aside as James leads me to an old clapped-out Ford Escort and shoves the alpha in the back.

He climbs into the driver's seat and rips the wires out from underneath the dash.

Climbing into the passenger side, I ask with a snicker, "*You* know how to hot-wire a car?"

He gives me a grim look, tinged with amusement as he sparks the wires together and the car starts. "I wasn't always the responsible arsehole you know and love," he says and glances over his shoulder briefly, before turning back to face front and setting off at a reasonable pace so as not to draw attention to the car.

"Well, well, well. James St. Stevens, the rebel."

He snorts. "Guess we are both exposing more of our hidden selves today." I ignore his pointed look and stare innocently out of the window.

"Head towards home and I'll direct you from there."

"Thanks," he mutters.

We don't speak again until I tell him where to go.

Chapter Fourteen

Rayne

It feels like my brain has given up and left the building. Or at least the part that can think and feel. Actions are coming easily enough. The trembling of my hands won't quit, which is seriously annoying and is shaking my bag which is housed on my lap in front of my chest. The further we get away from the house, the more returns to me though.

Blinking, I turn my head to the side, then I reach out and grab Spencer by his shirt. "Richard. We have to go back for him."

With a kind smile, he unpeels my hand gently from his shirt and places it on the seat between us, before he lets go. "James has got him. Don't worry. He is your...mate?"

He can't hide the curiosity behind his innocent tone. It draws me in. I shake my head.

"No. But he was trying to save me. Even though he didn't stop them from abducting me in the first place."

I see the spark of rage in Spencer's forest green eyes and shy away from it, but it's gone in a flash. "He did what?" he croaks out.

"Doesn't matter," I say with a sigh, rubbing my wrist where Richard bit me. "He redeemed himself. I feel terrible leaving him there."

"It's okay, I promise you. James and Cameron know how to take care of themselves, and each other."

I nod slowly, not really believing him. There were so many nasty alphas at that house. The three of them are probably dead now because of me.

My shoulders slump and my back arches in mental defeat. The car swerves abruptly to the left, shunting me over the seat to crash into Spencer.

"Sorry," I mutter and scoot back.

"Will," Spencer snaps. "Be a bit gentler, please."

"Tail," the giant named Will replies.

I glance over my shoulder, but don't see anyone. "Please don't let them take me back there," I cry out suddenly.

"We won't," Spencer says soothingly. "You are safe now."

"I need to ring my parents," I wail, the emotions that were absent earlier returning in full force.

"Before you do that, can I say something?" Spencer asks cautiously.

Going still, I nod again.

"What's your name?"

"Rayne."

"I'm Spencer and that's William."

"Uh-huh." I already knew that.

"Can you tell me what was going on back there?" His tone is light, but insistent.

I shudder and clutch my bag tighter. Licking my lips, I say, "Mick, that douche canoe, lame-arse alpha wanted to use me to tie some loose packs to him as their leader. He assumed they would all fall in line if he offered me up for pack mating."

"Jesus," Spencer mutters. "Who are you?"

"Rayne."

"No, I get that," he says with a small smile. "I mean, *who* are you? Why did he think you had this power?"

Power.

"Rayne Halstead. My father is..."

"Chief Justice of the Inter-pack Parliament," he finishes for me. "I see. Perhaps ringing your parents isn't such a good idea, right now...or at least, you can ring them but don't tell them what happened. I fear that this may have been about your dad as much as it was about you."

"What?" I don't understand what he's saying. "Who are *you*?" I snap. "What makes you such an expert? Are you planning on doing the same?" My voice has gone shrill and weak. I can't run again. I'm too tired. But Richard trusts them. I have to believe that I can trust them as well.

"Absolutely not," Spencer says firmly. "However, we know a thing or two about politics. We are the St. Stevens pack."

I blink rapidly. "Yes, I've heard of you. The most powerful pack in England next to the St. James pack. You have not one but two seats in Parliament." This knowledge is coming back to me from poring over my dad's books.

"That's right. James, our prime alpha is the MP for Kensington and Chelsea. I sit on the backbench."

"Yes, yes, yes..." I keep nodding like one of those annoying nodding dogs, but I can't seem to stop the action. "I know this."

"We are going to take you to our home in Chelsea, where you can contact your parents. Where are you supposed to be right now?"

"With my cousin in London."

"Okay, good. Tell them that you're safe, which you are with us. If you lure your father out and into the middle of this, things are going to get ugly. We've been increasing our efforts on the loose packs to arrest and prosecute. Your father is in the very midst of it. His location is a secret for a reason."

I don't know what to think right now. It sounds plausible, but maybe he is just trying to separate me further. And secret location? Since when? I search Spencer's eyes and see no sign of deception or fraud. Have I been living a lie this whole time, oblivious to everything around me?

Heaving a sigh, I look away. It wouldn't surprise me. All of dad's hushed meetings, why he never leaves the house unless he absolutely has to, the video calls in the middle of the night.

Oh, Rayne. You're a dumb fuck.

"Why can't you just take me home?" I ask, my lower lip trembling with the effort of holding onto my tears.

"We have several tails," William says from the front. "I keep shaking them, but more keep finding us. This is going bigger and wider than we originally thought. If we lead them back to your home, we are being idiots."

"Oh," I whimper.

I feel that I have no choice but to believe them.

"Here," Spencer says and hands me his phone, unlocked.

I stare at it and scrape my teeth together as I think. Eventually, I shake my head. I'm in no fit state to speak to my parents and make them believe everything is fine. "Later," I mutter, but feel marginally safer knowing he offered. It goes a long way to making me believe they mean me no harm.

Moments later, we pull up outside a fancy mansion in Chelsea and William gets out first. Spencer watches him through the window and then opens the door. He gets out and holds his hand out for me. With only a slight hesitation, I take it, drawing in his fresh lemony scent. He helps me out of the car and with a protective arm around me, he rushes me up the few steps that lead to the front door and into the house with William right behind us.

"You'll be safe here, Rayne," William says softly. His voice is deep and growly. I think he is being quiet so as not to scare me anymore than I already am. I give him a weak smile and inhale a shallow breath so I can take in his scent. I nearly groan with hunger when I catch the faint aroma of freshly baked biscuits.

"There's a room upstairs where you can rest, and maybe take a shower," Spencer says, leading me through the white marble entrance hall and up the white carpeted stairs.

"I don't have a change of clothes," I say, shaking my head, mortified. I try to get a sneaky whiff of my pits in case I stink of sweaty fear-BO.

"You will soon enough. Jones, our go-to beta, has gone back for your car."

"Oh," I say in surprise, still feeling numb and out of it. "Thanks."

Spencer smiles and then leaves me in a pure white room, all alone and wondering what the fuck my next move is.

It only occurs to me seconds later, how did they know where to find my car?

Chapter Fifteen

Rayne

Figuring that Richard must've told them where my car is, which makes sense and also reassures me that he is okay, or alive at least, I disappear into the beautiful en-suite, which is all black, the exact opposite of the gorgeous pure white room. I flick on the light, and it illuminates the room in a low-level brightness, which my tired eyes appreciate.

Dumping my handbag on the countertop, I glare at myself in the mirror and then my gaze drops to the bag. "You are fucking amazing, my friend. You were worth the four hundred quid and more." Feeling idiotic, but not caring, I give the bag a hug. Opening it, I fish around for my watch and lay it on the counter, then my bangle and then after a panicked root, I find my ring in the bottom corner attached to some fluff. I blow it off and lay it down as well. Since Spencer told me about my dad and his secret location, my brain has done nothing but recall small details. The ring, given to me four years ago when Dad suddenly declared we were moving from our modest 4-bedroom, detached Victorian house in Hillside to the country manor in Lakesview, a good half an hour's drive away.

I pick it up and turn it around.

It was a payoff, so I didn't ask questions.

I remember gushing over it as the movers came in, quick and efficient, packing up our house late on at night so we moved the next day. I thought it was weird at the time, but figured my dad was doing well in his job and wanted to give us nice things.

I slip the ring on my finger and pick up the watch. My eighteenth birthday present. I'd mentioned to Dad after my A-Levels that when I left school, I wanted to go to Uni and learn the law like he did.

Days after I got my exam results, which I'd aced like a boss and got into fucking Cambridge, I got this watch and a trip for me and my friends to Ibiza for the month of September, thus missing the start date. Figuring I'd take a gap year, which was suggested by Dad when he offered to extend my holiday with a shopping trip in Prague, two weeks on the Amalfi Coast, through Paris for more shopping and returning home via Oxford Street in London.

"Jesus, Rayne. You are the worst kind of woman alive. Distracted by shiny things."

Shaking my head at myself, I put the watch back on then pick up the bangle.

The gold, Cartier bangle. I clasp it to my wrist, wincing as it rubs over the bite that Richard gave me. Dad gave me this four months ago, before I made my appointment with Doctor Fredericks for my heat suppressants. He was proud of me for making this decision because I was unmated, and he didn't want me knocked up with no pack to love me.

But I see what it was.

He was relieved that I hadn't found a pack yet. That I'd started to be a bit withdrawn when most of my friends ditched me and went off to Uni. He wanted me at home where he could keep an eye on me as his job grew more and more dangerous. Firstly, shipping me away and then keeping me close as the situation with the loose packs changed, swapping my cars every few months and being really anal about social media.

The Porsche. I was talked out of liking it, I know that now.

I wish he'd told me the extent of the danger. I was always careful. It was drummed into me as a child. I'd thought it was just one of those things with being the daughter of such a powerful man.

I feel like such an idiot, but more than that, I feel used.

Almost as a punishment, I don't want to call my parents and tell them I'm safe. *If* I'm safe.

Pressing my lips to the bite mark on my wrist, I sigh. Half of me wishes Richard had given me a mate bite now. It would anger Daddy, and I really want to hurt him right now.

It's mean, and the thought quickly vanishes. I really hope Richard is okay and on his way here.

Sighing heavily, I reach for my bag and open it, peering inside for the small zip-up pouch in which I'd stored a weeks' worth of the heat suppressant injections. Not finding it immediately, I frown and root around some more, scrabbling to find it.

When I don't, even in the depths of the handbag, I tip it up on the counter, my heart pounding in panic.

"No, no, no, no, no!" I exclaim as the contents scatter across the black granite. Everything from various tubes of lip gloss, to a half-eaten packet of Polo mints, an open packet of pocket-sized tissues, some gum, my purse, a roll-on deodorant, some perfume, more fluff than I care for... but no pouch.

"Fuck!" I roar. "Fuck!"

It must've been part of the stuff that fell out on the pavement when I was struggling with Tree-man.

I lean on the counter, tears pricking my eyes. This is bad. Really, really bad. My twenty-first birthday is next week. I'm supposed to be doubling up my injections for the next few days to ensure their success at suppressing what is, naturally, a very powerful part of my biology. Without them, the build-up over the last three months is for nothing. They will fade and I will enter my heat, maybe a bit late, and probably not so intensely, but the suppressants will fail.

I *need* to get home. There are no two ways about it.

I scoop up all the crap and dump it back in the bag, glad that I've carried around so much junk. If the bag had been lighter, it wouldn't have saved my arse earlier.

Marching out of the en-suite and through the white room, I gather up my courage. I'm going to have to tell these alphas to get knotted, and that I'm going home.

Leaving the room and heading down the stairs, I find Spencer sitting on the third to last, flicking through his phone.

"Going somewhere?" he asks with a droll tone that

despite my fear, anger, disappointment and whatever else I'm feeling, I smile at.

"Home."

"Yeah, nope, BM. Can't let you do that?"

"BM? And why not? Am I a prisoner here?"

"Blueberry-muffins is a bit of a, err, mouthful," he says, looking over his shoulder at me with a dazzling smile that really lights up his eyes. "And no, of course not, however, if you fancy your chances with the three cars of loose alphas out the front there, be my guest. Train station is on Sloane Square."

I hesitate. "Three cars?"

"Yep."

"And you are just sitting there checking the football scores?"

"Chelsea played a friendly at home," he replies.

"Why aren't you doing anything?" I shriek.

"They haven't done anything. What would you like me to do?"

"They were going to..."

"Going to isn't the same as doing...our hands are tied. We are biding our time. As soon as one of them sets foot on the property, they are toast."

"Ugh," I groan, scrunching up my nose as I flop down next to him on the stairs. "These must be such a bitch to keep clean."

"That's why we usually insist that guests remove their shoes."

I stare down at my white Vans and cringe. They are pretty scuffed up after the day's events. I kick them off with a sigh. "So, I'm stuck here with you or I'm omeganapped again by them."

"Looks like. And by the way, there are worse people to be stuck with." His mildly insulted tone makes me giggle like a stupid fool.

Hysteria.

Definitely hysteria setting in.

I let out a loud guffaw and slap my hand over my mouth, meeting his amused gaze. "Sorry," I cackle. "I have no idea what's so funny."

"You're in shock, probably. You should rest."

"I can't," I say, sobering up as everything comes crashing back down on me. "I'm hungry, upset, angry, tired..."

"Hangry."

"What?"

"You're hangry. I can fix that." He stands up and holds his hand out for me.

Hesitantly, I take it and let him help me up. "Why are you doing this? You don't even know me."

"You mean something to Richard," he says evasively, avoiding looking at me. "That's enough."

I take it at face value and follow him down the marbled hallway and into a clean, modern kitchen, where he sets about making me some food.

Chapter Sixteen

James

Pacing up and down the front room of this large town-house in Mayfair, I wonder how such a prominent doctor fell so far down the ladder that he takes on dodgy clients in the middle of the evening at his home.

I cast a glance to Cameron, who is seated in an armchair, his ankle on his opposite knee, flicking through a magazine.

"How do you know him again?" I ask, wildly curious that enthusiastic Cam has a dark side.

"Went to Harrow together," he replies, not looking up from his flicking. "Saved his face a few times."

"Huh," I murmur and then look up as Philip, last name not given, enters the room, covered in bloody scrubs.

I gulp.

"He's going to be fine, but he should be in a hospital."

I shake my head. "No hospitals."

"I get that, but I have to say it. He could do with a blood transfusion."

"Okay," I say, rolling up my sleeve.

"What's your blood type?"

"A positive."

"Ah, good, a match. Follow me."

Cam's gaze follows me out of the room. His own curiosity is well beyond piqued, but he knows me well enough to know that he won't get answers right now, so he doesn't bother asking.

Entering the room right behind the front room, I stare at Richard. He is awake, just about, but completely unrecognisable.

"You're a dick," I inform him loftily.

"Grrrrnnn," he groans, holding his left side where the bullet went in.

"What was that?" I ask, cupping my ear and being a complete twat.

He grimaces. "Never gets old."

"Unlike you, you're a mess."

"Fuck you, cuntweed."

"Nice. I see your new pals have taught you some lovely new insults."

"Don't," he warns me as I sit down and look away from the needle that is about to be jabbed into my arm.

I'm not squeamish, but...okay, yes, I'm squeamish. Not at the sight of blood as a whole, just my own when it's being sucked up a tube with a gross gurgling noise that makes me want to vom.

Richard snorts through his busted nose and then yelps with pain. "Some things never change."

"Fuck off."

I keep looking in the opposite direction. "The omega..." I pause because I have no idea how to ask him. I don't even know how to talk to him anymore.

"Is she safe?" His words tumble quickly through his split lips.

"Yeah, Spence and Will got her home. She's fine. Scared and confused, but safe." I'm not telling him that she's been asking about him constantly.

Growing a pair, I blurt out, "What's she to you? Your mate?"

"I wish," he grits out, shifting to get more comfortable but not finding it. "She deserves better than me."

"Don't," I snap, getting pissed off suddenly. "Don't go looking for pity from me. You're a fucking bellend."

"I know."

"No, you don't. You just fucking left, not a word in over eight years. There are *no words* to express how much of a cuntweed *you* are."

"You're not telling me anything I don't already know, Jay."

"Fuck. Off." I give him the middle finger and then inhale sharply when the doctor, who I'd forgotten was even there, removes the needle from my arm, having sucked enough blood out of me.

He sticks a plaster on the jab wound and I roll down my sleeve. Standing up, ignoring the headspin, I growl, "We've been searching for you for years. Seeing you now, I wish we hadn't bothered."

"Fuck off then and leave me alone, arsehole. I never asked to be found."

I resist the urge to punch him in his already battered face. Instead, I stalk out of the room and out of the house, Cameron, scrambling to catch up with me.

"So, we're just leaving him?" he asks as I fire up the stolen Escort.

"Get in and shut up or stand there yapping to no one."

Without hesitation, he gets in and I shoot off at break-neck speed in the direction of home. This day has gone to the dogs, and I need a stiff drink. Also, I need to find out more about this omega and what in the hellfire she was doing entangled in this mess. Her accident was definitely set up, but why? Did they target her or just any unmated omega? Spence has been very tight lipped about anything she's told him, saying he will have that conversation with me and Cam when we get home. I get it.

We need to have a big old pack meeting about all of the events that unfolded today.

To say that I'm not looking forward to it, is a vast understatement, and once again I curse Richard for being a selfish prick.

Pulling up outside our house in Chelsea about twenty minutes later, I get the distinct impression that *someone* forgot to mention that the house was being staked out.

"Fucking Spence," I growl. I turn on Cam. "Did you know about this?"

He shakes his head, taking in the three strategically placed vehicles outside our home, as blindingly out of place on our exclusive street as this jacked Escort. Cam and I stay where we are as I pull out my phone and ring Spencer.

"You nearly back?"

"Spencer," I state in my most businesslike voice. "Did you know that the house is being watched?"

"Yep. Didn't you get my message?"

Frowning, I pull my phone away to check. "Nope," I growl.

"Oh, hang on."

I wait impatiently while he checks. "Oops, forgot to press send."

"Fucking hell, man."

"Sorry."

He doesn't sound sorry at all.

"How is our omega?"

"Rayne is okay. Can you get inside before they beat you to death?"

"Probably not."

Cam taps his fingers on the dash. I can tell from his impatience, that we are going to try regardless of our impending death or not.

"See you in a few," I mutter and hang up.

Giving Cam a brief nod, we both open the doors at the same time and launch ourselves up the steps and at the front door, which Spencer opens suddenly, and we fly through it, crashing into each other and ending up in an inelegant heap on the marble floor as Spence leans over to kick the door closed.

"Why didn't we get a house with a driveway and big gates again?" Cam asks, rubbing his head. "This pavement to door shit is absolute bollocks."

"Next time," I grit out, getting to my hands and knees and then seeing a pair of small feet in white trainer socks in my view.

I look up to see the omega, standing in front of me with a tub of mint choc chip ice cream in her hand, sucking a spoon with a twinkle in her eye.

"Richard!" she exclaims. "Wow, you look a lot better than I thought you would. I'm so fucking glad you're here and you're okay." She drops to her knees and envelopes me in a tight embrace that I return with envy building up inside me for my twin brother.

'Ouch' doesn't even cover it.

Chapter Seventeen

Rayne

Richard pushes me away gently and stands up, helping me up as well. I blink a couple of times and then squint at him.

"Not Richard," he says, his hand on his chest.

"Yeah, I see that now. Hmm...you are?" Drawing in his pineconey scent, I frown.

"James St. Stevens. Prime alpha of this pack."

"Rayne Halstead."

"As in Chief Justice Halstead?" he asks, squinting back at me.

Casting a glance across to Spencer, I see that he didn't mention this. I guess he was waiting for everyone to be here. Makes sense.

"Is Richard okay?" I ask, peering around the men in a show of where-the-fuck-is-he.

"Yeah, fine. We need a pack meeting. Where's Will?"

James asks suddenly, glaring at Spencer. He stalks past me and bellows, "Will?"

I turn my attention to the cute light blonde-haired man, with the most remarkable hazel eyes, who got out of the car earlier, who smells like forest rain.

"Hi!" I say, awkwardly giving him a wave.

"Hi!" he responds enthusiastically. "I'm Cameron."

"Rayne..."

"Mmm." The delicious murmur sends a shiver down my spine.

"Cam," Spencer says, giving me a sassy look. "Come with me." He grabs the younger man and hauls him down the hallway whispering furiously and gesturing wildly.

"Uhm...am I supposed to come to this pack meeting?" I call out, feeling like that popped out left tit again.

When no one replies, I shrug and shovel more ice cream in my mouth. I saunter after them, wondering why Richard left this pack with his twin and younger brother. I'm also left wondering and concerned about where he is *now* and if he is really okay. That was left a bit up in the air.

Walking past the door that leads to the kitchen, I hear the men in a room a few paces away. I follow the noise and peek around the door to see a large sunken lounge with huge, squishy white leather couches and a massive TV on the wall. The glass doors at the opposite end, lead out to a courtyard where I can see a patio set and barbecue, along with some big pots of colourful flowers.

"Rayne."

I look over at James, and venture further into the room.

"Come in, sit down," he says, gesturing to the squishy couch.

I linger in the doorway like a fart in a thunderstorm. Dithering and debating about whether I should make myself at home or not.

He gives up on me in the end and carries on talking. He is telling William and Cameron about his twin brother, and how they have been estranged for eight years after Richard just left in the middle of the night.

"It wasn't until a few months ago that Spencer and I made the decision to find him again. We figured leaving him to his own devices would make him see sense, and life gets in the way, but eventually it became clear that we needed to go to him. Finding him today was no coincidence. We knew he would be at that house."

He slides his gaze across to me briefly before addressing his pack again. "We took him to a doctor that Cam knows, and we got into an argument. I walked out. I'll go back for him tomorrow." He heaves a heavy sigh. "I hope we can integrate him into the pack, as he belongs here with us."

"So he's really okay?" I ask into the silence that falls.

Those blue eyes that are exactly the same as Richard's, search mine. "He'll be fine." Moving his gaze back to the alphas sitting on the couch in front of him while he stands in front of the TV, he asks, "Any questions?"

When no one says anything, I raise my shaky hand like the nervous new kid in school. "I need to go home."

"No can do," James says. "You know about the cars out front. Spencer very briefly told me the situation and I've connected the rest of the dots. You need to stay here for your own and your family's safety. We believe you were targeted for a reason and until you are completely safe, we cannot in good conscience let you leave."

"But there is something that I need," I say desperately.

"We can provide you with anything you need. Jones is also picking up your car and taking it to get the tyre replaced. He will bring your belongings as soon as he has figured out a way into the house undetected."

"No, you don't understand," I persist. "It's medication."

If it was possible for the room to go even quieter, it just did.

"What kind of medication?" James asks.

My cheeks flame. "Well, that's a bit personal," I fluster.

"Is it lifesaving?"

"Well...err...no..."

"Then we can get you whatever it is in a few days."

"That's too late!" I exclaim. "I need it *now*. Today!"

"Is it not in your belongings?" Spencer asks.

"No, I think I lost it on the side of the road when I was grabbed earlier." I'm starting to get wound up here.

"I'm sure we can sort you out with another prescription..."

"No! There isn't a single doctor in the country that would prescribe it to me again so soon. It's restricted. Fuck!" I run a hand through my hair, only just remembering about the ice-cream that's now melting and gloopy.

"Oh," James says, understanding dawning on his Richard-looking features. "Oooooh."

I make a 'uh-huh' gesture with my whole body, hands, head, the works, threatening to slop ice-cream all over the gorgeous wooden floor. I look for somewhere to place it down, but the carton is all drippy and wet and the closest piece of furniture to me is an antique-looking sideboard. So

I continue to hold the drooping carton as all four alphas look at me in varying degrees of interest.

I've thrown them for a bit of a loop, it seems. Clearly, they have never met an omega who suppresses her heat before. Or not to their knowledge, at least. I find it curious, and a bit intriguing, but also, I feel like a bug under a microscope now.

"Ahem." I clear my throat out of a lack of anything to say, but needing to say something.

It jumpstarts them into action and they flap about, throwing suggestions at me. Well, three of them do. William, the big biscuit man, locks his gaze onto mine and says over the din. "We'll ring Jones and see if he can find them near your car."

"Thank you," I say relieved. "They're in a black zip up pouch. There is only a few days' worth. I was meant to be staying with my cousin and then heading back home. I can't stay here indefinitely, so we are going to have to come up with a plan to remove those arseholes from the front of your property. I mean, come on. You live in one of the most exclusive neighbourhoods in the country. Surely the neighbourhood watch or whatever it is, will shift them on their way soon?"

"You would think," James scoffs, "But unfortunately, they haven't done anything other than pull up and stay in their cars."

"Well, they did more than that," I reply heatedly. "Can't I ring the police and tell them?"

"That would give out your location and then your dad would find out, come for you and with them waiting outside, he would be jumped before he knew what was going on. As much as I hate to be the arsehole here, no, you can't."

I glower at him with open resentment. But a small part of me knows he's right. I'm stuck here until we figure a way out.

"How about over the neighbour's fence?" I put that out there.

"You mean the ten-foot-high solid brick wall that borders two multi-million-pound properties with more security than you can shake a stick at? You would be arrested for trespassing and then you would be fair game. We can't protect you in jail."

"Can't you explain and ask them to allow me over?" I spit back. "They might be amenable if they knew what was going on."

"You don't know the neighbours," he growls, and I shut up.

Lowering my gaze and my chin, to stare at my feet. I try not to cry.

"Rayne," he says, in a much kinder voice. "Leave this with us. We have connections. We can sort this out. It's just going to take time and the *right* way. We won't keep you here any longer than we have to."

"Unless you want to stay," Cameron says, bouncing up and down on the couch like a buoyant puppy.

I can't help but give him a smile. "Please ring your man and ask him to pick up my stuff from the pavement, if it's still there. I'll be upstairs, I guess."

Turning to leave, I feel their eyes on me. I keep going, stopping by the kitchen to dispose of the wet carton. I slope up the stairs, feeling very despondent and not even having my phone to ring anyone to tell them I'm okay. I hope the alphas use all of their heavy political sway to make this right and soon because one thing is very clear to me. If this Jones guy doesn't find my injections, there is no way I can be here when my heat inevitably hits.

Just no way in hell.

Chapter Eighteen

Spencer

"We have to tell her," I say as I loiter in the doorway of the TV room, watching her progress down the hallway to the kitchen, and then up the stairs.

"That would ruin the illusion that we're actually the good guys," James says with a sigh. "She is starting to trust us and if she knew we'd been after her all this time, what would that do?"

I sigh. For some strange reason, I seem calm and composed around her. Even with her in this house, the need for aggression is lessened. It is very weird. I'm not used to being so chilled.

"I know and believe me, I don't want to build up any walls that have started to crumble. She's been through hell today, and yet she is still standing. Somehow. I've never known anyone quite like her before."

"You and me both."

"Too bad she's more interested in your twin than you." Cam's innocent jab came out with its fists flying towards James.

"Jesus," he snaps. "Do you mind?"

"Just saying...you want him here so bad, use her to get to him."

Three astounded gazes cut to the preppy puppy. "You what?" I blurt out.

He rolls his eyes. "Okay, that came out worse than how it sounded in my head. I meant, use her presence here to draw him into the fold."

James and I exchange a glance. "Maybe," he mutters. "Isn't it just more deception? We are supposed to be caring for her, not the exact opposite of that."

"We are and we will, *but*...there are two birds here and we have one stone. Why not knock them both down at the same time?"

"He has a point," I venture, firmly on the side of not deceiving her any more than we have to. I like her. A lot. She has fire and is gorgeous and sweet and obviously loyal to a fault. By all accounts, Richard was in the car when she was grabbed, but he redeemed himself by trying to save her at the eleventh hour. It could be that she has a slight case of Stockholm's or whatever, but I think it's more than that. She connected with Richard in the way that she is supposed to connect with us. We know she is our mate. At least, James and I do. Her scent has been driving us nuts for the last three months. The rut that didn't happen a few weeks ago was proof that something wasn't right. Two of us went into the rut and two of us didn't. Namely James and me. We were attached to our future mate, and nothing was getting in the way of that. It made for a hellish few days. It was like all the pent-up frustration that you can usually fuck away with a hot omega bouncing away on your slicked-up dick was still there and getting increasingly worse as the days went on. Neither of us were bending though, and tempting fate. Neither of us took an omega to bed to try to force the rut.

Fuck.

We are whipped by a short, curvy omega with bouncy, light brown hair, eyes the colour of a rainstorm, tits big enough that you can drive your cock in between the pushed-up mounds, and a fortitude that would put many alphas to shame.

In a word, she is everything.

To tell her all of this, would definitely ruin the small amount of trust she has in us, but not telling her is wrong.

I fix James with a defiant stare. "We need to tell her that you and I spotted her outside the doctor's office three months ago and were trying to find her. Christ knows, maybe she'll be flattered."

William snorts with what comes across as angry mirth, if there was ever such a thing. "I think you are living in a fantasyland there, Spence. But we have lost sight of the bigger picture here. We need to ask Jones if he found her stuff on the pavement. If not, we need to try to accommodate her somehow. She has her reasons for wanting to suppress her heat and that's none of our business until she tells us. *If* she tells us. Secondly, we need to get rid of those dicks out front. You two have to keep your noses clean.

You've already risked too much by getting involved in that shitshow before. Cam and I, however, are not in Parliament. Leave it to us. And thirdly, if you are sure you want to bring Richard into the pack, then we have what he wants." He stands up after that shockingly long speech. I don't think I've even heard that many words from him the entire time I've known him.

Six years.

Six years of grunts and one to two word sentences.

He's quite articulate and reasonable. Who knew?

"Agreed," I murmur, staring at the giant man with a new level of respect. "James?"

He is staring off into the distance. I know exactly what he's thinking. I've known all along how hard this would be for him, since we first decided to find Richard and bring him home. But there is no going back now. We know where he is and as much as we can tell ourselves it's gross to use Rayne to bring him to us, it will work. And on the flip side... bringing Richard here will keep Rayne with us as well. There is no downside to this, except the deception. It will have to be something that we come clean about soon or it will eat my insides away until there is nothing left but a ball of anxiety and tension.

"Jay?" I prompt him when he doesn't answer.

"Agreed," he says eventually. "We will tell her after Richard is here. Let's try and secure that before we go about ruining the best thing that has happened to us."

"You feel that strongly about her?" Cam asks warily.

"Don't you?" I ask, not giving James a chance to answer.

"I feel...something. Her scent, it's alluring. Pretty and

sweet. She is gorgeous and I can see her strength. I'm not quite where you are, but I guess you've had longer to work on that." His slightly confused look concerns me.

"Will?"

If he is in the same confused boat as Cameron, then we have a small problem. The pack cannot be divided in choosing a mate. Granted, she has to agree to be with us, but the four of us, five if you count Richard, need to be on the same page first.

He grunts at me.

Great. Now he decides to go backwards.

"What the fuck does that mean?" I'm getting agitated, but I'm *still* not looking to smash any faces in. Weird. Fucking weirdy-weird.

He shrugs. "Give me a day or so to figure it out. Maybe speak to her on my own a bit like you have."

I nod slowly. "Fine. You can show her where the landline is and tell her she can ring her parents and cousin. I assume her phone was taken from her by the loose pack or she'd have contacted them already and we'd be on our way to the job centre or worse."

James snickers, despite knowing I'm right. If Chief Justice Halstead in any way finds out we were anywhere near his daughter and her abductors, we will be tarred with the same brush and sent down without a trial. He isn't called Hard-arse Halstead for nothing.

"I will go to her now," Will mutters and disappears through the door.

"I guess someone had better ring Jones."

"I'll do it," James says. "Hopefully he found her stuff

and doesn't have to go back for it. He's already at National Tyres in Wimbledon."

I nod and sit back down, leaning my head on the back of the couch, exhausted from this day already.

Chapter Nineteen

William

Making my way upstairs to the bedroom that was assigned to Rayne, I pause at the top, seeing the door open. Slowly, I approach, clearing my throat so she knows I'm coming.

Stopping outside, I lean against the doorframe casually and see her lying on her stomach in the middle of the bed, a bunched-up pillow under her chin.

She looks despondent and tired.

"Can I get you anything?" I ask quietly. Maybe too quietly, as I don't think she heard me.

"For this day to never have happened," she replies a few moments later.

I click my fingers and the sharp noise makes her look up and across to me.

"Sorry, it seems like my powers of time travel are on the fritz." I give her a small smile.

She giggles. It's a cute sound, and it makes me warm inside.

"Gingerbread man is a funny guy."

I tilt my head.

"Sorry, you smell like biscuits to me, and I love gingerbread."

"Me too."

Her smile warms even more, and she sits up. Finding common ground with her will go a long way to helping her trust in us. I'm surprised that James agreed to Spencer's suggestion that I be the one to help her contact her parents. She will see that as a big gesture.

"Do you want to ring your parents?" I ask her, still casually leaning in the doorway.

She blinks a couple of times and then sighs. "And say what, exactly?"

I push off from the doorframe and regard her closely. "Have you spoken to them at all since you left the house earlier?"

She nods. "Yeah, Mick the prick said I could ring them. I said I was at my cousin's and that I'd check in later."

"What did you tell your cousin?"

"I texted her and acted like a big, fat slapper," she says with a groan, stuffing her face into the pillow.

I frown. "Pardon?"

"Ugh! I said I was going to be delayed because I'd met a hot alpha at the services. Christ knows what she thinks of me. I didn't have my phone to see her reply."

I stifle my snicker. I'm fairly certain that she is not a slapper, even though I don't know her. She hasn't thrown herself at any of us and we are a reasonably attractive pack as far as that goes. Holding my hand out for her to take, I say, "Come, I'll show you the landline."

"Jesus," she mutters, but climbs off the bed anyway. "Landline? What is this, the nineties?"

"Like you'd know," I chide her. "You are what? Twenty-two, three?"

"Twenty," she says with a huff. "It's my birthday in five days' time."

She takes my hand, but she doesn't know what she has just done to me. Something deep inside, in that dark place that rarely sees the light of day, has sprouted. I understand her in that moment. I empathise with her predicament. She is desperate to delay her first heat because she is unmated and the last thing she wants is to be here without her meds. It has fired up my protective side like it has never been before. I will now physically attack anyone who tries to go near her. It's a strange feeling, but one that I could definitely get used to.

"Don't worry," I murmur. "We will make sure you are safe and protected."

Rayne looks up at me with those eyes that I only just noticed now are a cloudy blue and so pretty. She laces our fingers together as we head towards the stairs.

"Thanks," she says quietly. "I feel like such a fool."

"Why?"

"For losing something that is so important."

"You didn't know you were going to be abducted."

"No, but I knew something felt off. I should've been more with it."

"You have nothing to feel foolish about. You were taken

advantage of and that is not acceptable. Those who did this to you will pay."

She nods and we carry on in silence until I lead her to James's office and show her the phone. She giggles again when she picks it up and then frowns. "Err, dammit."

"What?"

"All of my parents' numbers are saved in my phone. I can't remember them off the top of my head."

I don't hold back the snort this time. "Oh. That's a problem."

"No shit, Sherlock," she mumbles.

"Hey, that's my line," Spencer says as he enters the room. "What's the sitch?"

"Rayne doesn't remember her parents' numbers."

"Ah, the issue with mobiles. Can you sign into your account on the laptop and retrieve them?"

"Yes," she says with a grateful smile. "Thank you."

I watch as Spencer sets up the laptop for her and then steps back. Her father's numbers are strictly confidential. No one knows them. The fact that she is going to use an outside, unsecured line to ring him now isn't really how it's done. I know this and I'm not even part of the Parliament. They didn't really have this issue when my grandfather was Chief Justice many moons ago, but I remember always being told as a child, never to tell anyone where he lived.

Rayne gives us both a glare when she picks up the phone again and we back out, giving her some much-needed privacy. If she is anything like me, telling a lie is hard enough when you are by yourself and ten times worse when you're saying it in front of others. As much as I hate lies, there are times, like this one, when it is needed to protect the people you love. Honesty has its place in the world and it's a big, important place, but even I can understand that it's not always the best policy.

"We'll be in the TV room if you need us," I murmur.

She smiles, a slightly wobbly, but genuine smile. "Thanks."

That one word, with her brave smile despite her perilous situation lands me on the same page as James and Spencer.

"I knew she would work her magic on you!" Spencer laughs and slaps me on the shoulder. "You have fallen like a skydiver out of a plane."

"Hmm." I just hope I have a parachute because I have a feeling that this fall with Rayne, isn't going to be as easy as her accepting to be our mate today, tomorrow or even the next day. She needs to know the truth behind why we were at that house earlier.

Something tells me she will inform us that we can get knotted before the end of the conversation, and, honestly, I wouldn't blame her if she did.

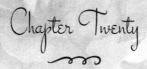

Chapter Twenty

Rayne

With a shaky hand, I dial my dad's mobile number. Then quickly, I slam the phone back down before it starts to ring.

"Shit." Is there a way to withhold your number on this ancient contraption? I turn back to the laptop and leave it to good old Google to inform me that yes, there is.

Picking the phone up again, I dial 141 and then the number I retrieved from my iCloud account.

"Hello?"

My dad's deep voice resounds through my head like a bass drum.

"Dad, it's Rayne."

"Ray-ray? Why are you ringing me from a withheld number?"

His suspicion makes me a bit annoyed. Before, I

wouldn't have thought twice. Now I know about all the danger, it pisses me off that he never told me.

Okay, here goes. "My phone battery died, and I can't get it to charge now."

"Oh," he says, his relief evident. "Do you need me to arrange to have another one sent to you? I don't like you wandering around without it."

"Yeah, to arranging, please, but I can go and pick it up at the shop in London."

"Oh, are you going shopping with Morgan?"

"Mm-hm." I cringe, my eyes tightly shut, glad my phone has been stolen so I don't have to video call, and he can see the lies on my face.

"Leave it with me. Should be sorted by tomorrow. Everything else okay?"

The loaded question leaves my mouth dry and my pits sweating and exuding the BO stench of lies and deceit.

"Yep."

"Okay, I'll let you go. Have fun in the city."

"Dad?"

"Yes, love?"

"Is everything okay there, with you and mum?"

"Of course," he replies. "All good in the hood."

I roll my eyes. "Fuck off with that, old man," I chortle, making him laugh and it's like the great divide that I suddenly know about isn't there. "I love you."

"Love you too, Ray-ray."

"Dad?"

"Mm?"

"Don't let Andy back into the house, please, okay? I've

heard some things and I don't want him hanging around me anymore."

"What things?" he snaps, suddenly not fun-Dad anymore, but Chief Justice Halstead.

"Just some shit, getting drunk and spreading rumours. It's nothing bad, but I don't want to know him anymore."

"Consider it done. I can have him detained and questioned if you want me to?" I hear the twinkle in his voice and giggle.

"As much fun as it would be to see Scrappy Doo piss himself, no, leave it and him. Uhm, one more thing before I go..."

"That doesn't sound good..."

"I'm going to actively start looking for a pack while I'm here. It's time."

Silence.

"Oh? What changed your mind?"

"Well, it's not changed, Daddy. I've always wanted a pack, but you know I wanted to go to Uni and study law like you first."

"Ray..." His world-weary sigh brings tears to my eyes as I interrupt him.

"But, I've decided, I don't want that anymore," I lie, doing my best not to sob as I give up my dreams to keep him from having to worry about me. "I want to mate and have babies and live a good omega life, happy and secure." I brush the tear away, that fell from my eye unexpectedly and then I pull my big girl knickers on and smile. "It's what I've always wanted, you know that."

"Are you sure?" He tests the waters expecting to be bitten by a Great White.

"Yes, I'm sure."

"I'll put the word out, see if I can find you some options. There are several packs I know about who will be searching for an omega and they won't find anyone better than my little girl."

"Thanks, Daddy," I whisper, hearing how happy he is. Like, I've never heard his voice so light and relieved and excited. I know I've done the right thing, and who knows… maybe once all the dust settles and I've got my pack and my babies, I can go to night school, or whatever. I'm still young, I can still make this work, I just have to be a bit more creative, that's all, and creativity is one of my strong suits.

"Pick up that phone tomorrow and let me know when you've got it," he orders.

"Will do. Bye."

"Bye, Ray-ray."

We hang up and I hope to fuck this Jones fellow can head to the mobile phone shop tomorrow and pick up my new phone for me. If that phone call has done anything, it's convinced me to stay here, with my head down and not make waves for my dad.

I won't be the reason he is targeted and possibly hurt. No fucking way.

Deciding to make the best of a bad situation, I at least know I will see Richard again tomorrow. That thought excites me. He is just the right amount of sweet mixed in with the bad boy. His vulnerability is sexy, and it brings out the mother hen in me. I want to cuddle him, well, air cuddle him, and make him see that he is worth more than he thinks about himself. Yes, he did me wrong, but he immediately tried to fix it when he noticed the connection between us. Had that not been there, Christ knows where I would be now, but that is something I can't dwell on. It *is* there and to be quite honest, I felt something when I hugged his twin, as well as when I was sitting next to (I think he must be) their younger brother. Could I have unwittingly landed in the middle of the pack I'm supposed to mate with?

How does that work?

Fate?

Destiny?

Some fucked up luck?

"Or maybe it's just you projecting and trying to make this situation less shite, you dumb fuck," I mutter to myself.

But I know. Everyone else might think I'm being hasty and silly.

But time will tell.

And Christ knows, that's all I've got right now.

Time to know them, time to figure this shit out and hope that it all works out the way I think it will.

On that note, instead of heading back upstairs, I walk down the hallway to the TV room and this time, I don't float about like a fart in a bucket. I march straight up to Cameron and Spencer, sitting side by side on the big, squishy white couch and flop down in between them. Grabbing the game controller from Cameron, I proceed to kick the shit out of Spencer's avatar, to their utter shock.

Yeah, that's right, bitchachos. Hot Omega's got game.

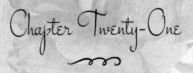

Chapter Twenty-One

Richard

My eyes snap open.

I take in the unfamiliar ceiling and blink.

It is unstained, clean and white with expensive, fancy coving.

I try to sit up and then groan. "Eurgh." Slapping a hand to my side, I proceed to prod gingerly and remember the events from yesterday.

Shots were fired and a bullet grazed my side, deep, but still not that bad, straight through, Doc said. Rayne is safe, though. That's all that matters to me. I really hope that someone called the police and Mick has gone down for possession of illegal weapons along with all the other crimes he has committed.

"Fucker." I wish I'd never gotten involved with the Jets, but I was in a dark place, alone with a lot of pent-up aggression to let loose. It was the obvious fit. Now, I regret every single second of my time with them. Meeting Rayne has fundamentally changed me. It's bizarre. There is no other word for it. I lived my life with an unyielding pressure until I walked out and became the exact opposite of what was expected of me. All I want now is to be good enough for the omega who crashed into my life and turned it upside down. The omega who has made me feel things, I didn't think was possible.

But I'm not good enough.

She deserves to find happiness with a pack who can love her, adore her, treat her like a princess and worship her body like she deserves. I can do none of that.

James can give her everything.

Gritting my teeth, I make a decision. I know my twin. He is a relentless prick, and he will be back here soon. It's still early out. I can disappear again and make sure this time he doesn't find me.

Struggling to sit up from the too-comfy bed, I swing my legs over the side and hoist myself up. The carpet sinks under my feet and for one brief, gut-punching moment, I miss my old home. Shaking my head and taking a step forward, I ignore the head-spin and slight nausea that rises up as I reach for my jacket.

"Where do you think you're going?" The light, cultured voice of Doctor-I-don't-think-I-got-his-name rings out, as he appears like an apparition in the doorway. "You should be resting."

"Places to be, people to *not* see. You get my drift?"

He nods his light blonde head and takes a sip of his coffee. "He cares about you. He will be back."

"All you have to do, is tell him I was gone when you woke up."

"You sure you have somewhere to go? That wound needs to be kept clean and dry."

"I'll take care of it." I grunt when I take a step forward, but push past the Doc. "Thanks," I mutter as I head down the hallway and out of the door.

He doesn't try to stop me, for which I'm grateful. I'd hate to have to kick the arse of the man who patched me up and ruin all the hard work he did.

I open the huge wooden front door and peer out into early morning Mayfair and wonder how the hell I'm supposed to get back to my digs in Croydon. It's not much. Actually, it's a fucking dump, but my stuff is there and clearly, James and Spencer have no idea about it, or they would've found me ages ago. I'll be safe from Mick and everybody else, and I can collapse there for a few days while I heal up and mourn the loss of the only woman I've ever been attracted to. Knowing it runs so much deeper than that, hurts too much to think about. All I want to do is forget. But I can't push the feel of my teeth sinking into her flesh away. Her delectable, creamy skin that made me want to run my rough hands over, just to feel the silky smoothness before I kissed and licked every inch of her.

Closing my eyes briefly as I hobble down the street, I stifle the whimper that is bubbling up. It wasn't a mating bite, but it was enough to latch me onto her and now I'm pining. I know it deep in my soul. I wonder if she is missing me too. Or if she has already jumped into bed with James and the rest of them and forgotten all about me as they ravage her for hours on end.

The thought makes me feel sick to my stomach.

Coupled with the pain from the wound and my face being all fucked up, it gets too much. I bend over a wooden pot full of pansies and throw up a mouthful of bile that my empty stomach complains viciously at.

Straightening up, I ignore the horrified expression of the dapper man walking his dapper dog and stagger onwards, knowing I've got at least a four-hour walk ahead of me, more in my current state, unless I find enough loose change on the way to pick up a bus further down the route.

My guts are telling me to go back and wait for James to inevitably rock up so I can return home with him, but my heart can't do it. I can't do that to Rayne. I will only drag her down when she should soar. It's not fair to her for me to be thinking about her.

So, with every ounce of strength I have, I clench my jaw, hold my side and lift my head up. This is one day of sheer horror and then I can go back to my life as I knew it before yesterday.

Assuming Mick and his crew don't catch up with me before then. I completely fucked up their chance to force a mating with Halstead's daughter and they will be gunning for me if they're still on the street.

I drag my phone out of my jacket pocket and unlock it. The first thing that pops up makes my stomach curl up in disgust. It's the notification I sent out to let the other loose alphas know we had Rayne and to meet at the house in Southall. She thought we were on a scavenger hunt and that we would let her go. She had no idea the danger she was really walking into, and I wonder why I ever agreed to be part of this plan in the first place.

Making a noise of revulsion, I flick the screen off and bring up maps. I need some direction as I have no idea where the fuck I'm going out of this fancy neighbourhood, which is too close to Chelsea for my liking. No, I need to get back to the South side of London and the sooner the better.

I pick up my pace, pushing past the pain.

It's only when I pause to look up so I can cross the road, do I notice the car that has pulled up just a little bit behind me.

Moving as quickly as my battered body will let me, I cross over the road and keep going. It doesn't stop the car from swapping lanes and pulling up in front of me. Just before I can turn back, the rear car door opens, and a head pops out.

"Richard St. Stevens? We need to talk. Get in."

I gulp and try to run, but two guys who are way bigger than me are blocking my way. I have no idea where they came from, but they weren't there a minute ago

Or were they?

My brain is fuzzy and I'm tired.

I don't even try to fight as they usher me up to the open door and practically shove me in as the occupant slides over the back seat to the other side.

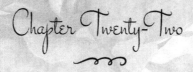

Chapter Twenty-Two

James

It is still fairly early, but I intend to get back over to Mayfair before Richard has a chance to make an escape. I know he will try, but hopefully he was too drugged up last night and stayed where he was. I'm frustrated with myself for leaving him there, but he just makes me so mad and there are so many issues I can't get over. Seeing his face again, didn't lessen that in the slightest, only aggravated it.

But I've searched and searched and finally found him. I'm not letting him go again. I will drag him back here by his knot if I have to.

Sneaking out nice and early without Spencer, I make it to the bottom of the stairs and then there is a loud knock on the front door.

Grimacing at it, I cross over quickly, knowing who it is already from the official sounding rap.

Opening the door, I discover I'm not wrong.

"James St. Stevens?" The Police Constable gives me a thorough once-over.

"Yes, what can I do for you?" I try to surreptitiously peer around the two of them to see if the loose alphas are still outside.

"We are investigating an incident that happened over in Southall yesterday afternoon. Can you confirm your whereabouts?"

I pin his gaze with my own, letting him know that he has just made a big fuck-up. "I beg your pardon?" I spit out. "Do you know who I am?"

The gaze wobbles slightly, but he doesn't back down. "I do, but I still need you to confirm your whereabouts yesterday afternoon."

"Humph," I mutter. "I was on some family business. *Personal* family business."

I know I'm being overly ornery with the PC, but he is standing between me and getting my brother back. Also, I still can't see if the cars have gone yet. They were still there last night.

"Did this family business have anything to do with Richard St. Stevens? He was spotted at the scene of a crime yesterday."

I blink once, taking that in. I understand that he has offered up that information out of respect for me and my position in Parliament, but he is still pissing me off.

"No," I lie. "Can you tell me what you want with my brother?"

"We would like to talk to him in connection with Mick Savoy. We believe he may try to make contact with you. We'd appreciate it if you could let us know if he does."

"Will do," I say, crossing my arms.

He glances over his shoulder before his steely gaze lasers into mine again. "Did you know that some of your neighbours called in an incident last night?"

I shake my head.

"There were some unsavoury characters parked up outside. We moved them on about eleven o'clock last night. If they come back, please do let us know. Your safety is paramount, of course."

I uncross my arms and give them a tight smile. "Of course."

Bobbing their heads briefly, they back down the steps that lead to the front door. I watch as they get into their car and drive off, making sure that the street is clear of dodgy looking cars. It is. Even the stolen Escort has vanished, probably by one of the alphas who were staking out the house.

I close the door with a heavy sigh. If the police are looking for Richard, things just got a lot more complicated. Although, I'm not surprised with the amount of dust that was kicked up yesterday at that house. Half of me is very wary about who ratted him out. Why him? Was it one of Mick's crew? Or Mick even? Probably.

"Everything okay?"

Rayne's quiet voice interrupts my musings.

I turn to see her standing at the top of the stairs, out of view from the front door.

"Why were the police here?"

"They were looking for Richard. But it appears they moved our unwelcome guests along."

"So, I'm free to leave?" she asks, coming down a few steps.

"No." I give her a smile. "We don't know who is lurking in the shadows. But nice try."

She giggles. "Yeah, I figured. I just wondered if you had thought of it. Are you going to go for Richard now?" Her innocent expression belies the storm in her eyes.

"No, I'm going to have to send Jones. They probably won't be watching him."

"Did he bring my car and stuff back yet?"

"He's on his way. He stayed away last night so he could also stop by the phone shop undetected to pick up your new phone as requested." I check the time on my watch. It's nearing 9.30AM.

"Oh, thanks." She chews her lip.

I can see she feels bad for making him stay out and do her errands, but it's what he's there for. Sort of.

I step back as the door opens and Jones strolls in laden down with bags and boxes.

"Did you find the pouch?" Rayne demands rudely, zipping down the stairs in her haste to get to him.

The middle-aged man gives her a cautious glare before he says, "No. Unfortunately, it wasn't there."

"Dammit!" she spits out, running her hand through her hair. "I'm sorry. Sorry. I'm Rayne. Thank you so much for picking up my car and stuff." She gives him a honey-coated smile and he accepts it.

"I should go and sort out this phone and text my dad to let him know I've got it."

She gives me a soft smile. "Will you let me know when Richard is here, please?"

I nod and return her smile. She goes off struggling with her bags and new phone.

"Richard?" Jones asks, his eyebrows raised.

"Yeah. I need you to go back out there and pick him up. I'm being watched. Actually, you might be now as well."

He shrugs. It doesn't concern him. He never met a tail he couldn't lose. "Where to?"

"Mayfair." I give him the address of Cameron's doctor friend.

"Okay. I'll take little missy's Merc. Stay off the radar."

I laugh at his description of Rayne. "Thanks, Jones. I know these last couple of days have been a shitshow."

He grunts. "Well, I've not made it easy, sending you all over the place. Will he come willingly?"

"Probably not, knowing him."

He lets out a loud guffaw. "Don't worry, Jay. I've got this. I doubt anyone will be looking for me or him in the Hot Omega-mobile."

"Thanks," I say again, trying not to chuckle.

I watch him leave and climb back into Rayne's Mercedes and take off back down the Square, wishing I was going myself, but there is no way I'm leading the police straight to Rich. I may have some serious issues with him, but I'm not that much of a twat.

"Are we free and clear?" Spencer asks, strolling down the stairs, freshly showered and dressed in just his grey joggers. He's such a fucking show off.

"Yeah, for now, and Rayne is in her room, not down here, so go and put a shirt on."

He snickers. "Yeah, nope. Be grateful I've got pants on."

He glances conspiratorially up the stairs. "Did Jones find her...you know...?"

"No, someone probably picked them up and they're being sold on the black market as we speak. She is, unfortunately, going to go into her heat unless we can figure something else out. And before you say it, no, *we* aren't going to purchase them on the black market. There is another way, and we'll find it."

My phone dings for an email before he can reply, so I pull it out of my pocket and read it.

"Oh," I murmur, walking into my office and shutting the door quickly before Spence catches on that something is very, very wrong. "Oh, fucking hell."

Chapter Twenty-Three

Rayne

Dumping my stuff on the bed, I try to calm my nerves. If I'm being quite honest with myself, I half expected this Jones guy to arrive without the heat suppressants. The items that fell out of my bag in the struggle were left on the side of the road for hours. Anyone coming by could have grabbed them. Yes, there were only a few, but adding them to another stolen batch and then cutting the meds in half to double the dose and then distribute them is not only dangerous, but totally something someone shady would do. The problem I now face is what the hell do I do? I've already missed yesterday's second dose and this morning's first one. If I don't sort something out by tomorrow, then it's hello heat and hellooooo big, strong alphas with their sexy knots.

"Fucking hell," I mutter, distracting myself by setting up the new phone.

As soon as it's all ready to go, I message my dad and then fire off another message to my cousin asking her to ring me when she's got a minute. I'm going to have to come clean to her and hope that she won't go straight to my dad with this information.

Waiting for my dad to message back, I'm a bit surprised when he doesn't.

Ten minutes later, after I'd unpacked my few belongings, and when neither one has gotten back to me, I decide it's time for some breakfast. I've been up for hours, but felt a bit shy going downstairs and making myself some food while they were all still asleep. It seems a bit cheeky, but my stomach is growling so I head downstairs and run into Spencer in the kitchen.

My heart beats a little bit quicker when I see him staring into the open fridge, dressed only in joggers.

"Morning," I murmur.

"Hey," he says, turning to face me. "You hungry?"

"Yes," I say quickly. "I can make you something. What've you got in there?"

He steps back to show me a full fridge, but I quickly land on the carton of eggs. "Scrambled okay?"

"Definitely," he replies with a smile and sits at the kitchen island. "Any food someone else makes is my favourite."

"Oh, tell me about it. But I don't mind cooking. My mum taught me. Uhm, you get me the utensils, and I'll do the cooking," I add when I realise I have no clue where anything is kept.

"Deal," he says, standing up again and sorting me out

with a mixing bowl and whisk, a frying pan and wooden spoon, a knife for the butter and some plates.

He sits back down and watches me. I feel like he wants to say something and to be honest, I'm starting to feel a bit awkward, so I ask, "Something wrong?"

He shakes his head, his green eyes clouding over. "Actually, yes, there is."

I stop whisking, my hands going cold. I stare at the half-whisked eggs. "Have I done something wrong?"

"What?" he says. "No, no, it's not you. Rayne, look, there's something I need to tell you, don't say anything until I've finished, okay? James and I..." he barrels on, not giving me a chance to say anything. "...we saw you about three months ago, outside a doctor's office in the village of Lakesview. We watched you go into the chemist and caught a whiff of your scent and we fell for you like dumbfucks. Then Jones rang James to say he'd spotted Richard back in London, after he'd sent us up to Lakesview in the first bloody place, and we lost you. I mean, you left the chemist and drove off in your flashy black Porsche and that was that. We tried to find you, but man, you are one Hot Omega that is difficult to track down." He gives me a sassy smile, letting me know he knows my licence plate number. "We understand now. You're Halstead's daughter. It all makes sense why we couldn't find you. We were on our way back to Lakesview yesterday when I spotted you on the side of the road. When we turned around, you were already gone, but Will, he's a bit of a clever clogs on the sly, had the reg number of the A8, so Jones managed to track the car to Mick's address in Southall. Finding Richard there wasn't so much coincidence because we knew he was hanging out with the Jets. Fuck. Does this make any sense? Are you mad? We should've told you right away, but there kind of wasn't the right time and you were shaken up, understandably..." He trails off as I just stare at him.

What the fuck?

"Uhm," I say, scrunching up my face and pushing the eggs away. "What?"

"I know," he groans, dropping his head into his hands. "We were at that house for *you*, not Richard. We wanted to find you and explain to you what we felt and hoped that you would feel something too. Our ultimate goal was to ask you to mate with us. I'm sorry, Rayne. This is all so fucked up and getting to know these little slices of you the last day, has made me *need* to tell you this. Please don't be mad. Well, be mad. We fucked up. Big time, we know this and right now everything has gone to hell in a handbasket."

I lick my lips as he rambles on, not quite sure what to think. "What were you going to do if you'd found me in Lakesview?"

"Not abduct you, if that's what you're thinking. As much as we wanted you and were not prepared to give up on that dream, we would have given you a choice, obviously."

"You and James were there?"

He nods.

"Not William or Cameron?"

He shakes his head.

"So you two just decided?"

"James decided and I followed pretty quickly. If they'd

been there, they would've followed too. They have now. They want you. Shit. Fuck. I didn't mean..."

"Stop talking," I say, shaking my head. "This is... UGH!" I give him a furious glare and pick up the bowl of raw eggs. I march over to him and dump the contents over his head. "This is unbelievable!" I roar, trying not to laugh as he wipes eggs from his eyes.

"I know. I'm sorry."

Inside, I'm shaking, but not with anger. I'm not angry, not at all. I'm not scared that they're big stalkers, or psychotic lunatics.

No.

I'm relieved because now I *know* that this is fate.

There is absolutely no way on God's green earth that this story could be anything except destiny. It's too fucking crazy, too much of a coincidence.

But never let it be said that Rayne Halstead didn't enjoy a good grovel from some sexy alphas.

"You all owe me a fucking apology!" I thunder at him. "Come and find me when there are gifts to go along with the sincere words of remorse."

Fixing him with a death stare for a moment, I then stalk past him, still starving, but determined to make my point. I'm not a fucking pushover. I'm not going to just forgive them. While it's a little bit confusing and more than a coincidence that our lives got entangled in such a way, it doesn't change the fact that they kept this from me. I don't doubt that this has anything to do with my father and my abduction. But they did use it to their advantage. For that, there will be penance.

"Hopefully in the form of some food," I grumble as I storm up the stairs, hissing at Cameron as I pass him and scaring him half to death. I slam my bedroom door and wait for things to get apologetic around here.

"Bellends. Utter Bellends."

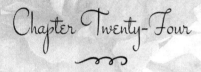

Chapter Twenty-Four

Cameron

Startled, and a little bit turned on, I shove the kitchen door open, a demand to know what's happening on my lips, but stop dead in my tracks at the sight in front of me.

I let out a loud laugh, which Spencer does not appreciate. He is over at the sink, cleaning his face and hair under the tap.

"Wow, you seriously pissed her off," I comment.

"No shit, Sherlock," he growls.

"What did you do?" I try to straighten my face, but it's difficult under the circumstances.

"I told her the truth." Spencer grabs a fresh tea towel out of the drawer and wipes his face with it.

I pause, my blood going slightly cooler. "You did what?"

He fixes me with a glare of epic proportions. "I told her

the truth. All of it. To say she is annoyed is a slight under-statement."

"What did she say?"

"Not much. It was me who had the verbal diarrhoea."

I make a fake retching noise, which he rolls his eyes at. "So what do we do now?"

"For starters, we need to tell James that she knows, and then find William and tell him. After that we owe her sincere apologies with gifts and I'm guessing food, seeing as she didn't get to finish making her breakfast." He gestures to the empty bowl of eggs.

I start to snicker again, but I'm saved from his wrath by William's voice.

I turn to the door, when he says, "I've got gifts covered."

He is so quiet for a large, burly man, I didn't even hear him come in.

Spencer comes closer when William holds up a flat-ish black velvet box about the size of a small box of chocolates.

"Oh?" I ask, trying to snatch it from him to see what it is.

He holds it up over his head where I've no chance of reaching it, being a good eight inches shorter than him.

"Fucker."

He glares at me. "Not for you. These are for Rayne."

"What are they?" Spencer asks slowly.

"Heat suppressant injections."

Silence descends.

"James was very clear about not getting them on the black market," Spencer starts carefully.

"I didn't."

"Then where?" I ask, curiosity getting the better of me.

"Let's just say, I owe my little sister a favour with which she is thinking over and will no doubt involve all of us."

"Willow got them?" I ask.

I don't know much about William and his family. He is quite close-lipped, but we know he is close with his younger sister.

He nods. "I asked her last night to make an appointment with the family doctor this morning. They've just been delivered."

"That was fast," I murmur.

"Rayne needs them. I wasn't leaving it to chance that they were still on the side of the road."

"You feel strongly about her suppressing her heat. Worried?" I add, without thinking, but not really meaning anything by it. I'm just being a dick.

He growls, drawing my full attention to him. "I feel strongly about her having a choice over her body."

"No, I get that," I murmur. "It's totally her choice."

"Humph," he mutters under his breath. "Gifts are covered."

"We need more," Spencer says. "I will make breakfast. Cam, dig through the pantry, see what you can find in the way of chocolates, and then maybe go cut some flowers from the garden. Then find James and fill him in."

"Yes, sir," I drawl, giving him a mock salute. He can be such a douche sometimes.

Giving me a fierce glare, he points emphatically to the empty bowl. I look at it again and start laughing.

135

"I wish I had been here to see it."

"You would've gotten off lightly. She knows you weren't there at the beginning."

I blink, taking that in. "Hmm." Perhaps William and I won't be in the firing line as much as Spence and James.

Turning from him and sobering up slightly as I open the huge walk-in pantry, I scan the shelves in the dim food cupboard. There is a small window high at the top of the wall, offering enough light to see, but not enough to ruin the food stored inside. Moving over to the big plastic tub on the middle shelf, I pop the lid off and root through. Coming up with a multi-pack of two-finger KitKats, I cry out in jubilation.

"Yes!" Who doesn't love a KitKat? Also, the whole 'have a break' aspect has a nice chill vibe to it.

I replace the lid on the tub and then grab some scissors from the drawer on my way out of the kitchen, ignoring Spencer as I go in search of some flowers. I've never been big on chocolatey/flowery gifts for women. Omegas especially. It seems too trite for the creatures with whom we are dependent on to appease our alpha needs and desires to mate and breed with. They are fascinating, gorgeous creatures and none more so than our curvy little brunette upstairs, who clearly, has a fiery temper and a sense of showmanship in how that is displayed.

Poor Spence.

I can't help but chuckle again, glad I wasn't on the receiving end of what will forever be known as the Humpty-Dumpty incident.

Leaving the KitKats on the coffee table, I open the

French Doors at the back of the TV room. I step out into the bright, summer morning and breathe in the scent of the flowers scattered in large tubs around the paved courtyard. Wondering what colour Rayne likes, I immediately search for some bluey grey flowers, but there aren't any, so I go with pink. I think she seems like a 'pink' girl. Pale pink, I bet. Bright pink is too garish.

I find some kind of flower, who the fuck knows what kind, and snip a few off, adding in some yellow at the last minute because yellow is a happy colour. No one can stay mad when confronted with sunny yellow flowers, right?

Deciding I'm right, with no one here to challenge me, I bunch them together and then grab my phone out of the back pocket of my joggers and frown at it.

"Phil?" I ask, when I answer. "What's up?"

"There is a very large man here who is inquiring about your friend," Doctor Philip Walstow clips out dryly.

"Oh? What does he look like?"

"Tall, menacing, scar on his forehead..."

"That's just Jones. Hand Richard over."

"I would, but as I've informed your friend, he isn't here. He left early this morning."

My face falling into a frown, I shut the French Doors behind me and cross over to the coffee table. "Uhm, what do you mean left?"

"Left. Walked out. Disappeared. I can't be clearer," Phil snaps.

"Weren't you supposed to be watching him?"

"I gave him enough painkillers to knock out a small elephant. How the hell was I supposed to know he had the constitution of a massive bull? Besides, I'm not his keeper, and if you think I'm getting into a punch-up with him, you obviously don't remember Harrow that well." His huffy tone makes me smile, but I bite my lip so I don't laugh.

"I see. Put Jones on."

"Cam?"

"You might as well come home. Phil doesn't have him."

"Fine."

"Cameron," Phil barks at me again. "This is the last time. I could lose my license over this. He was *shot*."

"I know, I know. I'm sorry. Thank you for all your help. You won't see me in your doorway again."

"I'd better not," he growls, but then adds, "Don't forget it's Maisie's birthday next month. We've got that barbecue planned."

"I'll be there."

"See you then."

"Bye, Phil."

We hang up and I sigh. This is going to send James into more of a strop than Spencer telling Rayne about their obsession. This day is going to get worse before it gets better.

I snatch up the KitKats and then fumble around in the junk drawer for some Sellotape. I wrap it around the stems of the flowers, taping them to the chocolate biscuits and then throw the roll back in the drawer.

Making my way to James's office, assuming that's where he is, I knock and wait for him to call out.

"Yeah?"

I hesitate.

His tone is pissed off. Why me? Why do I have to be the one to tell him his brother is gone?

With a sigh, I push the door open and see James slumped over his desk, his hand in his hair, a look on his face that is a cross between scared shitless and excited at the same time.

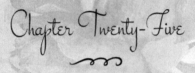

Chapter Twenty-Five

James

"We have a bit of a problem," I say, glancing up at Cameron, who also appears to have a bit of a problem. "What did you do?" I eye up the KitKats and flowers with a dubious expression.

"Me? Nothing," he replies, but then glances down at the offerings in his hand. "These aren't for you. These are for Rayne. Your idiot brother blurted out the truth to her and she's a bit pissed if the eggs are anything to go by."

"Huh?" I'm more confused now than ever. "Eggs?"

He waves his hand dismissively. "Truth was told. Rayne is pissed, and on top of that Phil called. Richard is missing."

"What?" I thunder, taking that last bit in and processing fully. Standing up, my chair rolls back several feet and hits the wall behind me. "Missing? How? When?"

"I'm guessing he walked out the door, and since early this morning."

"Fuck!" I bunch my fists and shake them at nothing, before I kick out at the same nothing. It's only then that the rest of what he said crashes down over me. "Spencer told Rayne we were looking for her?"

"Apparently. She's expecting gifts, apologies, food..."

"Double fuck!" This time I aim for the wastepaper basket and kick it over to the other side of the room.

"What's got you so wound up?"

"Get the others. We need a pack meeting."

"Here," Spencer says, hovering in the doorway behind me with William towering over him. "Guess you know."

I fix him with a withering glare. "You just told her, with no warning?"

"How was I meant to warn her? Besides, I feel guilty. She's lovely, and we shouldn't be leaving this bit of information out no matter how it might hurt us."

"I know," I grit out. "But I was hoping I could be there to tell her together. Now she probably thinks you're the hero, and I'm the wazzock who didn't come clean."

"She definitely doesn't think he's a hero," Cam snorts with laughter.

Spencer's face goes dark, but he doesn't say anything.

"Anyway," Cam says in between bouts of laughter. "William has just the thing to appease her anger enough for her to hopefully forgive us for being stalkery dicks. Well, you two mostly."

"Yeah, I know," I mutter. William came to me a little while ago after the injections arrived. We are going to owe Willow *big*. "Listen up, the Richard thing and the Rayne thing aside, we have a small dilemma."

"What's that?" Spencer asks.

"I received an email this morning from Jeremey Halstead. Apparently, his daughter has declared she is actively looking for a pack and he has decided we would be a good match for her."

I let that sink in and watch their surprised faces turn jubilant.

And then I ruin it.

"We obviously can't accept that offer. Not just yet, anyway. I mean, what are we going to do, meet with him and lie to his face, knowing his precious Rayne is locked away in our mansion? Or worse, tell him where she is? Yeah, big fat nope to both." I sigh and sit down again, only to land on my arse because my chair had rolled away.

"Fuck," I mutter as Spencer leans over my desk to see where I went, chortling away to himself.

"Jesus," he says. "What the fuck?"

"I know." I haul myself to my feet and snatch my chair back from the wall. I sit my arse firmly down this time and lean my elbows on my desk.

Spencer parks his butt on the edge of my desk. "So what are we going to do?"

"There is only one thing to do. We have to convince Rayne to go to her dad and tell her we are the pack for her. Assuming she's amenable, of course."

"What about Richard?" Cam asks.

Will, as usual, is silent, just listening until he has something to add.

"We go back to searching for him." The thought weighs heavily on me. I had him and, in a temper, I lost him again. Fucking bollocking nutsack. This day belongs in the pits of hell.

"Or we do what I said in the first place..."

I glance up and search Cam's eyes. "Use Rayne to lure him to us. She's not a tie. She deserves better than that."

"Yes, she does, but she also wants him. Is it so bad to give her what she wants, while getting what you want in the process? Plus, if he is part of this pack, she is more likely to agree to stay."

I hate to admit that he's right, but he is. "He bit her," I say quietly, still sore over that knowledge, but trying not to let it get to me. "He possesses her, and she feels it. I don't want to abuse what she feels for him. It feels wrong." I know I'm being a sap, but I see her eyes light up when she talks about him. I've seen her concern for him. In her eyes, he is her saviour. I make a decision. "Okay, somehow, we will use her to tie Richard to our pack again, but we are doing it for her. Not us. I would find another way if she wasn't here. I'm stating that for the record. Clear?"

"Crystal," Spencer says and stands up. "First things first, she is waiting for us to do some grovelling and also, we need to get those injections to her now. So, can we go? Brekkie is getting cold."

"Yeah," I say standing up and making another decision. I'm going to tell Rayne about her father's email and feel her out. I want to see her first reaction to her father's offer.

"We could just let her go back to her family," Cameron says. "And wait to see if she comes back."

I shake my head. "We can't risk someone following her back to her family home that is meant to be kept quiet. We would never forgive ourselves if something happened to her, or her family. As much as this looks like we have her locked away, we are protecting her, just like Richard asked. And for ourselves as well."

"Yeah, I know," he mutters.

Filing out of my office and heading for the stairs, where Spencer has left a tray of food, we head on up, quietly contemplating how the next few minutes are going to go.

I sincerely hope she isn't too pissed off about the deception, but honestly, who could blame her if she is?

Chapter Twenty-Six

Richard

I sit across from Jeremy Halstead in his big, fancy office in the Parliament buildings. We travelled here in relative silence after he introduced himself, so I have no idea why I'm here or how he tracked me down. Two things I intend to find out as soon as he looks up from his laptop.

I mean, leave a guy hanging, why don't you. Jesus. Like this day isn't shit enough. My side is hurting, my head is pounding, I'm hungry, but don't think I can eat, and my mouth is as dry as a camel's left bollock. Glaring out of the huge window of the fourth-floor office, I see the bright blue sky and wish I was stumbling my way back to Croydon so I could collapse and sleep for a week.

"So," Halstead says, finally looking up and closing his laptop. "You want to know why you're here."

It's a statement, so I don't bother replying.

"Two reasons. I know you are estranged from your family pack and that you've gotten involved with some shady characters over the last few years."

He glares at me, but I remain quiet. I don't know what any of this has got to do with him. If he's expecting an apology, he can get knotted.

"You show no remorse?"

I shrug.

He shakes his head. "Very well. I asked you here today to discuss a deal with you. I want Mick Savoy. I want him behind bars so badly, I will do almost anything to get him. Do you understand?"

"What's this got to do with me?"

"I know you've been running with him. I have you on CCTV from a few months ago. Then you all disappear and voila, a few months later, here you are, getting into illegal gang activity and getting yourself shot."

I groan inwardly. Doctor Mayfair. That bastard.

"I'm willing to look past it all if you help me get Savoy and his crew."

Blinking, I let that sink in. "How? I burned that bridge yesterday." I stop talking abruptly, suspiciously, but there is no way I can tell him why, or how. He will have me thrown in jail and the key will magically disappear.

His eyes, the same colour as Rayne's I note with a pang in my heart, narrow. "Oh? You are no longer associated with the Jets?"

"I never was, just to be transparent. But no, we got into a dust up and well, you know..."

"No, I don't know. How about you enlighten me."

Again, it's a statement. This guy seriously does not take his job lightly. He knows his sway; he knows one word from him and I'm a goner.

"I realised they are a bunch of pricks. End of story." I shift uncomfortably, wishing I was anywhere but here.

"Hmm, tough. You need to go back. Immunity for *your* crimes if you help me get him."

Okay, that gives me pause.

Big, fat, juicy pause.

I could stop hiding. I could just go about my life without having to worry about my past catching up with me, I could go to Rayne...

No, I can never go to Rayne. Her father would see me dead before he ever let his girl be with a loser like me.

"Immunity?" I ask to bide my time enough to shove Rayne from my thoughts.

Halstead nods and sits back in his chair. "While you think that over, let's talk about reason number two, seeing as I have you here."

"What's that?" I croak out. I feel it's not going to be good.

"Your pack, well *ex*-pack, I suppose it is."

"What about them?"

"Why did you leave?"

"That's not really any of your business," I point out, wishing I could get up and leave. But the carrot he's dangled is still there, swinging in the wind. I would be a fool to walk away from it.

"It is when I'm considering the St. Stevens pack for my daughter."

His words make my blood run cold. "Oh?" I practically whimper with the pain that has caused me. Even more than the wound on my side.

"Let me put it bluntly. I want to know if you ever intend to go back to them, because if that is part of your plans, then I can rule out the pack as a contender."

"Ouch," I mutter, feeling that punch of words right in my heart. "But you don't have to worry. I won't ever go back there. Your precious daughter will be safe from me, and my criminal ways." Every single word of that sentence squeezes tighter on my lungs until I can barely breathe.

"Good. Good. I will hold you to that. In case you hadn't gathered, your immunity is contingent on both of these things we have discussed here today. You need to decide now before you leave these offices, and potentially disappear again.

"I don't need to think about it," I say, knowing I'm making the right decision. Rayne is better off without me, and with the alphas who can treat her the way she deserves. "You have a deal."

Halstead nods, smug and jovial. "Glad to hear it. You can go next door and sign the contract Lisa has drawn up. Know that if you break the terms..." He makes a slashing motion at his throat.

Every cell in my body knows he means that in the literal sense.

I stand up, my legs shaking and turn to the door. As I reach for the handle, I say quietly, "Your daughter will be cherished by them. You couldn't find a more loyal, loving pack. I hope you endorse them. They are worth it."

He doesn't say anything as I leave with my heart smashed into a million pieces.

It's nothing less than I deserve, but part of me is glad I came here today.

Now I know it's truly over between me and Rayne, before it even really started.

Chapter Twenty-Seven

Rayne

Bewildered by the events that occurred in the kitchen earlier, I'm starting to feel warm. Too warm. I cross over to the window and open it, fastening the lock and then staring out over the road. The cool breeze drifts through the gap, lifting the tendrils of hair away from my hot forehead. I stayed away from the window last night, hiding under the duvet, despite the warmth. But now the arseholes are gone, I want to see where I am. There are rows of gorgeous multi-million-pound houses across the small green square in the middle of the red-bricked road. Summer is in full swing, with blue skies and a bright, hot sun. Taking the opportunity to take a cool shower and change, I disappear into the en-suite and strip off. Stepping under the rainfall of luke-warm water, I sigh in bliss as the soft splats hit my sensitive skin, cooling it down.

"That's better."

I know why I'm feeling so off. The lack of heat suppressant injections over the last two days is taking its toll. My heat is bursting to come out.

Squeezing my eyes tightly shut and trying not to think about it too much, I clean up, enjoying the water running through my hair as I wash it.

Several minutes later, I turn off the water and reach for a couple of towels. I wrap one around my hair and then another around my body. I dry off and slip back into my bedroom, heading straight for the dresser to pull out some underwear, a fresh bra, some white shorts and a tight white t-shirt.

I towel dry my hair and brush it out, cursing that I didn't bring my blow-dryer. I figured I'd just use Morgan's. Speaking of Morgan, I reach for my phone to check if she messaged.

I groan when I see a missed call from her while I was in the shower. "Typical!" I exclaim and immediately ring her back.

"Engaged? For fuck's sake!"

In a huff, I throw the phone on my sumptuous, white king-sized bed and get dressed, not too soon as there is a knock at the door.

My heart jumps. I wasn't really ready to face the alphas yet. I'm still trying to process this information. I mean, it's not *bad*. They didn't snatch me off the street. They were just looking for me. It makes sense they couldn't find me if my dad is so protected. I understand why it took them so long after that day. To be honest, if they hadn't come looking for me the other day, they would never have seen me on the side of the road. They wouldn't have been there to see the Audi and I'd probably be mated to a super-pack of loose alphas right about now. I shudder, the chill skittering over my skin.

"Rayne? Are you in there?" James's voice comes through the door.

"Yes," I say determinedly. They saved me as much as Richard did.

I hover in the middle of the room like a fart in a soggy box as the St. Stevens alphas file into my room.

"Food, gifts and sincere apologies," James says, a sheepish expression on his handsome face.

"Food first," I snap, not really that mad, but not wanting to let them off that easily. It's still a bit creepy regardless of them ultimately being there to rescue me.

Spencer places a tray with all the fixings of a Continental breakfast on the bed. I can't help the snicker. "Run out of eggs?" I ask archly.

He snorts, fortunately amused and not angry with me for dumping several raw eggs on his head. "Let's just say I'm traumatised."

The giggle that bursts out of my mouth downplays the seriousness of this situation, but I couldn't help it. After a few seconds, I clear my throat and cross my arms. "Right, boys. I've heard Spencer's side of this. Cameron and William, tell me about the day you saw me." I slide my gaze over to the breakfast tray and my stomach growls. I ignore it for one more minute while the two confused alphas exchange a glance.

"That was yesterday," Cameron says, clutching a cute, colourful bouquet of flowers taped to a multi-pack of KitKats.

"Was it now?" I tap my foot.

"Yes," William says in that too-quiet tone that I know he reserves for me. He doesn't want to frighten me and it's a bit too sweet. It makes me less mad when I want to be mad. Yes, I know that things could be taken in a stalkerish way, but I don't really get that impression. They saw me, fancied me and tried to find me. The thing I have the problem with is that they waited to tell me, when this could have come out at yesterday's little pack meeting. Not to mention Spencer just blurting it out, which makes me feel they were still trying to hide it.

"Hmm... James?" I drop my arms and lean over to grab a blueberry muffin from the tray. I bite the top off it and chew, suddenly overly aware of the sexual tension that just went up a few notches. I drop it back down on the tray.

My scent.

Spencer called me Blueberry-muffins yesterday on the stairs. Did they have these in waiting for me or to remind them of me?

"What Spencer told you is true. I may have made a declaration about wanting you as our omega, but I wasn't going to force you into it. We wanted to find you, court you and make an offer to your father..."

I choke on a bit of muffin. "Offer?" I scrunch up my nose.

"We do things right here, Rayne," he says, just this side of insulted. "Of course we would seek your father's approval."

I nod, taking that in. That's interesting and good to know. I'm glad he added that bit in. Perhaps, I should come clean myself about what I told Daddy. Trust is a two-way street after all.

"About my father. When I spoke to him yesterday, I told him I was formally declaring that I was actively seeking a pack. Perhaps, if you are serious about me and about becoming my mate, then you should get in touch with him. Plus, it will make it easier not to have to lie to him anymore." I throw that test out there and like what I see.

James nods enthusiastically. "If you are on board with that, then we are more than interested, and in the spirit of this frank discussion, I should tell you that your father emailed me this morning to discuss this very thing."

I swallow, a bit caught off guard by that. "He did?"

"He did."

Well, he did say he was going to have a think about it. I didn't know he was going to jump straight onto his emails and start contacting packs he thought might be suitable. However, it's a good thing he contacted the St. Stevens pack. Things are aligning as I feel they should be. All we need now is Richard here and all will be right. We can make our announcement to court and then move ahead with the mating.

"Is that okay with you?" James asks, slowly, carefully, anticipating my answer in case it's not what he wants to hear.

"We've gotten off topic a bit," I point out. "I'm going to need more grovelling for failing to tell me that you already knew who I was."

"In all honesty," Spencer says. "We didn't *know* who you were. We saw you and fell like idiots for you. We had no idea who you were. If we had, we'd have been able to find you a lot sooner and a lot easier."

Okay, that makes sense, but one last thing... "What if you discover I'm horrible and you don't want me after all. What then?"

"What if you discover *we* are horrible, and you don't want us?" Cameron counters.

"You first." I cross my arms again.

James drops to his knees, startling me. The rest of his pack follows. "Even if you are the biggest bitch known to man — which I highly doubt having interacted with you these last couple of days — we still want you," James says quietly. "Deep in our souls, we know you are our mate. Your scent affects us in ways that we can't even explain, you being here has made our pack feel complete. Well, almost." His eyes meet mine and I know what he means.

"You calm me," Spencer says, shifting my gaze to him. "Before you came here, I was a loose cannon. Always looking for a fight. Now," he shrugs. "I've never been so chilled and happy before. It's all down to you because you belong here with me, with us. Christ, William actually speaks in full sentences since you arrived, if that's anything to go by, you know how he feels too."

I press my lips together and glance at William. "Do you feel what they feel?" I ask quietly.

His dark eyes meet mine and I see straight into his soul. "Yes."

"And you?" I ask Cameron, focusing on the hazel eyes of the cute little pack puppy.

"I didn't at first. I was attracted to you, obviously, I mean, look at you, and your scent definitely drew me in, but it wasn't until this morning when you hissed at me, did I feel connected to you in the way that everyone else does. I think that's *my* issue, though. It's nothing to do with you."

"Famous last words," I mutter.

"No, really," he stammers.

"What he's trying to say is he was scared," James says with a soft smirk.

"Hey," Cameron spits out. "That's rude."

"But accurate."

"Fine," he huffs. "Might as well lay it all out there."

"Scared of what?" I ask.

"Being hurt."

His open answer makes me feel all sorts of things for him, especially all the warm and fuzzy things.

"Stand up, all of you."

They do as I say and Cameron hands me the chocolates and flowers. I take them from him with a smile.

"I think we've come to a deal," I say, sniffing the flowers gently.

"Wait!" Cameron exclaims. "Will has something for you!"

"More gifts?" I ask in surprise.

William steps forward, holding out a black velvet box. "I think this one will show you what you mean to us."

I take it suspiciously, lowering the flowers to the bed. It looks like jewellery. I'm not sure what to make of that.

But I lift the lid carefully and stare at the contents for a brief moment. "Holy shit," I mutter. "How?"

"Not the black market, so you are safe," Cameron pipes up.

"My sister got them all above board from our family doctor this morning," William says.

I meet his gaze. "Wow," I say, shocked and touched. "Wow." Tears spring into my eyes. There is nothing better they could've done for me, apart from taking me home and I know that's not possible right now. "Thank you. Thank your sister for me. I know that mustn't have been easy for her." I take one out and place the box carefully on the bed. Without waiting for them to leave, I rip the cap off with my teeth and lift my t-shirt. Squeezing my flesh together, I jab myself, injecting the suppressant into me, relief making me light-headed.

"We'll leave you to eat and rest," James murmurs and they back out just as William's phone rings. He takes the call quietly, disappearing down the hall and James closes the door.

"Well," I say, picking up my discarded muffin and shoving it into my mouth with less grace than my mum would care for. I take the velvet box and place it carefully in the bathroom, throwing the needle in the bin, remembering to ask them for a sharps box at some point, but now seems a bit ungrateful. I pick the bin up and take it into the bedroom, putting it up high on a shelf in the wardrobe out of everyone's way.

"I'm impressed pack St. Stevens. Very impressed indeed."

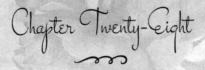

Chapter Twenty-Eight

William

"Willow," I say quietly into the phone as I head downstairs, relieved things worked out with Rayne. "Everything okay?"

"Yep. That guy you told me about yesterday. He's here."

I frown. "What?"

"Richard St. Stevens," she hisses quietly. "He's in with Lisa right now signing a contract of some kind."

"What is he doing there?"

"I dunno. He just had a meeting with Halstead. The bullpen is taking bets on what it was about."

"Huh," I murmur. "Can you keep him there?"

I pass Jones in the entrance hall and gesture for him to give me the keys he is about to place down on the side table.

"These are for the Merc," he whispers.

"Doesn't matter," I whisper back and take them, heading out of the door without mentioning anything to anyone. I don't want to get James's hopes up.

"How?" Willow asks. I hear her shuffling around. She works as an MP aide while she gains enough experience to run a campaign to get her elected. When I spoke to her last night, I told her about Richard and James's idea that he wants to re-integrate him into the pack and my concerns about the balance of it. I never expected her to take his name and remember it to the point where she's now calling me with this information. We are close. Very close. We only had each other growing up, with our parents too busy with their careers and pack life to notice us much. I will be the exact opposite when I become a parent, and I know Willow will too.

"I don't know, stall him somehow, I'm on my way." I squash myself into the Merc, regretting the choice, but just needing to move.

"How long till you get here?" she whispers.

"I'll try for ten minutes." Placing the phone in the holder, I switch it to speaker. "Follow him if you have to. Stay on the phone."

I fire up the engine and set off, immediately stalling it. The pedals are too close together for my big feet. "Fuck's sake," I mutter and try again.

Lurching off through the square, I head in the direction of Westminster. Cursing the traffic, I switch the Satnav on and get a faster route out of Chelsea.

"He's leaving," Willow says a few minutes later.

"Follow him."

"He'll see me!"

"He doesn't even know who you are."

"I can't just leave."

"Go!" I roar at her. I am *not* losing the one other thing that Rayne wants. I may be concerned about how things will work once he re-joins the pack, but I know she needs him. That's all that matters.

"Okay, okay," Willow grumbles and I wait as she shuffles about and then says, "He's going down the lift."

"Take the stairs, then." I let out a noise of exasperation, but it's not aimed at Willow. I'm just eager to get to Richard and bring him back to the pack and to Rayne.

I hear her panting as she races down the four flights of stairs. "I..see..him..." she rasps, "He's going outside."

"Stick with him. I'll be a few minutes yet."

Her breathing slows down and I hear outside noises.

"Which way are you going?"

"We came left out of Parliament."

"Okay," I murmur. That's good. That means they are going with the flow of traffic.

A couple of minutes later, I see my sister's bright blue dress, the one with the big pink flowers on it that I got her for her last birthday. "I'm right behind you. You can go now. Thanks, Willow. You're amazing as always."

"Ooh, compliments from the taciturn arsehole. Noice."

"Fuck off," I say gruffly.

She laughs and hangs up.

I push the button to slide the passenger window down and slow to a roll next to the scruffy looking man with the beat-up face. It has to be Richard.

Flicking the hazard lights on, I call out, "Richard?"

He turns his head to me, his eyes telling me he's pissed off. "Oh, fuck off. I'm not getting into any more cars today or ever."

Well, I don't know what I was expecting, but his attitude is as rough as he currently looks.

"My name's William St. Stevens. Will you get in now?"

He pauses and peers in the open window. I press the brake, coming to a stop by the curb.

"You're part of his pack," he sneers. "He couldn't even be bothered coming to find me himself."

"Actually, I'm here for Rayne. She wants to see you. Will you get in?"

That hits him right where it hurts. The flash of pain in his eyes is palpable. He straightens up and starts walking again. "Not interested," he growls.

I set off again at a crawl. "Richard."

"I said fuck off," he snaps. "I'm not interested in going back to the pack."

"Forget about the pack," I say patiently, ignoring his repeated attempts to get rid of me. I'm as stubborn as a mule, and I'm not going anywhere. "Come back for Rayne."

I watch as his face scrunches up. "No. I can't. Leave me alone."

"She needs you. She needs to see for herself that you're okay. Five minutes and then you can leave."

"Do you think I'm fucking stupid? As soon as I get there, James will tie me up and keep me."

"Is that so bad when Rayne wants you there?"

"She's still with you."

His flat statement belies the torment on his battered face.

"She is still in danger. She is safe with us. You know that."

"I can't go there."

"Not even for her?"

"Especially not for her."

"You're being a selfish dick," I comment, trying to rile him up enough to justify my next action.

His furious gaze pins mine as he bends down again to glare at me. "And what do you know about it?"

"I know that I've asked you to come back for Rayne and you won't. You bit her, and she is feeling your absence. Now, I've tried to be nice about this, but this is how it's going to go down. You are going to get in this car under your own steam, or I'm going to pull up, and stuff you into the boot."

"Please," he scoffs.

"Have you seen the size of me?"

That gives him pause. He stops and glares at me again. I stop the car. "The boot is tiny, but I will make you fit if it kills me."

"You're a fucking bellend, you know that, mate."

"Takes one to know one."

"Jesus, does nothing faze you?"

"Not this. Rayne wants you, if you think I'm letting you go, you have another thing coming. I promise you, I will make James let you go if that's what you want, but you are coming back with me one way or the other."

His anger turns to desperation. "I'm no good for her. She should forget all about me."

"She can't while she has your bite."

"Fuck," he growls. "Fuck." He looks back over his shoulder, as if he's expecting someone to be there. He leans down again and looks through the open window. "You don't understand, I really can't go."

"Right," I say, undoing my seatbelt and opening the car door. "You leave me no choice."

I march around to the boot and open it, then I storm over and grab the alpha who is darting away, but is slow and injured and easy to snatch.

"Last chance to get in by yourself."

He closes his eyes and breathes in deeply. I know he can smell her faint scent on me from being in her room and in her car.

"Jesus," he moans and yanks himself out of my grip. He opens the car door and slides inside, slumping down as he slams the door closed.

Hastily, I make my way back around, closing the boot and then stuffing my huge frame back into the car.

"You promise me I can go as soon as I've seen her?" he asks quietly.

"James won't make you stay if you are so adamant to leave."

He nods absently and stares out of the window.

I set off and make my way back in the direction of Chelsea, neither of us saying a word, until we pull up outside the pack house.

Richard just sits there.

"Come in and clean up before you see her," I suggest. "You're a bit of a mess. You can use my room." We gave away the only guest room to Rayne, so if he does change his mind and decide to stay, fuck knows where he's going to sleep.

"Thanks," he mutters and with a woeful sigh, he gets out of the car and slopes up the steps. I follow him, hoping that I've made the right decision in bringing him here. Not for Rayne, that's a given, but for our pack.

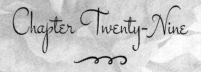

Chapter Twenty-Nine

Rayne

After finally talking to my cousin and explaining the situation as best I could, with her promises not to tell her dad or mine, I close up the dishwasher. Bending down to see which buttons to push to set it running, I hear the kitchen door open. Inhaling the fresh pinecone scent of James, I smile.

"I've finished cleaning up in here. Give me a few minutes to nip to the loo and then I'll make lunch for everyone."

"Rayne."

The gruff voice freezes my body, only my heart is beating faster and faster. Not daring to believe he is finally here, I turn around, half expecting James to have developed a rougher tone.

"Richard," I breathe out when I see his poor battered

face, but all nice and cleaned up, fresh from the shower it seems, going off his damp hair.

I rush forward when he stays in the doorway, but then remembering his preference, I skid to a stop and just look up at him with a smile, hugging him with my eyes, if that's even a thing.

It must be, because his tormented face collapses into a smile and he opens his arms carefully before crushing me to him with a pained grunt.

"You're here, safe and perfect," he murmurs, tangling his fingers into my hair.

I wrap my arms around him, clinging to him as I inhale deeply, filling my lungs with his scent. I notice it's just slightly different to James's. More earthy and feral. I shiver as the lust descends on me, causing me to produce a fair amount of slick, that he responds to with a low growl. I let go of the purr that is vibrating in my throat. Running my hands up his chest, I gaze into his deep blue eyes. My lips part, but then he pulls back, making me stumble awkwardly forward.

"How are you?" I ask lamely, trying to cover up the hurt of his rejection. It shouldn't pain me, knowing what I know about him, but it does.

"I've been better," he mutters.

"Same," I murmur, even though he didn't ask.

"Are you okay?" His earnest expression relieves some of the tension that has been building.

I shrug. "Yep. I mean, I wish I could go home, but the whole thing with my dad...Did James fill you in?"

He nods slowly. "About your dad...look, Rayne. I can't

stay. I came here to let you know I'm okay and to see with my own eyes that you are, but now I have to go."

I rear back as if I've been slapped. I don't know what I was expecting, but outright rejection wasn't it. Not after everything that happened, not after the *bite*.

"Why?" I ask, my voice breaking.

He sighs and runs a hand through his hair. "Your dad knows who I am. He's told me in no uncertain terms to not go anywhere near this pack, or you. Seems he's picked them out to be your mates, and that's good. They will treat you like a princess. But not me. I've got to go."

He takes a step back, as if he is actually about to walk out of my life. It fires up the panic that was bubbling under the surface ever since he walked in here. I knew something was off.

"No!" I snap, grabbing his arm. "You can't leave me."

"I don't have a choice," he says desperately. "You will be ripped away from this pack if your father finds out I'm here. I won't do that to you. I need to leave you where I know you will be looked after. Please understand, Rayne. I have no choice."

"There is always a choice," I spit out and shove past him. "I'm going to ring my dad right now and tell him he can get knotted. He can't do this. He has no right."

"Wait!" Richard calls out, following me down the hallway and up the stairs when I keep going. "You can't say anything to him. Rayne, if he knows I'm here, he is going to throw me in jail. It was all part of a deal. You can't tell him."

"What?" My heart is hammering against my ribs. "Jail?"

"Jail. He knows about my ties to Mick and the others. He has offered me immunity if I help bring them down and stay away from this pack. He doesn't want me anywhere near you."

The bitterness in his tone, breaks my heart. But there is no way Daddy is getting away with this.

Shaking my head, trying not to cry, I march over to my bed and bend over, scooping up my phone.

"Rayne, stop." Richard's deep voice resonates behind me. I feel his body pressed up against mine.

My breath hitches.

I straighten up, clutching the phone. Turning around, his chest comes into view, and I tilt my head back to look him in the face.

"Richard," I purr again, his closeness driving the omega inside me to the point where I'm about to pounce on him.

He reaches out and cups my face, a look of sheer amazement on his. His fingers tangle in my hair and he tugs gently before he drops his mouth to mine.

I drop the phone on the floor and fist my hands in his black t-shirt, wanting to claw it off him so I can touch his skin. His kiss bruises me, tearing at the wounds on his lips to bleed again. I taste it when I flick my tongue out and let out a soft purr which makes him growl into my mouth as his tongue twists around mine in a kiss so deep, so full of emotion, I want to cry and cling to him forever.

His hands reach for the hem of my t-shirt, and he pulls it up. We break apart long enough for him to yank it over my head. His eyes drop to my breasts, encased in a lacy bra.

"Are you sure you want to do this?" I ask in a small voice, knowing his concerns about touching and sex.

"I have never been more sure of anything in my life," he replies before he kisses me again, drawing in my scent at the same time so he sucks the breath out of me. I pant, gasping for air as his mouth devours mine. I tentatively reach for the button on his sexy black jeans and flick it open, ready to stop the second he tells me to.

But he doesn't.

He removes his own t-shirt instead.

I take in his hard, tanned body and mewl like a kitten, kissing his chest and sliding my tongue over the rough flesh.

Skating my fingers over the side where he got hurt, I slide down the zip on his jeans and then shove them down to expose his hardening cock.

"Christ," he murmurs when I pull away. "I never knew it could feel like this. Rayne..."

I drop to my knees in front of him and take his weighty cock in my hand. I let out a moan of pure, unadulterated lust when I see his reverse Prince Albert piercing.

"Oh, fuck," I gasp and close my mouth over his tip.

He groans, shoving his hand forcefully into my hair.

I suck him off, wrapping my tongue around his shaft, unable to resist the urge to flick the ring piercing his cock. My deep "mmm" sound makes him groan and gently pulse his hips. I let him fuck my mouth, knowing he won't be rough with me. I run my tongue up and down his length and over the tip, enjoying this immensely.

So is he, if the noises he's making are anything to go by.

"Fuck, Rayne."

Suddenly, he withdraws his cock from my mouth and pulls me gently to my feet. "If you keep that up, I'll come in your mouth and that will be such a waste."

"Fuck, yeah, it will," I murmur, trying for a sassy smile, but I think it came off more sad than anything else. I don't really understand what's going on here. He pushes me away, tells me my dad is going to throw him in jail if he's caught near me and then he kisses me. I want to question him, but I'm scared he will stop what he's doing. I don't want that. If he is truly going to leave and never come back, I want this time with him. I *need* it.

He brings my wrist to his mouth. He places his lips over the bite he gave me and kisses it gently. "This makes you mine," he growls softly.

"It could be so much more."

To my surprise, he whimpers, his eyes closed. He lowers me to the bed, shaking his head. He leans over with a grunt, and quickly undoes my shorts, pulling them down my legs and dropping them on the floor. He does the same with my g-string, leaving me only in my bra.

He drags me gently down the bed until his cock is in line with my pussy. With a wicked smile, he takes his cock in his hand and rubs the pierced tip over my clit.

I arch my back and cry out as the pleasure that built up during our kiss and after, shoots straight to my pussy. I gush slick, soaking his cock when he drives it inside me, a wild growl on his lips.

"Rayne."

He pounds into me, slamming his cock in and out of my drenched pussy, bringing my climax closer and closer.

It hits me suddenly, fiercely, like a bolt out of the blue. Fireworks explode around me as I climax intensely, clutching his cock possessively, never wanting to let him go.

"Fuck, Rayne," he groans. "This is..." He chokes back a whimper.

Coming down from my orgasm, I look up at him and

see spots of blood welling up under his bandage. He is overexerting himself and is going to end up in worse shape than he already is.

I wiggle away from him and sit up. Reaching behind to unclip my bra, my heavy breasts tumble free, drawing him to me instantly.

"You are so beautiful. The way I feel about you..."

"Ssh," I murmur and push him gently back to the bed.

I climb on top of him and treat myself to some more pleasure from the Prince Albert. Trembling with my need, I slip him inside me and ride him slowly, lovingly, showing him what making love is like. He has only ever fucked out of a primal need. Never for desire. He has no idea how amazing, how beautiful, how *right* it can be.

Rotating my hips slowly, he grasps them. He lets out a soft groan as I bring him to the brink of the best orgasm he will ever have had.

I know it.

He knows it.

And he doesn't disappoint me.

Digging his fingers into my hips, he starts to thrust quickly, deeply, filling me up in ways that no alpha has ever managed to do before. He has taken over my soul and I know that there is no way I can let him go after this.

It's what I was afraid of, but now I don't care. No one is going to stop me from claiming him.

He grunts loudly and with one long, hard thrust, he detonates inside me, mingling his cum with my slick to form a delicious nectar that I want to lick off his cock.

"Rayne," he pants. "Fuck, Rayne." He gathers me to

him, pulling me down onto his chest, his cock still buried deep inside me. "Don't move. Let me savour this."

I kiss his chest and rest my cheek over his hammering heart.

For the longest time, we lay wrapped around each other, until I hear his breathing go heavy.

He's fallen asleep.

I look up and gently disentangle myself from his embrace, feeling his cock slide out of me and mourning its loss.

Creeping off the bed quietly, I snatch up my phone from the floor and slip into the bathroom.

There is no way my father is taking this away from me.

I ring him, but it goes straight to voicemail.

Grimacing, I don't bother leaving a message. This is a conversation we need to have in person. Well, as 'in person' as we can get.

I quietly climb back into bed. Richard turns towards me in his sleep and wraps his arms around me. I lay back with a smile and close my eyes.

This is perfect, and I will not lose it or him.

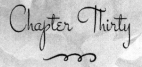

Chapter Thirty

James

"So, you're just going to sleep with her and then leave?" I ask Richard, who I've caught just about to sneak out of the front door.

I'd been waiting for it, if I'm honest.

When William told me he was here, I threw some clothes at him and told him to go and see Rayne.

I expected them to fall into bed, it was pretty much a given over everything I've seen from her in the last few days, but this is just typical Richard.

"Fuck off," he growls, not even turning back to face me. "You don't know anything."

"I know you're a selfish dicksplash that is going to leave her heartbroken."

He spins around, anger etched into his face. "She knows I can't stay."

"Then why get in so deep with her?" I'm furious now.

I'm really starting to care for the omega upstairs and he is treating her like dirt. It enrages me to the point where I have to cross my arms to stop myself from kicking his arse.

"Leave it alone, Jay," he snarls. "She knows my reasons. Don't try to stop me and don't try to find me."

"You're such a fucking wanker!" I spit out, dropping my arms and marching up to him. "Use her and leave her. Fucking nice, arsehole prick."

"Shut it, Jay." His face goes dark, and he clenches his fists.

"Do it," I taunt him, knowing he is dying to throw the first punch. "Christ knows I've been dying to kick your arse since you walked out and left me here to run *your* pack."

With a loud growl, he lunges. I let his fist connect with my face, so I've got the excuse to retaliate. I draw back and feeling only slightly bad about it, I hit him so hard in the face, he goes down.

That's a first.

But he is already damaged.

Regardless, I take the victory, but it's too soon. He swipes out with his feet, knocking me off mine to land flat on my back on the unforgiving white marble floor of the entrance hall.

"You fucker," he roars, launching his battered body at me.

I roll over and shove him forward, so he falls face first to the floor. I push him over and straddle him, bunching my fist in his shirt.

"You're the fucker," I shout, punching him again and not holding back. "You fucking abandoned me. You were my big brother and you just left without a fucking word, leaving me here to deal with all of this shit that should've been your responsibility. This wasn't my destiny, arsewipe. It was yours!"

"Why do you think I fucking left?" he thunders. "I didn't want any of this! Cursed by positioning to be the one born first by two minutes. Two minutes that ruined my life forever."

I growl loudly, ready to hit him again, but he shoves us over and then rolls off me, to sit up panting and feeling his bruised face.

"You don't know what it's been like for me all these years, Jay. I'm no leader and being groomed to take over the pack as prime alpha made me miserable. Everything that goes with it was a weight heavy on my shoulders."

"How do you think it's been for me?" I spit. "Do you think it's been easy stepping up when you bailed? It's been hell."

"I'm sorry," he whispers. "I really am, Jay, but you don't understand. I'm an alpha that can't bear to be touched. The thought of mating with an omega to get her pregnant and have my children made me physically sick. How could I run a pack with that hanging over me every hour of every day?"

His words have floored me. Okay, I was already on the floor, but now I'm even lower. "What?" I pant, catching my breath when the adrenaline of the fight wears off.

"I'm asexual, James. I don't feel a sexual desire to anyone at all."

I blink, at a complete loss for words.

"I never told anyone," he whispers. "I didn't know *how* to form the words or even know what it all meant. I thought I was broken, but when I looked into it years later,

I found out who I am. I knew then that there was no way I could come back, even if I missed your fucking face and Spence's dumb arse. I'm no prime alpha, Jay. I'm no alpha at all. I needed to leave. I needed you to take the reins and bring the new pack members in. Take this pack and make it strong and powerful. You did."

"The fuck?"

I'm so confused, I shake my head. I ignore the praise he's doling out and focus on the most important thing he's said.

"I know you just had sex with Rayne. I can smell her all over you, for a start, but Christ, this house isn't that big. What you're saying doesn't make sense unless you just what? Gave her what she wanted?"

"No," he croaks out. "No, I would never do that. I couldn't. It's not a choice, Jay. It's a fundamental part of who I am. But with Rayne...she makes me feel all the things that I never could before. I'm scared to stay in case it goes away, and I have to reject her. But more than that, I can't. Her father has me over a barrel, and I won't hurt her by staying. I guess there must be another term for what I am. I don't know. I'll look it up when I get over the hurt walking away from her is causing me."

"Rich," I murmur, all of my anger washing away at his utterly defeated attitude. "Why didn't you just tell me? We could have worked something out. I'd have taken over as prime to save you the pain, but you just left. You left *me*. It hurt, still does. I'm hurt that you didn't think you could trust me to help you."

"I didn't want help, James. I wanted out."

"What does her dad have on you?" I change tactics. Surely, we can work this out.

"Everything. He knows exactly who I am and what I've been up to the last few years. He offered me immunity to help bring down Mick and his crew."

"But that's a *good* thing," I interrupt him.

He shakes his head. "It's also contingent on me not re-joining the pack. He wants you for his daughter, but not me. I signed a contract. It's done." He hauls himself to his feet and staggers towards the door. "Take care of her for me. She deserves everything you can offer her."

"Get your arse back here," I growl, standing up. "You aren't going anywhere."

"I have to."

"How can you just walk away from her?"

His sudden sob as he reaches the door, takes me aback. "It's what's best for her. Tell her I'm sorry."

"Rich," I call out, but he's gone. I can't force him to stay, as much as I want him to. I really thought Rayne would be enough to make him stay, but he's throwing himself on the sword to protect her.

"Fucking prick," I mutter and then spin abruptly when I hear her voice filtering down the stairs.

"So he really left?"

Our gazes meet, hers cloudy and sad, mine furious and confused.

"I'll get him back," I state. "He doesn't get to walk out a second time."

She nods slowly, a tear falling down her face. She runs down the stairs, dressed only in a white fluffy towel and flings her arms around me. "Please," she begs.

I hold her close, falling for her even more as she places her trust in me.

"I'll get him back," I say again, pulling back slightly to look into her eyes again.

She blinks, the tears that were pooled, spilling over and onto her cheeks. I'm frozen in place as our gazes lock. She rises on her tiptoes, placing her mouth to mine, flicking her tongue over my lips.

"Rayne," I moan, using every ounce of willpower that is inside me to push her away.

"James," she whispers, biting her lip.

I shake my head and turn away before I ravage her, forcing her onto my knot that I can feel throbbing at the base of my cock. She has just thrown me into the rut.

I need to get away from her as quickly as I can before I turn her world upside down and rip it apart at the seams.

Chapter Thirty-One

Rayne

Mortified by my actions, I turn and run up the stairs, my hand over my mouth. What was I thinking throwing myself at him?

I thank God, he pushed me away and didn't take me right there in the middle of the entrance hall. Although, that wouldn't be the *worst* thing. I do fancy him, and there's that whole alpha/omega mate connection that I want to explore more once I know them a bit better, but it hardly screams classy on my part, now does it.

Racing to my room, I snatch up the yellow sharps bin that was left outside my room and run in, slamming the door behind me. I hastily dispose of the previous needle appropriately and then I grab another from the bathroom and quickly jab myself, ensuring that the double dose is well and truly underway for today. I can't see missing one teeny tiny dose is going to cause irreparable damage.

Whisking off my towel, I dive into the shower and clean up. I have business to take care of. I am determined and taking this bull by the horns before things spin completely out of my control. I will not cower in this house a day longer, nor will I go out there brazenly and place my family at risk. There is a middle ground here, and while I will get it in the neck from Daddy, it's tough.

Big girl knickers time.

Getting dry and dressed a few minutes later, I carefully choose my outfit from the sparse collection I brought with me. I go for my skin tight black jeans, black ballet flats – in case I have to run – a black vest top and my lightweight black denim jacket. I cringe at the denim-on-denim look, but I'm not convinced it overlaps to black. But I want to be covered up, sassy, bold and also denim doesn't tear as easily if I do end up being attacked. Hopefully, it won't come to that.

Brushing out my hair, I tie it up in a high ponytail, circa 1990's.

Then I grab Old Faithful – my handbag, of course – and head out the door, calling Daddy as I go.

"Rayne?" he answers after the first ring.

"Are you at the office?" I ask without pleasantries.

"I had an important meeting, so, yes," he replies carefully.

Now I know shit is hitting the fan. He doesn't leave the house for the office unless it's in the middle of the night, or as the bird's call it, 4AM and back before morning rush hour. I always thought it was because he was an early bird, but now I see it for what it really is. Moving about undetected.

But since he didn't answer his phone at home, and after Richard's confession, I took a stab in the dark. Or light as the case may be. It's early afternoon, so I have time to go and say my piece before returning here before dark.

"I'm popping in," I inform him. "Expect me in about half an hour."

I hang up before he has a chance to try to talk me out of it.

"Not this time, Daddio. My life, my rules."

I'm all fired up over losing Richard, and it's Daddy's fault. He is in for an arse-kicking when I get there, along with the shock of his life.

Gritting my teeth as I reach the entrance hall, I scoop up my keys from the side table where I spotted them earlier, and then come to a screeching halt as Spencer dives in front of the door.

"Going somewhere?" he asks.

"Out." I tap my foot impatiently. "Move."

"You aren't safe out there, Rayne," he starts, but my mocking retching noise forces him to trail off.

"Rayne," James's voice barks at me from the left. "Where are you going?"

"To sort this mess out," I spit. "Now, you either let me go, or I swear to God, I'm going to start swinging this bag, and in case you weren't aware, it's got a strong strap and is full to the brim with junk. Ask Mick *and* your brother how much it fucking hurts when it smashes into the side of your head."

"Whoa!" Spencer says, holding his hand up. "No need to get violent there, Muffins. We're just looking out for you."

"Well, I don't need it. I know what I want and I'm going to get it. Now out of my way, Dumpty, or you will regret it." I grip the bag tighter, my threat absolutely a promise, as Cameron lets out a loud guffaw.

"Dumpty!" he cries. "Fucking, yes, Hot Omega! I knew we were on the same wavelength!"

I try not to smile at him and ruin my air of menace, but man, Spencer's face is a picture.

"Fuck you both," he snaps.

"Let her go," Cameron says between bouts of laughter. "I wouldn't *egg*nore her if I were you!" He practically shrieks with hilarity.

I have to press my lips together not to laugh along with him.

"Rayne," James's less than amused voice rings out over the laughter. "Please can you explain."

Well, I guess I owe him that much. With a sigh, I say, "I'm going to meet my dad. He's at Parliament. I'm going to sort out this shitshow and then I'll be back, hopefully with Richard. Either let me go, or it's bags for you." I take it off my shoulder and swing it gently.

"We aren't letting you go alone," he counters.

I shrug. "Whatever, follow me if you must but I'm going and I'm going now." I march forward, fully expecting Spencer to move, which he does. Giving him a grim glare, I yank the front door open and then skip down the steps to my waiting Mercedes.

I slip inside and fire up the engine. I set off before the alphas even have a chance to get their shoes on. Slamming down the accelerator, I zip out of the square and quickly finding the Inter-pack Parliament address on the Satnav, I gun it towards Westminster, hoping that no one is on my tail, I ignore the nerves that are turning my stomach into a ball of anxiety. This is exactly what needs to be done, and I *will* see it through for my happiness, Richard's and the rest of the pack, I know I want to spend the rest of my life with.

Chapter Thirty-Two

Spencer

"Well," I comment as we watch the fiery omega shoot off out of the square like a bat out of hell.

"Guess we should follow," James says with a sigh and leans over to the side table to grab the keys to the Range Rover.

"Wait," I say and turn to him with a serious expression. "Is it just me, or do you feel that?"

"I feel it."

"She threw us into a rut?"

"Pretty much."

Turning to the other two alphas, I raise my eyebrow in question.

They confirm that they are also feeling it.

"What are we supposed to do?" I ask, at a bit of a loss, for once.

"Beg her to sit on our knots until we get some relief?" Cameron pipes up.

"Something tells me that won't work," James replies dryly. "Come on, we have some catching up to do."

He heads off down the stairs while I rush to slip my trainers on, as do the other two. James is a serial flouter of the shoe rule, but he rules the roost. Or does he? With Richard making a short, but meaningful appearance, will things change around here?

Leaping into the car, in our respective places, James sets off.

"Is anyone going to let us know what the fuck is going on here?" Cam asks as we set on the road to Westminster.

"Short version," James says, "Richard is being black-mailed by Rayne's dad to give him Mick, with immunity, if he doesn't come back to this pack. He wants to allow Rayne to mate with us, but not Richard because of his criminal past."

"Oh, wow. What are we going to do?"

"About?" I ask.

"All of it."

"Not sure yet. I'm thinking Rayne is going to confront her dad about Richard, which is not going to go down well. But we have her back, so here we are."

"About the rut... do you think she feels it?"

"She felt it with Richard, and that is what has caused this. Yes, she knows. She feels it," I say quietly. I know she does. She is our mate through and through and we all know it. Richard set us on this course. He is integral to this pack and to her. We have to get him back now for all of us. There really is no other option.

"We have to make this work," Cameron says quietly. "I don't want to lose her after knowing her."

"We won't," I say adamantly. "Her dad might kick our arses and threaten to take away our seats in Parliament, but we will fight for her. She needs us to. She needs to see we are as loyal as she is, and wow, does she have a loyalty that runs deep. It's a massive turn on. Whatever she demands, we will give her."

"I'm down with that. Will, if she wants you to recite Shakespearean prose over breakfast, you can't refuse."

Everyone in the car, except for Will, snickers at that. He gets his own back, though when he says, "And if she asks *you*, Spencer, to sing nursery rhymes at bedtime, you can't refuse her either."

"Dammit," I growl. "Cam, you tattletale."

With the mood lightened, James takes no notice of us as he guides us towards our destination in the heavy afternoon traffic.

We quieten down as the Parliament building swims into view.

"What exactly is *our* game plan here?" I ask tentatively. "I mean, I know we go in and protect Rayne at all costs, but how? Barge in?"

"If that's what it takes," James replies. "Rich and I had words earlier. I get where he's coming from now. He wants to come home, Spence, but Jeremy has him over a barrel. We won't let him down again."

"Again?" That has me curious. As far as every day has gone since Richard left, it has been *him* letting us down. Now, it's the other way around? "What did he say?"

"That's for him to tell you if he wants to. But he

belongs with us. Will, I know you have concerns, and we will find a place for him, all of us as a pack, once we get him back. I just need you to trust me. Can you do that?"

"Of course," he says gruffly. "I don't want to lose Rayne either. If Richard is part of the deal, then we stand together with him. It has to be said, he's a bit of dick, though."

I snort with amusement. "Turned on his charms, did he?"

"He needs a serious attitude adjustment."

"He will once he's back home. He's been living with a lot on his mind," James says quietly.

The car goes silent again when we pull into the underground car park of the IPP building.

Many minutes later, when our identification has been verified a thousand times, we pull up into James's parking space and clamber out, heading straight for the lift to take us to the first floor, before we head up again to the fourth. It's been a long time since I've set foot in the admin part of the building. Longer still since we heard the Chief Justice was in situ. Something tells me that the stringent checks at the gate are only just the beginning.

I'm not wrong.

As we are basically strip-searched before being allowed past the security team to the internal lifts, I contemplate what it will mean having Richard home again. I remember living in his shadow. His and James's. They were inseparable when we were young kids. I was always trying to tag along, and they'd find a way to ditch me. James looked up to Richard, but there was always a cloud over our older brother. One that I just assumed was because he was trying to be responsible while James led him astray. When Richard left, James turned to me, and we became the inseparable pair. How will Richard coming back affect that? Will I be cast to the side again? The thought of it makes me sad and mad and disappointed in James, even though he hasn't done anything. I hope that James will stick up for me and that Richard will have to find his place again, not just be handed it on a silver platter.

If he comes back.

This situation sounds dodgy as fuck, and dangerous to boot. If Richard is supposed to get back in with Mick and the Jets after he betrayed them over Rayne, I don't like his chances. Somehow, we are going to have to fix this mess before that happens. But if I remember Richard, he doesn't sit around waiting for shit to happen. He is a doer, and if he thinks this is his only way out, he will take it and deal with the consequences later. He has already been beaten up and shot by these thugs. What will they do to him when he goes back to them?

It is something we have to prevent, while also still securing our place with Rayne as her mates.

This is going to be a fun afternoon.

Fun, fun, fun.

Chapter Thirty-Three

Rayne

Fortunately, even though I basically shouted to my dad that I was stopping by, he called it down and I'm let through without too much hassle.

As I reach the fourth floor and the lift dings open, I'm greeted by a friendly face I haven't seen in years.

"Hi!" Willow says, waving at me.

"Hi!" I exclaim and wave back before we hug a little. "I *love* your dress!"

"Thanks," she says, smoothing it out. "My idiot brother gave it to me for my last birthday."

"He has great taste."

She eyes me up and agrees, "Why, yes, he does."

I pause, wondering what she is talking about. Her dark eyes, fixed on mine, look suddenly familiar and the penny starts to drop. "Willow."

"That's me."

"St. Michaels?" I scrunch up my nose. I'm sure that's her last name.

"Yep." She gives me a bright smile.

"Wait! You're William's sister!" I click my fingers. "Small world!"

"For my sins," she says with a giggle.

"Wow. Thank you," I blurt out. "For what you did earlier. I owe you my life."

She shakes her head. "Nope. You don't owe me jack, hunny. We omega's gotta stick together. The guys on the other hand? Oh, I'm going to have fun making them pay!" She giggles in delight.

I join in. "That sounds like too much fun."

"I'll be sure to fill you in before I drop by. I hear you are being courted."

"Well, that's what I'm here to clear up," I point out. "Wish me luck."

She holds up her crossed fingers and with a smile, I take my leave of her and make my way to my dad's office.

I knock once and then enter when he calls out.

"Rayne," he says sternly, leaning back in his chair. "What on earth is this ruckus all about? You know you shouldn't be here."

"Well, neither should you at this hour," I retort, jabbing my Rolex fiercely.

He has the grace to look slightly chastised, but not by much.

"Anyway," I state and clear my throat. "I wish to report a crime. Do you have somewhere we can discuss this?"

He sits up suddenly, his interest in my being here goes from a mild annoyance to massively intriguing.

"A crime?" he asks. "What do you mean?"

"Not here. This is an official statement."

I turn around and march out into the bullpen. Daddy follows me and grabs my arm.

"Rayne," he growls. "What is going on here?"

"Get your official statement taking guy, and you'll find out."

I gulp when he gives me a glare that is so hard, and so fearsome, I nearly back out. But it's too late for that. Plus, I really need to do this for everyone I'm starting to care about.

He leads me to an empty room with an uncomfortable looking chair and a bare table, gesturing to someone on the way. I sit down and cross my legs and arms, keeping my bag close by. They are not taking this as evidence. No way.

A beta man strolls in, notebook in hand and fixes me with a glare that lets me know he isn't pleased to be in here.

He will be as soon as I start talking, though.

Jason, Daddy tells me is his name, closes the door and sits down opposite me, while Daddy stands in the corner, his arms folded.

"What is this about, Rayne?" Daddy barks out.

"I wish to report a crime," I say again. "Yesterday morning..." *God, was it only yesterday,* "...I was run off the road on the way to London from my house and abducted."

"WHAT?" Daddy roars, his arms dropping to his sides as he marches forward, his face furious and red.

"I'm fine," I say to calm him down, but there is no chance of that. He blusters and expostulates, swearing and carrying on as a dad would do, not the Chief Justice.

"I'm fine!" I shout over his yelling. "Look, all good in

the hood." I stand up and make a show of how fine I am. "But I wouldn't have been if it hadn't been for Richard St. Stevens. He saved me. He risked his own life to get me out of the situation and I thank God he did, because if it wasn't for him, I would be mated to a super-pack of nasty alphas, chained up and gang raped."

That stops my father's tirade dead.

I continue into the silence as Jason hastily starts writing all of this down, now that things have proven worthy of his time.

"Richard St. Stevens saved my life and fought bravely while his brother's pack, the *St. Stevens* pack, got me to safety. I have been staying with them this last day to recuperate from my ordeal, but also to keep you safe, Chief Justice Halstead." Calling him 'Daddy' now probably would go against my credibility.

"Me?" he spits out.

"Yes, you. They targeted me to get to you, we believe. I may have been held up for ransom at some point or worse, just used for my position with you. I didn't tell you because I didn't want you running to come and get me, putting yourself at risk, nor did I want to come home and have them potentially follow me. Mick Savoy and his men were at the centre of this plot, and I can prove it. They still have my phone and with my testimony, we can convict them and send them to prison where they belong."

I inhale deeply and then sit down, my hands on the table, shaking from the confrontation and the reliving of what happened to me, what *could* have happened to me if Richard hadn't been there.

"Richard St. Stevens," Daddy growls, that seemingly

the only thing he has taken in. "Is a criminal and belongs in prison with the rest of them."

"Not in my book," I state firmly.

"You lied about where you were and what you were doing," he accuses.

"I had to. Did you not hear a word of what I just said?"

"Rayne," he snaps. "I am your father. It is up to me to protect you, not the other way around. Jesus wept!" He turns around and punches the wall in a previously unseen display of rabid temper.

In the next second, he lunges towards me, hauling me to my feet and throwing his arms around me. "My baby girl," he whispers. "What did they do to you?"

"Nothing," I choke out as he squeezes too tightly. "Because of Richard."

He holds me at arm's length and grabs my wrist. The one that Richard bit. "They tried to possess you?" His disdain is overpowering.

"No, Richard did it to save me. I gave him my permission." I pull my arm back.

"Richard," he sneers, shaking his head. "And the rest of them? The St. Stevens pack? What have they done to you while you've been in their house?"

"Nothing. They have been lovely and welcoming. They have *protected* me. I know you contacted them about a mating. I choose them. Along with Richard. He belongs with his pack. I know you've blackmailed him, and I won't stand for it!"

I bite the inside of my lip. I hadn't meant to reveal all of that yet.

"You won't stand for it?" he bellows as Jason takes the

opportunity to slip out, so he isn't a party to this family brawl. Doesn't matter. He has what he needs to arrest Mick.

"No, I won't," I growl. "He is my future mate. They all are, and I will not sit here and have you rip that away from me. I've given you everything you need to arrest Mick and his men and leave Richard the hell alone. He is coming back to his pack and to me. End of story."

"Rayne, you are walking on thin ice here, my girl. You don't tell me how it is. I tell you."

"I don't think so. I know all about your little manipulations over the years, Daddy," I say, grabbing my bag and slinging it over my shoulder. "All the gifts and cars to keep me in line. Well, no more. I am twenty-one next week. I'm adult enough to know what I want and to accept responsibility for my own actions. I will be mating with the St. Stevens pack *including* Richard, and there isn't a damn thing you can do about it. I know Mum will agree with me when I tell her everything as soon as I leave here."

"He signed a contract," Daddy says quietly. "I can have him thrown in jail right this second for breaking it."

"Try it," I snarl. "You always said you admired my loyalty, well, admire this. You go after Richard, and you go after me. If you never want to see me again, then be my guest and make good on your little contract, but know that I will fight to the death for him. For all of them. They have given me something so special in the little time I've known them, and I'm not giving up on any of them. They need me as much as I need them. You can take what I've given you about Mick. I will sit here and discuss the ins and outs of it with you like adults, so you have everything you need to send him down. But you leave Richard alone. I'm not saying it again, so nod your head if you understand me."

My heart is pounding as I talk to my father in a way that I would never have dreamed of before this moment.

"You're choosing him over your own family?" he scoffs.

"He *is* my family," I counter.

"I will see them all burned to the ground," he hisses, beyond furious with me.

"Why?" I ask, confounding him into stepping back. "What is the point of this?"

"To protect you," he replies calmly, even though his eyes are still stormy. "You are my daughter, Rayne and you deserve better than a low life criminal."

"Even if he wants to change? Even if he knows he has done wrong and wants to make amends for that? Who are you to judge a person so harshly?"

He doesn't answer me.

He can't.

There is nothing he can say that will convince me otherwise, and I think he realises that now.

"If you walk out of that door and go to them, you won't be welcome in my house anymore," he says eventually.

His words stab me in the heart, but they don't change my mind. "I'm sorry you've said that, Daddy. I thought this was about justice and getting the bad guys, but really, it's just a vendetta against a man who is lost. I hope you change your mind. You know where to find me if you do."

I stalk past him, clutching my bag strap tight enough to turn my knuckles white.

"Rayne, I'm warning you..."

"Don't," I say, holding my hand up. "You want to disown me, then you don't get to warn me about anything. Richard saved my life. James, Spencer, William and Cameron, took me into their home to keep me safe, to keep *you* safe, and this is how you repay them? Shame on you, Daddy. Shame on you."

Eyes straight forward, I walk out of the small room, feeling light-headed and sick. I didn't want this to happen. I didn't even think it *could* happen. What actually just happened? Did I fight for the men I've chosen and lose my dad? Is that what just happened? How? Why? What fucked up shit is this?

This is all Mick's fault, and I will make sure he pays, one way or another.

"Rayne," Daddy's voice rings out, but I ignore him. "Don't do this."

"Same to you," I call back, but don't stop walking.

When I approach the lift, the doors slide open and there are the men I've just fought valiantly for. Well, most of them.

They take one look at the tears in my eyes, and they gather around me, giving me the reassurance and love that I need right now.

It gives me the strength I need to say the next words. "We're going back to that house to find Richard, and we are bringing him home."

Chapter Thirty-Four

Rayne

James gathers me to him, embracing me and giving me the comfort I so desperately need. I try not to sob into his chest. Drawing in his pinecone scent, it immediately soothes my ravaged soul. I turn my face and press my cheek over his heart. Listening to it beating steadily, I pull myself together as the lift dings to open.

"Let's go," Spencer murmurs, placing his hand on my back.

"Rayne, wait!" my dad's voice rings out over the bullpen.

James lets go of me and steps in front, barricading me from my dad. "I think we're done here," he says, folding his arms over his chest and planting his feet.

"Move," Daddy says in a tone that can only be described as frightening.

"No." James's tone mimics my dad's, and I can see this going tits up in the middle of the Parliament building.

"Rayne," Daddy says, calmly. "Let's talk about this."

"There is nothing to talk about, unless you want to carry on asking me questions about Mick and his men in order to arrest him and let Richard off whatever hook you have him dangling from."

"Yes."

I blink in confusion.

"Yes, what?" I ask, peering out from behind James's muscular bod.

"We will talk about it," he grits out. "I am not having you walking out over this. Clearly, you have strong feelings about it, so we will talk more." He turns on his heel and marches back into his office.

"You don't have to follow him," James states.

"Yeah, I do," I say with a sigh. "He's my dad for a start, but secondly, he needs to see that Richard is not the enemy here."

"Are you sure?"

I nod and give him a brave smile even though my insides are withering away over the previous confrontation. I don't think I have it in my little omega soul to have a round two. I said my piece and I walked away. Going back in now might destroy me completely. If that's Daddy's plan, then I will officially cut him out of my life for using what he knows against me.

Most of me tells me that he won't, but there is that tiny part of me that isn't sure, and I don't like it. A few days ago, I would never have even thought my father would be so manipulative. But now I know differently and that knowledge hurts.

My mouth is dry as dust, but I force myself to move forward. The alphas follow me closely and my brave smile strengthens. They have my back.

"Here," Willow whispers as we pass and hands something to William.

He quietly removes the cap and hands me a bottle of water. Gratefully, I take it and gulp down a couple of mouthfuls.

"Thanks," I mutter and hand it back to him.

Reaching my father's office, I pause and turn to give them each a smile. "You don't have to wait. I'll be okay."

"We're not leaving," James says.

"Don't worry about anything, except what you came here to do," Spencer adds.

I nod and enter the office, closing the door quietly and turning to face my dad.

He is sitting in his chair, his head in his hands. "How did it come to this?" he asks quietly.

"You won't listen to me."

"I'm listening now."

I gulp. Now I don't have anything left to say. The adrenaline I was riding has run out, and left me drained. I flop down in one of the chairs opposite his desk and immediately catch a faint whiff of earthy pinecones.

Richard.

He was here in this chair.

It gives me the strength and courage I need to see this through. "I know it seems strange," I start. "That these alphas have taken over my life. But they have. They are sweet and kind and thoughtful. They have been perfect gentlemen and even helped me out of a situation that they could easily have taken advantage of."

"Explain," he croaks.

I bite my lip. Discussing my heat with my dad is a bit weird, but he already knows about my heat suppressants and the reasons why.

"I lost my supply of heat suppressant injections in the struggle on the side of the road. When they found out, William asked his sister to help me out by getting some for me. Yes, I understand that it's not exactly legal," I hasten to add when he looks up. "But I was desperate. They could easily have left me to go into my heat and taken advantage of that. They didn't. They want to court me as much as I want them to. All that I told you on the phone was true. I'm ready, and I'm ready because of them. But that includes Richard. I know you see him only as a felon, but he is *so* much more than that to me. Can you accept that?"

With shaking hands and bated breath, I wait for his answer.

It takes a long time to come.

So long that I start to panic. My stomach curls up and clenches, nearly forcing my breakfast out.

The clock on the desk ticks away.

I sweat in my denim jacket, wishing I could take it off, but I can't move. I'm frozen in place.

Eventually, he sighs.

"They really mean that much to you that you would walk out on me to be with them?"

"That's not fair," I croak.

"No, I don't mean it as a nasty thing. I'm asking you outright. You would choose them over me?"

"I don't want to..."

"Rayne," he says, exasperated.

"Okay, yes. I would. But I don't want to. I don't see *why* I should."

"You don't have to. I was thinking only about the small, immediate picture. You have a depth to it that I couldn't see until you walked away from me and to them. I'm not losing you over something so ridiculous, Rayne. You deserve a pack who will love you and take care of you. Clearly, the St. Stevens pack is enamoured with you that they defied me to protect you. I could've had their seats for that."

"But you won't, because that is a dick move," I point out, gaining some of my sass back, because he's acting like my dad again, sort of, and not the Chief Justice.

"It is a dick move, and I try hard not to be a dick." He smirks at me, and I relax.

We are back in familiar territory now.

"But Richard...he may be trying to change, or has changed, or whatever, but the people he has been associating with are dangerous criminals, Rayne. Can *you* understand where I'm coming from? My job as your father is to protect you at all costs."

"I do understand. I also know that Richard would never put me in harm's way. None of them would."

"Not intentionally, maybe."

"But that's why I'm here, Daddy. To give you my statement, so you have the information you need to make arrests."

He nods slowly.

"You don't need Richard to risk his life going back there and threatening him to stay away from me is cruel."

I nail it home now he is back on my side.

"I see that now. He, *they*, are your future mates. Anyone with eyes can see that. Even your old dad."

We exchange a shaky smile.

"Give the rest of your statement. As many details as you can about who, how many, where, and we will use that to take these loose, packless alphas down and clean up our streets."

With tears in my eyes, I jump up and dart around to give him a hug. "Thank you, Daddy."

"Are you sure they didn't hurt you?" he whispers, pulling back. "I need to know, Ray-ray."

"No, they didn't. Apart from a couple of bruises, I'm fine."

"And Richard saved you from them? The truth will come out if you aren't being entirely honest about that." His stern tone doesn't scare me one bit.

"He fought like the prime alpha he is supposed to be. He would have died if it meant getting me to safety. He nearly did. His pack brothers will corroborate all of the details."

Daddy nods. "I'm still concerned about his past, but I know James and Spencer are remarkable, stand-up alphas. It is why I contacted them about you in the first place. They were my first choice for your pack. Have been for a while. I was waiting for you to give me the go ahead."

"Cameron and William are pretty remarkable as well," I say with a smile.

"I will make it a priority to get to know them better. All of them."

"Thank you," I say again. I cross over to pick up my bag. "Where do you want to do this?"

"Back in the interrogation room. I'll call Jason back." His world-weary sigh makes me smile and I follow him out, giving my alphas two thumbs up and an excited smile behind his back.

My alphas. I like the way that sounds.

They chuckle and follow us to the small, stuffy interrogation room.

I sit down, while they surround me, not leaving my side for a second.

Chapter Thirty-Five

Rayne

Staring at Jason across the table as he makes his little notes, I give him everything I can think of starting from seeing the Audi, to swerving off the road, my torn tyre, the wait for the RAC and then Tree-man approaching me.

"Tree-man?" Jason inquires, scrunching up his nerdy face.

"I don't know his name," I point out. "He was built like a tree and smelt like cedarwood, hence Tree-man."

"What did he look like, his features?"

"He has a face like a box of frogs," I state.

"Uhm, what?" Jason asks as Cameron laughs so loudly, my dad gives him a fierce look that threatens to kick his arse if he doesn't shut it.

"A box of frogs," I enunciate clearly. "You know, fugly."

"Fugly..." he murmurs. "Anything specific?"

"A broken nose, I think? It was a bit skew-whiff. Seriously, he looked like a bag of spanners."

"Jesus!" Cameron howls. "You are slaying me! Do you talk about us that way?"

I give him a sassy smile and shake my head. "Nah, none of you have faces like boxes of frogs. Pretty spring baskets of easter chocolate, maybe."

"Eggs, you mean?" He shoots a wicked smile at me.

"Fuck off with that," Spencer growls, earning a throat-clearing from my dad.

"Ray-ray. You need to be more specific. Hair colour, how tall, scents, eye colour even, Anything you can give us will help us identify the right people connected to your abduction."

"I'm trying! Box of frogs is accurate."

After Cameron finally quietens down, Jason fixes me with a piercing stare. "And you say Mick Savoy was in the car with you. Did you know who he was at the time?"

"No, I gave him the name Burnt-toast because that's what he smelled like to me. I only found out his name later. Richard said it. Oh, wait. Bryan. One of them was also called Bryan. Don't know who. Tree-man or driver-guy. I didn't see him. Or smell him. He probably had a face like a bag of spanners as well."

More snickering from my alphas.

"So this Tree-man took your phone, but allowed you to ring your parents?"

"I spoke to mum."

"She said," Dad murmurs. "She was surprised you rang, but we didn't think anything of it. We are terrible parents. We should've known..."

"Stop right there. You are not bad parents. There's nothing you could've done. Anyway, I also texted my cousin to tell her I was delayed."

Dad lets out a sudden noise. "Morgan! She'll be worried sick."

"No, I've spoken to her, she's up to date with everything."

"Oh." He goes quiet again.

"Then we drove to this house in Southall, while Richard and I got...close."

"Close?" Jason queries.

"I knew what he was straight away, what he was trying to hide. It was obvious to me, because I know who he is to me now. He didn't want the other alphas knowing. He was lost and just trying to blend in. But he knew as well as I did, that there was something between us. That's when he started helping me. When we got to the house..."

"The one where the riot broke out and shots were fired?"

I nod. "Yes, Richard told me everything, and I allowed him to bite me on my wrist to try to save me as much as he could."

I take a sip from the bottle of water William placed in front of me when I sat down and then I tell them everything else that happened, including how my bag saved my life.

Dad peers at it, parked next to my feet. "I'll get you another one," he murmurs.

"No need, this is like an old friend now. And now I guess you need to speak to these four."

I take another sip of water as Jason questions the pack, feeling content and happy. I also feel the strong urge to go home, well, to the house in Chelsea and curl up in a comfy nest. I know that if I wasn't on the suppressants, I would be entering my pre heat now. I don't feel overpowered by the yearning, but it's there, nonetheless. My skin feels more sensitive to outside factors. The denim of my jacket is rubbing roughly over my arms. My feet feel a bit swollen and sweaty in my shoes. My hands are desperate to reach out and stroke the alphas while I draw in their masculine scents, riding their cocks until they knot inside me...

Whoa. Where did that come from?

But the answer is obvious. Even though I'm not going to have a heat, as such, the mate bond won't be denied. The alphas have gone into rut. Their scents are pungent in the small room, a delicious aroma of a pinecone in a rainforest, scattered with lemons and biscuits. It is turning me on in ways that are highly inappropriate right now. I wave my hand in my face like a make-shift fan.

"Do you feel okay?" James asks, interrupting himself to check on me.

"Yep," I squeak, avoiding his eyes. I can't give away the fact that I'm thinking about his cock and if it's pierced the same as Richard's is.

That was some hot dicking he gave me earlier.

"Perhaps a bit of fresh air," I stammer and stand up, not even stopping to pick up my bag. I hightail it out of the room and directly to the fan that is placed on Willow's desk, oscillating beautifully and lifting the damp tendrils of hair off my forehead and neck.

"It's hot today, isn't it?" Willow asks, conversationally.

"You have no idea," I murmur, eyes closed in bliss.

She snickers. "Oh, like that, is it?"

My eyes fly open, and I shake my head. "Not exactly. I figured the suppressants would squash it completely, but it's there...lurking."

"Aww, hun. I know what you mean. I was on them for a while before I met my pack. You'll be fine though. They'll work. You'll just feel a bit warm and nesty for a few days."

I nod slowly.

Problem is, I'm not sure I want them to work now.

I shake that errant thought from my mind, wondering where it came from. "Nesty is right. I can't wait to get home."

"I think they're done," she says, looking over my shoulder.

I turn and see the pack leaving the room with Jason and my dad. "Thanks," I murmur and head over to them, feeling a bit more in control of my lustful thoughts. Until Cameron hands me my bag and our fingers touch. I snatch my hand away like I've been electrocuted, ignoring the deepening desire that has filled his intense gaze.

"If you can wait a few minutes, Ray-ray, I'll finish up here and take you home."

"No," I say, shaking my head. "I'm going back with them."

He purses his lips. "You are not mated yet."

"I don't care. It's where I want to be."

He chews his lip, but eventually he sees that we will get into another argument over it if he presses the issue, so he nods.

But then he ruins the illusion of being adult about it when he grabs James by his shirt front and growls, "You touch one hair on her unmated head, and I will eat you for breakfast with the rest of your pack for dessert. Got it?"

"Got it," James says quickly, knowing a rabid Daddy alpha when he sees one. "But you don't have to worry, Sir. We all only have Rayne's best interest at heart. She is our everything."

He smiles at me, and I return it, tears pricking my eyes again. Stupid emotions. Where has all of this come from?

As we turn to leave, I suddenly remember something. "Andy!"

"What?" James asks, his face creasing into a frown.

"Andy," I say again to my dad. "He was the one who told Bryan about me. Richard said he got drunk and told them all about me and you. He is the root of this whole thing."

"Fucking little prick," Daddy growls so fiercely, we all back away. "I allowed him into my home, allowed him near you. I will…"

"Just arrest him and if he pisses himself while being interrogated, please video it and send it to me," I say with a smile.

"Oh, I'll make him piss himself. I'll make him shit himself and throw up at the same time!"

I giggle at the thought of it. "Okay, calm down there. A stern word will make him cry."

"Who is this Andy?" William growls, startling me with his jealousy.

"No one you have to worry about," I reply reassuringly, patting his rock-hard chest. Saliva fills my mouth and I practically drool all over his shoes. I need to get out of here and into my nest *now*.

"I'll see you back at the house," I murmur and with a quick kiss to my dad, I scarper back to my Mercedes and climb in, nearly jumping a mile when the passenger door opens, and someone slides in.

Chapter Thirty-Six

Richard

"Fuck's sake!" Rayne shrieks at me, clutching at her bag.

I duck, holding my hands up over my head. "It's just me!" That bag is fucking lethal. I've still got a bruise on my head from where she clocked me the other day.

"Jesus! Are you trying to give me a heart attack? What are you doing here? Thought you left?" Her tone has gone from shrill to downright frosty.

"I deserve the chill factor, but can you just drive? We need to talk."

"Humph," she mutters and shoves her bag in my footwell, over my feet, and starts up the car. I let her manoeuvre out of the underground parking before I say anything.

"Rayne, I'm sorry I left. I'm sorry I took your dad's

deal. I should've fought for you. It wasn't until we...you know..." *Christ, man. You can't even say the words.*

"Had sex?" she snaps.

"Yes," I reply calmly. "That I knew I'd made a mistake. I left to try and fix it. I was going to come back. I've been walking around, trying to figure out how to get Mick to trust me again, but then I knew I was going round in circles. I came back here to speak to your dad again, maybe see if he had any ideas."

"You did?" Her face creases and she gives me a quick glance. "It doesn't matter, anyway. I've taken care of it."

My blood runs cold. "What do you mean?"

"You are off the hook and free to come back to the house in Chelsea, if that's what you want?"

I can hear the hopeful note in her tone, and it floods me with relief.

I take her hand carefully off the steering wheel and kiss her knuckles, revelling in the delight I feel to have my lips on her skin. "I want that."

"Good, because I got into a huge fight with my dad about this. I put us first, *all* of us and took a huge risk. But it paid off. Daddy is on board. I gave a statement about everything that happened and how you saved me."

"And your father accepted that?" It seems too good to be true.

"He did after a while."

I nod slowly. "Okay, so where does that leave us?" I'm more confused now than ever. I had hoped to see her again, kiss her one last time and try to tell her how I feel. This has surpassed that. Rayne has surpassed every expectation I had of her and this relationship.

"It leaves us free to be together. To get to know one another on a deeper level before we mate. If that's what you want, of course." Her murmured last words squeeze my heart.

"More than you know. But I'm still a bit confused. Are you sure your dad isn't going to come for me?"

"I'm sure. He knows how I feel about you." Her voice has gone low and husky.

"And how is that?"

"My soul aches without you. A part of my heart feels empty."

"I feel the same. You have touched a part of me, Rayne that I didn't know was there. I don't think anyone will ever be able to bring this out in me ever again. I want it. I don't want to lose this feeling. I don't want to lose *you*."

"You won't."

She gives me a bright smile, but I can see the strain under the happiness.

"What's wrong?" I ask quietly.

"Nothing, I'm just supposed to be going into my pre heat. The suppressants are fighting with my biology and the last few days have been exhausting."

"Suppressants?" I murmur, worry coursing through me. I've seen what those things can do when bought on the black market.

She nods. "I made the decision a while ago when I wasn't mated and approaching my twenty-first."

"Oh, so they were prescribed?"

She nods to my relief. If anything ever happened to her, I wouldn't be able to carry on. I was prepared to go on living knowing she was safe and happy with James and his pack. But if she wasn't here, then I would wither away. This bone-deep, *soul*-deep connection that I have to her is mind blowing and I want to keep exploring it. I didn't think I would ever have a chance to.

"Rayne," I croak.

She glances at me before turning her gaze back to the road.

"I don't know what love is, but I think this is it." There, I've said it and I don't care how desperate or foolish it makes me look. I needed her to know.

"I don't know either," she replies like the beautiful, sweet goddess that she is. "But I'm really looking forward to finding out with you and the rest of the pack."

I sit back, the feeling of happiness washing over me. It's something that I thought was far out of my reach, that I didn't deserve it, or need it even.

There is just one dark cloud in my sunny sky.

"What about Mick and his crew?"

"Daddy has enough to start making arrests today. He won't stop until he has every one of them. Maybe, though, to be on the safe side, you should stay inside for a while? Come back to Chelsea and just stay there until the streets are clear. I don't want anything happening to you. Anything *more*."

I grunt at the reminder of my gunshot graze. It's still oozing blood, but I'm not going back to the doctor who ratted me out to Halstead. Although, I see why he did, it doesn't change that my trust issues have trust issues and that didn't help.

"Deal, but James gave away my bedroom."

She snickers. "I'd offer for you to share mine, but that

will lead to nookie, and I really need to build a nest when I get back."

"I'm sure James will find somewhere for me," I murmur, wondering if the couch is comfy. I could sleep for a week. It took everything I had to get up and walk out of Rayne's bed, *my* old bed earlier.

We spend the rest of the short drive in silence, but a peaceful one, and I know that despite the hell I've lived for years, I finally see the light at the end of the tunnel. I hope James and I can come to an agreement about the pack and that things work out with Rayne the way I hope they will.

One thing I know for certain is she's right. Until Mick is behind bars, I cannot show my face on the streets. I won't put Rayne through the agony of losing me, when I know she feels the same as I do. We are tiptoeing around it at the moment, but I know. I can feel it vibrating between us as we sit here in silence. She is my mate. I am hers. We belong together and nothing will come in the way of that.

Chapter Thirty-Seven

Rayne

When we pull up to the house, I pause, chewing my lip. "Do you think it's safe to get out?"

Richard opens the door and climbs out, slamming it shut in the process. He makes his way around to my side and opens the door. "Come on. Let's get you inside."

I take his hand and grabbing my bag, I let him pull me up out of the car. I close the door and lock it, before we hurry up the front steps to the door. Jones opens it and we pile in, with the rest of the alphas right behind us.

"I'm leaving now, unless you need anything?" Jones says to James.

"No, we're good. Thanks, pal. You've gone above and beyond. Go back to your family and say hi to Marie for us."

"Will do," he says and waves before he disappears.

Spencer closes the door and locks it, also sliding the bolt across and putting the chain on.

"Is that all necessary?" I murmur as the pack take in Richard, hovering uncertainly near the side table where the keys are kept.

"Rather safe than sorry," James mutters. "Rich. Are you back or just here to cause more shit?"

"Back," he replies. "If you'll have me."

I beam and snuggle into him, not being able to resist touching him. He cuddles me back with a smile down at me, his poor battered face bruised and cut. "I want him here," I state just in case anyone wasn't aware of my feelings about this.

"We want you both," James says. "But, Rich. Rayne has your room, so you'll have to bunk with me until we figure something else out."

"Oh," I murmur, my cheeks going warm. "Sorry, I can sleep on the couch."

"Absolutely not," Spencer insists, giving Richard the stink-eye for some reason.

"No," Richard agrees. "You keep it. I will fit in wherever."

Feeling a bit bad that I've taken his bed away from him, I pull away and murmur, "I need to go and shower and change. It's hot out there."

"We'll find you later when there's food," Cameron says.

I nod and make for the stairs quickly, kicking off my shoes and scooping them up before I head up.

"Thank you," Richard says before I hit the first one. "For what you did. It should be me looking out for you. You are amazing and brave and all the things that make me *feel* something. Sorry, I'm not very good at this."

I turn to see he is looking down, almost embarrassed by his words. "That was perfect."

He looks up and grins.

I return it and continue on my way, making sure to give a sexy sway to my hips as I can feel all of their eyes on my arse.

Once in my room, I close the door and rip my jacket off, flinging it onto the small armchair in the corner. I pad blissfully barefoot over to the wardrobe and shove the sliding door open. Turning to the bed, I yank the duvet off and hold it to my nose, breathing in Richard's scent from when he slept here briefly earlier. It sends a beautiful shiver across my skin, giving me goosebumps. Pulling it away from my nose, I lay it on the wardrobe floor and then grab the pillows from the bed. Kneeling down, I arrange the duvet to my liking and then lovingly place the four pillows encased in the most amazing, cool, white cotton covers, artfully scattered for maximum comfort. Once satisfied with my little nest, I stand up and move across to the window, opening it further to allow more air into the spacious, minimalist room. Pulling the curtains half across, I strip off and shove my sweaty clothes and jacket into the laundry basket in the bathroom. Removing the tie from my ponytail, I scoop my hair up and wrap it into a bun, snapping the tie back around the bunched-up hair. Stepping into the huge power shower, I turn the taps on and revel in the cool water hitting my slightly fevered skin. I worry a little over what a full-on heat will feel like if this is a suppressed one. Will I be able to cope with it? Maybe over winter when it's freezing, and the warmth will be welcome. It would be unbearable in this August heat.

A few minutes later, having cooled down and washed up, I turn the taps off and step out, dripping wet, enjoying the breeze from the open bedroom window against my damp skin.

I reluctantly dry off, and then slip into the cream silk shortie pjs, which are the only ones I brought with me on my trip to see Morgan. Shrugging that it can't be helped, it's not the end of the world if the alphas see me in this over dinner. In fact, it might go nicely with dessert.

Giggling at my rampant sexual thoughts, I grab my phone and text my dad that I'm here safe and sound as I crawl into my nest. With a heavenly sigh, I curl up, flicking through my phone and landing on the news website. I keep the tab open, hoping to see news of Mick and his men's arrests in the morning before placing it next to me. Closing my eyes, I fall straight to sleep, happy and secure in this house full of my future mates.

Chapter Thirty-Eight

William

It's late. Nearing midnight. It's warm and cloistered, the humidity in the city making it difficult to sleep. Sitting in the armchair near the open window to try to grab any bit of breeze that may filter through, I focus on the book in front of me. It's a useless distraction. The rut is pretty much occupying all of my thoughts. The primal side of me wants to barge into Rayne's room and savagely take her body until I knot inside her, but I would rather rip my own cock off than violate her in any way. The others feel the same. It was something we discussed over dinner earlier with her absence.

We haven't seen Rayne since she left to shower earlier. Cameron popped his head in on her a while ago, when dinner was ready, but she was fast asleep in her nest, so we left her. She will wake and find food when she's ready.

Almost as if thinking about her made her appear, I see

her walking past my open door, yawning and stretching her arms.

"Oh, hey," she says, stopping in the doorway. "You're up late."

"Couldn't sleep." My gaze quickly flickers over her creamy skin exposed in depth by the scant pyjamas she's wearing.

"I did not have that problem," she giggles. "I missed dinner."

"Are you hungry?" I ask, motioning to stand up, but she shakes her head.

"Don't get up. I'll grab something and head back to bed."

"I want to," I insist, but stop midway to rising when she takes a step into the room. I freeze, my blood pounding in my ears at her nearness.

"What are you reading?" she asks, her voice low and husky from her deep sleep.

"Shakespeare," I say, sitting back down so I don't loom over her and scare her away. She is tiny. Fragile like a China doll. I don't want to break her.

"Wow, heavy stuff for nearing midnight."

I shrug. "I actually don't mind it." I'm not coming clean about studying English Literature at Oxford. She'll think I'm a total nerd. For some reason, I want her to think I'm manly and capable of protecting her. Shakespearean Sonnets don't exactly scream that.

"Me either," she says, dropping her tone even lower as she approaches me, standing directly in front of me in her little silk pjs. Her breasts are full and perfect from what I can see, even though I'm trying not to look at them.

I clear my throat and glare into her eyes.

She bites her lips and steps back. "Sorry, am I too close?"

"Not close enough," I growl.

Her eyes hood with desire and I throw caution to the wind. My cock is aching, and she is tempting me in ways that are previously unheard of. I have to conclude that if she didn't want me to look at her, she wouldn't be standing here half naked. Maybe that's being boorish of me, but that's where I'm at right now. I reach out and take her hand, drawing her closer.

"Is this okay?" I ask.

"More than," she breathes, inhaling my scent and letting out a little mewl.

It's more than I can bear. I drag her onto my lap, settling her close enough so that her hand rests lightly on my chest.

Her gaze on mine, she grinds gently down over my hard shaft, a soft purr escaping her lips. I growl in response and cup the back of her head, drawing her mouth to mine in a crushing kiss that leaves me breathless. She wraps her tongue around mine, rotating her hips and riling me up to the point where I don't think I can stop.

"Are you sure you want this?" I murmur against her mouth.

"Yes."

That one word is all I need. I slide my hands up her loose camisole top, pulling it up over her head to expose her tits to me. They are luscious. There is just no other word for it.

Dropping the top on the floor, I cup both of her

breasts, pushing them up into a delectable mound before I squeeze her nipples. She moans, throwing her head back and pushing her chest out. Her hand drops lightly in between us. She dips her fingers into the waistband of my loose black joggers before she tugs at the hem of my black t-shirt. I let her pull the t-shirt off and enjoy her raw noise of lust when she sees my body.

"Oh, yes," she whispers and leans forward to kiss my chest.

I want to do the same to her, but she has other ideas. She takes one of my hands and moves it to her shorts. I slide my hand up the inside of her thigh to her pussy and groan in response to the wet haven between her legs. Thrusting a finger inside her, hearing her moan of pleasure, I finger-fuck her, my gaze locked onto hers. She slicks up my fingers, a sweet scent filling the air as I arouse her.

I need more.

Removing my hand from her, I use my strength and grab the shorts with both hands, ripping the soft fabric away from her.

"Ah!" she cries out, now bare to me.

Her hands once again go to my joggers. She dips her hand in, pulling them down a bit so my cock can spring free. She gasps when she sees the size of it. I'm not a small man in any capacity.

"Like what you see?" I murmur, my hand cupping her cheek.

"Oh, yes. Do you?"

"You are a goddess."

She leans forward and kisses me again, turning my cock to iron in her hand. She rises up and guides it inside her.

I nearly weep with relief when I feel the slick coat me, her pussy encasing my length. Slowly Rayne takes me deep inside her, her breathing becoming a soft pant. She settles with my cock buried in her pussy and brings my hand back to her clit. I tease her, rubbing it gently, circling my thumb over the ripe nub. She starts to ride me, taking my breath away. Her scent fills my nostrils and I let out a cry of feral lust. Slick gushes out of her, covering my cock and balls so that we make a slurping sound as she fucks me deliciously slowly, rotating her hips one way, then another until I'm ready to burst.

Her pants are ragged, so I speed up the teasing of her clit. She cries out suddenly, convulsing on top of me, coming wildly, inviting me to pinch her nipples again as she shoves them in my face. I do one better. I lean forward and take one in my mouth. Grazing my teeth over the peak, I bite down sharply, hard enough to draw blood, marking her as mine.

"Christ, yes!" she cries, shuddering in my arms again as I claim her in a possessive way that she is here for, all the way.

"Not fair," a soft voice says from the doorway.

I look over to see James standing there, ready to pounce. Spencer and Cameron join him, called to us by the rut with our mate.

It's more than enough for me to grab her hips and thrust upwards, deep, forcefully, splitting her apart as my knot bulges inside her, a low, fierce growl escaping my lips.

She rasps when she feels me come, my cock jerking inside her, spurting out my seed to fill her up.

Then I'm surrounded by the other alphas, their hands reaching for her, ready to tear her apart.

"Room for one more?"

I glance over as Richard enters my room.

"Always," she cries out, her arms pulled out to the sides by James and Cameron.

Baring his teeth, James bites into her wrist, over the bite that Richard gave her, in a show of who is prime alpha here. She screams, weeping with the intensity of this assault to her body.

Spencer is at her back, leaning over her to bite her shoulder, drawing enough blood for it to slide down over her gorgeous tits, at the same time that Cam bites into her upper arm, marking her, claiming her but not as our mate. She is our possession for now. She is ours and anyone who comes for her will know it.

The mate will come. It will follow in a beautiful, spectacular moment when it's right for her. That time isn't today. She doesn't want it right now.

She wants this.

She wants us.

Chapter Thirty-Nine

Rayne

The alphas are tearing at my flesh. Blood is dripping down my skin in hot rivulets. It is hedonistic and erotic, and so far from what I've ever experienced before.

Vanilla sex.

It's the only way to describe it.

Vanilla sex with men who don't even deserve that title.

I cringe inside when I think that I allowed *Andy fucking Pandy* to take my virginity. What was I thinking when there are alphas like this out there? Where were they a few years ago?

Removing their teeth, they kiss me softly over the bites they've made that make me theirs in every way except as a mate. Under normal circumstances, I would baulk at the idea, be ashamed of these possessive bites, but not with them. I know it's temporary. We will mate, they are just waiting for me to say when.

Not now.

I'm not quite ready to do that yet. I want to sample their delights first. Have some fun before we get to the serious stuff.

Two down.

Three to go.

Who will be next?

I rock forward on William's knot, trying to force another climax. He is *very* good at getting my body to respond to him.

He chuckles and cups my face. "Eager, aren't you sweetheart."

"Mmm."

I grab the nearest hand to mine, James's, and place it over my pussy. He wastes no time in working my clit into a state of sheer pleasure. It pulsates under his fingertips, his low growl adding to the decadence.

Knowing he's pleased me, he leans forward and kisses me, this time taking full advantage of me.

"Are you ready for us, Rayne? All of us?" he asks.

"Yes. I need to please you."

His soft whimper tears at my heart strings. They have all been so protective and so sweet even though they are suffering through the rut with no omega to relieve them.

Well, they do now. I'm not letting any of them down. They can use my body for as long as they need, and I will revel in the debauchery of it until I can't take them anymore.

Turning my head to kiss Spencer, I gasp when his fingers pinch my nipple roughly.

"Beautiful girl," he murmurs. "Let me hear you

squeal." He tugs on the nipple that William bit and I cry out as the pain slices through me but it's not unpleasant. It's a need.

"Fuck, yes," I moan, feeling William's knot deflating inside my pussy. "James, take me."

He doesn't need asking twice. He whips me off William's cock and cradles me, carrying me back to my bedroom and laying me down in my nest.

I smile up at him for being sweet enough to bring me here.

"Can we join you?" he asks.

"Yes," I purr and watch him strip off, my mouth watering when I see that his cock is also pierced like his twin. "Oh, fuck, yes."

He chuckles, slightly embarrassed. "It was a dare," he snorts.

Richard joins in, stripping off and showing me his pierced peen again.

"Well, lucky me," I drawl and open my legs so James can tease my slippery clit with his tip.

The metal of the ring grinds against my clit, leaving me panting and in desperate need of a climax. It follows quickly. Ripping through my body at breakneck speed, forcing my blood to rush through my veins in a heated race straight to my clit.

"Fuck!" I roar, arching my back off the soft duvet, feeling my slick pour out of my hole, along with William's cum.

"I can't wait a second longer," James pants. "I need you, Rayne."

"Take me," I rasp. "Ride my pussy like a bareback stallion until you knot inside me. Use me to find your relief. Fuck me until your cum fills me up..."

"Jesus," he exclaims and falls on top of me, ramming his cock inside me as deep as it will go. "Jesus, Rayne. You are so fucking hot, so sexy. I need you. I need you. Slick my cock, baby girl. That's it, oh yes, perfect. Perfect. You are perfect."

Fucking hell!

His words are arousing me even more deeply than his cock riding me. I wrap my legs around him, lifting my hips up to meet his thrusts full on, taking his length and trying to claw at him to go deeper. My pussy clutches him, holding on as thrust after thrust he takes my body to a height from which I will freefall when my climax hits me.

Seconds later, I'm drenching his cock in even more slick, soaking the duvet underneath me, drawing in his pinecone scent as his gorgeous cock penetrates me harder and faster, the piercing rubbing against the inside of my pussy, bringing me to the brink.

"James!" I cry out, clenching around him, making him growl in response.

"Jesus, Rayne. That feels so good. Don't ever let me go." He kisses me wildly, his tongue as rampant as his cock until he groans into my mouth, knotting me with a bulge that makes me want to weep with joy. He shoots his load, mixing his cum with my slick and William's spunk. I cling to him, his heart beating next to mine as we rock together, locked in place.

"I'm yours, Rayne. Whenever you're ready, you can claim me as your mate."

"Soon," I pant. "Soon."

Chapter Forty

Spencer

Watching my older brother rail the woman I'm wildly attracted to is somewhat of a revelation. There is no jealousy, only a heightened arousal that is now off the charts with the rut in full swing. He leans his forehead on hers, panting as he knots her. Her delight in this is apparent and is making my cock ache. I will fight Cameron for her attention next if I have to. There is no way I'm not getting in there as soon as James's knot goes down.

With their breathing easing, I watch and wait until I can get my hands on her.

To my amazement, she makes me groan when she rolls them over and beckons me to her. I go in an instant. Wild horses couldn't stop me. I attach my mouth to the unwounded nipple, rosy red and inviting. I suck the peak into my mouth, swiping my tongue over it and enjoying the noise of pleasure she makes. Rayne runs her hand into my hair, fisting it tightly to hold me close. I can smell the blood on her skin and feel guilty for causing her pain, but she hasn't complained. Only the opposite. She has revelled in the assault to her exquisite skin.

"Rayne," I murmur, nipping her gently.

Lowering my hand to her clit, I flick it, careful to keep my fingers away from James's cock which is still buried deep inside her.

Cameron, on the other hand, has no need to stay away. He leans over and laps at her pussy, without a care in the world.

She trembles in our arms, treating James to another orgasm that he definitely appreciates.

"Ah!" she cries out and wiggles, rising up when she must feel the knot deflate.

That's when I leap into action because I know Cam is desperate to do the same. I flatten her to the floor of the wardrobe, regardless of the cramped nature with us all stuffed in here and bury my face between her thighs. My fingers slide inside her as I nip her clit, tugging gently as she writhes around on the soft duvet soaked with her slick. It smells like roses and chocolate and all the sweet, delicious things the world has to offer. She tastes like heaven. I can't get enough of her. Slipping a second and then a third finger inside her, I fuck her slowly, enticingly until a fourth finger goes inside.

"Jesus," she pants. "Spencer!"

"That's it, princess. Scream my name while I fist you."

"Ah!" she screams when I insert my whole fist into her

pussy, knowing she can take it. She shudders, coming for me, making my cock hard as iron for her.

"Good girl," I growl, my feral side rearing its head. "Take my fist and ride it like a cowgirl."

I hold still while she jerks her hips, giving me what I asked for.

"Oh, you're a dirty princess, aren't you? So precious, so sweet, so lovely, but underneath, so *diiiiirrty*."

"Spence!" she roars and clutches at my fist and wrist rammed up her pussy, her orgasm thundering over her, her slick soaking my skin.

When she's finished, I pull out and place my tongue at the base of my wrist, licking all the way up to my fingertips while she watches, sweating and feverish with desire.

"You taste like honey."

She purrs and I pounce, ramming my cock inside her without another second to waste. My knot is aching to be inside her. I know it's going to be hard and fast. In a frenzy, I ride her pussy, slick coating my cock until I burst my banks, coming deep into her womb as her walls clutch me tightly. My knot responds to the climax, bulging quickly, causing her to cry out in ecstasy when she feels it lock us together.

"Mine," I growl in her ear with my arms wrapped tightly around her.

"Yours!" she exclaims loudly for all to hear.

I nuzzle her neck, licking over her jugular and giving her a quick nip to make my intentions known. I know she isn't ready yet. I have a feeling she wants to take each of us without mating first, to get to know our bodies and how compatible we are with her. My best guess is, she wants to be in her heat when we mate, and that time isn't now. I can wait. I have marked her as mine. She is owned by me and my pack brothers. There is no escaping us now even if she wanted to, and her actions are screaming that she doesn't want to. She is right where she wants to be, stuck on my knot for the next ten minutes until Cameron takes her body and makes it his, and Richard after that.

And if she will have us all again from the top, this will make the most spectacular night of my life, even better.

"How do you feel?" I ask a few moments later, when I can speak again. My voice is hoarse and deep with my arousal.

"Purrrfect," she murmurs.

I chuckle and kiss her nose. "Funny, princess. You've got a sense of humour, don't you?"

She giggles. "What's the point in being serious all the time?"

"I couldn't agree more." I cast a glance over to James.

He is watching this intently, as interested to see her with me as I was to see her with him. We have never shared a woman before. None of us. I don't think Richard and James have, although I couldn't say for sure. James has certainly never said. I suddenly have the urge to see her railed by both of them, one in her pussy, one in her arse, impaling her on their cocks.

I groan softly and tear my eyes away from him. Will he think that's weird? Will Richard? It has nothing to do with *them*, but her. I want to see *her*.

"Have you ever had anal?" I whisper.

Her eyes go wide at the question, but I think she knows we are beyond personal now. She is stuck on my knot and intimate is where we are at.

"Once," she says. "It was awful."

"Would you try again? With us?"

She nods quickly, her eyes going a deeper shade of blue.

"Please tell me it wasn't with Andy," Richard drawls from his place, sitting on the floor outside the wardrobe, leaning against the wall.

"Yes!" she cries. "Ugh!"

"Andy? The one who your dad is going to make piss himself?" I snicker.

"I imagine that's the one," Richard says.

"I've pushed it to the dark recesses of my mind," Rayne spits out.

"I don't blame you," he says. "From what I remember about that night, he was a stuck up, entitle little prick who couldn't hold his beer."

She snorts and blushes fiercely.

"We will make it more enjoyable for you," I murmur. "I want to see them make you a twin sandwich."

Rayne's lips part with lust. James's sharp intake of breath is mimicked by Richard. It's all they can think about now.

Her pheromones are pinging all over the wardrobe, filling up my senses with her Blueberry-muffins scent. I bury my face in her neck, feeling my knot going down.

"Yes," she purrs. "I want that."

As soon as I unlock from her pussy, I roll over and let Cameron have his way with her. My heart is still hammering in my chest, my cock is still hard. I want another go, but I will have to wait my turn for now. Soon, she will accept us together, maybe more than two at a time. We can make it work. But for now, I will have to please myself by watching her with Cameron.

Chapter Forty-One

Cameron

"Last but not least," I say with a waggle of my eyebrows.

"Definitely not least," she giggles, her eyes on my stiff cock.

"Turn around," I murmur and watch her roll over onto her stomach.

I straddle her, pushing her hair over her shoulder so I can kiss the nape of her neck. It gives her goosebumps, which thrills me. I drag my tongue down a few centimetres, massaging her with it as I taste her skin. The sheen of sweat gives her sweet taste a salty edge to it. It is magnificent.

I run my hands down her body, over the side mounds of her tits which are squashed against the duvet. Down over her ribs and her waist, over her peachy arse and then in between her legs. I finger her clit gently, hearing her happy sigh. She opens her legs more for me and I can't resist leaning over to bite her bum. She squeals and laughs, enjoying the sharp pain before I kiss and lick it, easing the bruise.

"Pretty and sweet," I murmur, thrusting my finger inside her, crooking it and feeling her g-spot under the pad of my fingertip. I rotate slowly, until she gasps and shudders underneath me, her orgasm rippling over her slowly and steadily. She soaks my finger with her slick. I need to taste it.

I withdraw and lick it clean. "Spencer's right. Honey," I confirm.

She giggles again and wriggles on the duvet, letting me know she's ready for me. I want her to suck me off first, but I'm so ready, I'm fairly sure I'll come in her mouth, so I give her what she wants. There'll be time enough for blow jobs later.

Pressing my body over hers, I guide my cock into her from behind.

She moans softly as the change of angle from what she's used to gets to her. I brace myself on my hands and pump my hips slowly, rotating once and then thrusting, repeating this until she starts to pant.

"Harder?" I rasp.

"Yes!" she cries out. "Fuck me hard."

I ram into her, burying my cock as deep as it will go, filling her slicked pussy with my stiff dick.

"I want to see you give me a creampie," I breathe, withdrawing from her, my cock coated with her slick and the other alphas cum.

She turns over onto her back and bends her legs. I part the lips of her pussy, pressing down on her clit as she gushes the product of several orgasms out of her full pussy.

"Jesus," I groan. "Fuck, that's hot."

Spencer whimpers next to me, his eyes riveted to the scene of our omega creaming all over the duvet.

I grab my cock and shove it back inside her quickly before he gets any ideas. But I have one of my own. I roll us over, away from the wet spot, so she is on top. I grab her arse and pull her cheeks apart.

"Lube her up," I murmur to whoever is quick enough to get there first.

It doesn't surprise me that it's Richard. He shoves Spencer out of the way as William watches this intently from his position, also outside the wardrobe. Richard positions himself between my open legs and lifts Rayne up off my cock. He sticks his hand in between us and then up her pussy to scoop up a dollop of leftover cum and slick, before he grabs my cock and guides it back inside her.

I'm not shocked by the action, but curious.

He sets about lubing up her rear hole, his heavy breathing the only sound as everyone else watches intently.

I concentrate on her pussy, holding her hips in place as I thrust deep into her. When I hear her sharp intake of breath, I pause and let Richard sink his cock into her backside.

"Fuck," she moans. "Oh, fuck that feels good."

When he's settled inside her, I start to move again, my thumb going to her clit to give her the maximum amount of pleasure.

"How's that?" I pant. "Good?"

"Fuck, yes!" she cries. "Christ, ah, ah, ahhhhh..." She shudders and comes between us, which is more than I can take.

At the same moment that William squashes into the cupboard and inserts his ginormous cock into her open mouth, I shoot my load with a loud grunt followed up by my knot expanding and a feral noise ripping from my throat almost painfully.

"So hot," I rasp. "Fuck, Rayne, fuck."

She can't answer me with her mouth full of William's cock.

She rocks forward as Richard fucks her harder from behind, gripping her hips tightly.

Rayne removes her mouth from Will's cock just long enough to ask, "How does that feel? Do you feel it?"

"Yes," he pants. "Fuck, I love your body, Rayne. You do things to me. You make me feel hot and sweaty. You're gorgeous. Fuck, you're gorgeous. Jesus. I love you. Fuck, I love you." His low growl turns to a grunt when he comes inside her arse. Her nipples peak even more, turning to hard pebbles on her sumptuous, creamy mounds.

The silence that falls after he hastily withdraws so he doesn't knot inside her, is broken only by her deep purr that vibrates out from the bottom of her diaphragm, sending us all into a rabid tailspin and making this a night none of us will ever forget.

Chapter Forty-Two

Rayne

I awake from a deep sleep, naked, aching and thirsty. My stomach growls, letting me know I'm also hungry.

"Fuck," I murmur and open my eyes.

I'm alone in the wardrobe, with a fresh duvet and pillows that the alphas must've rolled in before they gave it to me because it smells like all of them.

Smiling, I roll over and wince as both my pussy and my arse complain vigorously at the movement. "Ouch."

I'm not used to so many dicks in either of my holes. Hopefully this will ease as time goes on.

I fumble around and find my phone leant against the wall on the outside of the wardrobe. "Bless," I murmur, loving the fact that they care about my stuff not getting broken. Getting to my knees painfully, I flick through it and see that my mum and dad have texted separately, wanting to know if I'm unharmed. Well, that's debatable. My nipple is stinging, and my arms are bruised and bloody with the bite marks from the alphas last night.

Groaning, I get to my feet and wince as I take a step forward, also cringing from the daylight shining into my gritty, sleep-deprived eyes.

As much fun as I had last night, I'm glad they left me alone to sleep though. If they hadn't, we would never have stopped, I don't think. Placing my phone on the bed as I pass, I stagger to the shower and climb in, blasting out hot water even though the day is warm, and my skin is slightly feverish. I curl my back and let the water hit the aches and pains before I turn around and squeak as the scorching water hits the bites, making them burn. After a few sweaty minutes of getting used to it, I pick up the sponge and soap and clean up, grateful that William gave me a bit of a spruce up after we were finished fucking our brains out. He is so sweet and caring for such a giant man. Richard seemed to slot in just fine and everyone was happy and content with the way things went. I'm not sure I can do round two, even though they are still in their rut. I might have to order in a sex doll or something to appease their needs while I heal up. I guess that's the problem when the alphas are in rut and I'm not in heat. It's something that has given me clarity on the suppressants. I need to find the men and have a frank conversation about what to do in the next few days. Come off them, or stay on for a few more months? It affects us all now, not just me. It's only fair that they get their say.

After a few more minutes of the hot water soothing my battered body, I turn the water off and get out, reaching for a towel. My phone is ringing, so I hasten over to the bed and pick it up.

"Rayne?" Daddy's voice comes down the line.

"Hi, Dad. I'm okay."

"No, listen...do not under any circumstances leave the house today. None of you. We have started the arrests, but the ripple effect has sent all loose alphas into panic. There is rioting and looting, and a whole bunch of nasty stuff..."

"Where are you?" I interrupt him, going into a panic myself as I hear background noise that sounds suspiciously like rioting and looting.

"Never mind that. Mick, we assume it's Mick, has told everyone it's you that's to blame. You are in danger, Rayne. Promise me you will not set foot outside that house until I tell you it's okay."

"O-okay," I stammer. "I promise. Daddy, be safe."

"Don't worry about me. Stay behind locked doors. The police are at breaking point, so they won't respond in a timely manner if you need help. I've texted you a number. Ring it if you need assistance."

He hangs up before I can say another word.

I quickly check the text and save the number he sent, wondering who it belongs to. Then I flick over to the news page and see that he is not wrong about the rioting.

"Shit," I mutter, running my hand through my hair. "Fuck." I need to go and tell the others about this. Tightening the towel around me and shoving the corner into the top to keep it up, I grip my phone and scamper across the room and out to the hallway. The next room down is James's.

Checking the time, nearing midday, I knock lightly and wait for an answer. When he doesn't reply, I hover around like a fart in a hot car and then make a decision. I reach out and turn the handle, pushing the door open gently and poking my head around.

"James?" I whisper into the darkened room.

The man has black-out curtains, and I can't see for shit after being out in the bright hallway. I squint and open the door further.

My breath catches in my throat when the sight before me is one to behold. All thoughts scatter off in a million different directions when I see James and Richard in the super king size bed, fast asleep, on either side.

My feet tingle and I move forward, climbing onto the bed and inserting myself in between them. Neither one of them budges.

I lie flat on my back and sigh. This is nice.

The calmness is ruined when Richard suddenly wakes up and leaps out of bed, his fists ready to pummel...something. Not me, because he drops them when he sees me. It's a bummer that he's got pj pants on.

"What the fuck?" he mutters. "Rayne?"

"Sorry," I murmur, waking James up.

He flips over and then leaps up as well when he finds an extra person in his bed. He's also covered up. Massive disappointment.

"I couldn't resist," I state boldly. "You looked so cute together."

They both let out a protesting growl about being called cute, and it brings me back to why I'm in their room in the first place.

"Bad news," I say, clearing my throat. I hold up my phone.

Richard takes it from me and groans, running his hand

through his hair and then placing it on his injured side. I notice that his bandage needs to be changed. I'll mention it in a minute after we get past the shit hitting the fan.

"Jesus," he mutters and hands the phone to James.

"Fuck's sake," he comments and hands it back to me.

"My dad rang and said we've all to stay inside. They know it was me. Someone ratted me out. I'm in danger. Thought you should know that before anyone comes beating your door down trying to get to me." I give them a sheepish smile.

"You're safe here," James says calmly.

"They will have to get through all of us to get to you," Richard growls, which amplifies their differences in one sentence.

"Sorry," I murmur. "I was trying to do right."

"You did," James says, sitting on the bed and taking my hand. "You absolutely did. You cleared Richard, and got the noose from around his neck, and you gave enough evidence to start rounding up these thugs. Do not apologise and don't be afraid. We will keep you safe."

"It's you as well. Well, *you*," I look at Richard briefly. "But you look like him, soooo..."

"We can take care of ourselves," Richard laughs, also sitting on the bed with us. "You are our first and only concern."

"Thanks," I mutter.

"We'd better wake the others and tell them to be on red alert. They know where we live. It's only a matter of time before they get here." James stands up and leaves me and Richard alone.

He gives me a shy smile.

I take the opportunity to mention his bandage.

He looks down at it and shrugs. "I'll change it later."

I don't want to push him, yet, so I leave it. I'll mention it again in an hour or so. Plus, there is something else on my mind. "When you grabbed Cam's cock, did you feel anything?" I blurt out, stunning him into backing away from me.

"Uhm..." His cheeks go red, accentuating his bruised eyes and nose.

"Sorry, it's none of my business. I'm just curious. You touched him and I wondered, that's all."

He deliberates for a moment, but then shakes his head. "No. I feel nothing, one way or the other. That's the way it is with me. You spark an excitement in me that I've never felt. Touching you thrills me, makes me want to cry and hold you, keep you close. Touching him is like it always was. Nothing."

My lips part with the weight of his words. "I'm scared," I admit eventually.

"Me too," he admits softly.

"Will you tell me if it ever goes away? Will you tell me, and not touch me feeling nothing?"

"Christ," he says, rubbing his face with his hand. "Rayne." The desperation in his tone adds to my fear. "I don't want this feeling to go away. I don't think it will. You are my mate. I know that. I feel it here." He thumps his chest. "That's the difference between you and everyone else."

"You haven't answered me." My voice is so soft, I'm not sure he heard me.

"Yes, I will tell you," he says just as quietly.

I nod and take his hand, kissing his knuckles. "Do you really love me?" I ask, scrunching up my nose.

He shrugs. "I don't know what else to call it. Is that okay?"

"Definitely. But can you wait just a little longer before I say it back?" My tentative question hangs between us before he smiles, a genuine, happy smile.

"I will wait a lifetime for you, Rayne."

Finding his answer perfect, I crawl off the bed and pull him up. "You won't have much of a lifetime left if that goes septic. Let's fix you up."

He nods slowly and lets me pull him into the bathroom, where I find everything I need to play nursemaid, and I'm not at all sorry when his cock pops into my mouth while I'm on my knees in front of him.

Slutty nurse always was my favourite Halloween costume, after all.

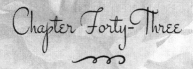

Chapter Forty-Three

Rayne

After I've settled Richard back in bed to get some much-needed rest, I stay until he falls asleep. It doesn't take him long, and it's not surprising. He looks worn out and last night would've aggravated his exhaustion.

I slip back into my bedroom and get dressed in my last remaining set of clothes. Black yoga pants and a loose top. Deciding that now is as good a time as any to do some laundry, I grab the basket, throw the towel in and head downstairs. I pause at the bottom of the stairs, watching the four alphas barricading the front door.

"They're here?" I croak, dropping the basket as my heart skips a beat.

"No," Spencer says, helping William move the side table over to the locked and bolted front door. "We are preparing to defend the stronghold."

"Oh," I squeak. "Can I help?"

He comes over to me as James wheels his chair out of his office and hands it to William to lift up and place sideways on top of the table.

"No, there's nothing for you to do except stay safe. Go back to your nest and we'll carry on down here."

I purse my lips at him and his slightly condescending words. "I can be useful," I snap. "I'm not going to stand around like a fart in a colander while you lot fortify the house because of *me*!"

Silence descends in the already quiet entrance hall.

"A fart in a colander?" Cameron asks, blinking at me, trying desperately to keep his face straight.

He cannot.

He bursts out laughing, easing the tension that ratcheted up a notch.

Spencer's lips twitch and he too starts laughing.

Trying to maintain my air of annoyance, I cross my arms and give him a fierce glare.

"Okay, Hot Omega, you win," he chuckles and peers at the basket. "Did you bring that to help?"

My cheeks go a bit warm. "Well, no. I need to do some laundry," I admit sheepishly. "But after, I'm soooo helping you arseholes."

With as much dignity as I can muster, I pick up the basket and head into the kitchen and through to the utility room at the back that houses the washer, drier and ironing stuff.

Pissed off, I shove my whites into the washer and search for the detergent. Finding it, I pour out a capful into the drawer and set it on a cotton wash.

"I didn't mean anything by it," Spencer says from

behind me. "I just meant that it is our job to protect you and we will. You don't need to help us do that."

In that moment, I see his statement for what it really is. Alpha protection mode activated. I've bruised their egos by offering to help. But it's tough. I'm a doer, and they're going to have to realise that and accept it.

"I want to help. This is because of me."

"Stop saying that," James snaps at me, shoving Spencer out of the way to storm into the small utility room. "This isn't because of you. If anything, it's because of Richard, but even that isn't one hundred percent on him. These arse-holes, who have taken it upon themselves to shun pack life and fly in the wind by themselves, trying to take what they think the world owes them are a bunch of entitled shit-heads, who need to be held accountable for their crimes. They are nasty pieces of work and you have gone above and beyond, Rayne. You are a victim – and don't get all shirty with me about that word, you are – and yet, you have done everything you can to help take them down. Do you know how much courage that takes? You are a fighter, loyal and brave. You will not blame yourself for this situation again. Do I make myself clear?"

His stern voice and expression are kind of turning me on in a way that is unexpected. I usually loathe being ordered about, and rebel against it. There are ways of asking people to do something and commanding or demanding don't work with me. This, however, mmm.

I adopt a sultry expression and focus on his stormy blue eyes. "Yes, sir," I murmur.

His eyes go wide and then narrow with lust. "Don't

make me come over there and smack your arse, young lady."

I turn around and stick my bum out, hoping for a naughty spank or two.

"Jesus wept," Spencer murmurs. "Please don't. My cock is about to burst, and we still have work to do."

"Later, missy," James says, jabbing his finger at me, which under any other circumstances, would annoy the shit out of me.

"Promises, promises," I drawl, and push past them both to make myself some food. I'm starving.

And because I'm not a selfish cow, I also make them each a cup of tea and some toast, which Spencer helps me carry out to the entrance hall like a little puppy with his tongue hanging out. He is hugely aroused, I can see the bulge in his pants, but my bits have gone on holiday and won't be entertaining his bits for a while.

As the men stop for a tea break, I check the news again and tell them about the number my dad sent.

"Do you know who it belongs to?" I ask, showing it to James.

He takes it from me and looks at the number, having gotten over his bossy attitude with a lovely cup of tea.

"No, I don't recognise it. Might be someone in private security."

I nod and take the phone back. "Anyway, if we need it, I'll ring." Something tells me texting won't cut it for this one.

Wanting to discuss the heat suppressants, but needing Richard here as well, I chew my lip, finding myself at a bit of a loss as to what to do next.

When William takes my cup of tea and says, "There's some chairs out on the patio, do you want to start bringing them in?" I nearly kiss him.

"Yes, I can do that," I say, giving him a bright smile and sauntering off to the TV room and out to the patio beyond. I pause, making sure that there is no one lurking before I grab the first chair and bring it in. It's wicker and lightweight and will do absolutely nothing against barricading the door, but I appreciate that he included me in the process. It's only when I get to the entrance hall, that a sharp pain pierces my side and I gasp, dropping the chair and doubling over against the pain.

"Rayne!" James shouts and races over, the others right behind him. "What is it?"

"Not sure," I rasp, clutching my side as the pain intensifies, but then disappears, leaving me breathless. "It's okay. I'm okay."

I straighten up and blink, feeling no more pain. "That was weird."

"Are you okay?" Cameron asks, hovering next to me, his hands outstretched ready to catch me if I fall.

"Yeah, yes, I'm fine. Just a sharp pain. It's gone." To show them I'm really okay, I pick the chair up again, but William whisks it away from me.

"Go and lie down in your nest, Rayne. We've got this. We overused your body last night. You need to rest."

"No," I insist. "I'm fine."

"Rayne, please." His dark eyes implore me to do as he asks.

I nod slowly and it's only when I look up to see Richard

making his way down the stairs, clutching at his side, that I feel the pain again.

I crumple with a cry of surprise, the knowledge that I'm feeling his pain, drowning out any rational thoughts on how ridiculous that is.

Surely that's not possible.

Right?

Chapter Forty-Four

James

Rayne falls into my arms, a cry of agony ripping out of her.

"Rayne," I murmur, lowering her to the floor and cradling her head in my lap. I lift her top to see if she's bruised or bleeding, but there is nothing there.

Richard hobbles over, looking ten years older than his thirty-six years, and kneels down next to us.

"What happened?" he asks desperately. His tone is panicked.

"We aren't sure," I murmur, looking at his hand clutching his side and then Rayne's clutching at hers.

Frowning, a thought pops into my head that makes my insides wobble slightly with the enormity of it.

Needing to test my theory, I reach over and prod Rich in his wound, hearing him grunt but focusing on Rayne's shout of pain.

"What the hell, man?" he growls.

"Open your eyes, you fucking muppet," I snarl. "She is feeling *your* pain. You did this to her."

"What?" His shocked expression makes it obvious that he didn't have a clue. He sits back on his arse, gobsmacked. He shakes his head. "No. No, that's not possible."

"Looks like it is," Spencer says quietly, also kneeling down next to us and stroking Rayne's hair absently. It's almost as if it's an automatic gesture.

"Rayne." Richard's strangled moan makes me feel bad about yelling at him, but if he hadn't gotten hurt, she wouldn't be in pain right now.

I ignore him and stare down into Rayne's astounded face. I think she realises what's happened here. "Let's get you back to your nest," I murmur.

She shakes her head and struggles to sit up, pushing Spence's hand away. "No, I'm okay."

"Rayne," I growl, fully expecting her to submit to me.

She does.

For about two seconds before she shocks me by growling back.

"No, I'm fine," she says and stands up.

"For fuck's sake," William mutters under his breath and steps forward, scooping her off her feet and cradling her in his arms. "Nest. Now."

"No!" She wiggles and squirms, but she is no match of the enormous alpha carrying her up the stairs. "Put me down, dammit!"

He ignores her, which makes her even more angry. I stifle the chuckle and turn to Richard.

"How has this happened?" he asks, still baffled.

"You are her mate. Her prime alpha mate," I state with as much finality as I can muster. "Get on your feet and go comfort her. You are no use to us while we fortify the house, anyway." I don't mean to be a dick, but he brings it out in me sometimes. He is so oblivious to everything and everyone around him, it infuriates me.

"Jay," he starts, but I shush him.

"Go to Rayne. She needs you next to her, not down here arguing with me." I turn from him and head into my office, shutting the door quietly to block out everyone's emotions that are running higher than normal. The rut is still nagging at me, but it doesn't seem to be as strong as a normal one. It must be because Rayne isn't in her heat. It's a bit confusing. I probably have been with omegas on suppressants before, but I just never knew it. They never said and I didn't ask. Does that make me a selfish cunt? Probably, but the interest just wasn't there. With Rayne it is different. I need her like I need to breathe. Being with her last night, knotting inside her, feeling her slick on my cock was the best feeling I've ever had. It was a high that I've never experienced before and will never be surpassed. The urge to mate with her is clawing at me, but until she is ready, all of us have to keep our teeth to ourselves. I will not pressure her or have any of the others even inquiring about it with her. We know she is with us; she chose us. That means everything right now. The rest will come.

A soft knock makes me move away from the door and call out, "Yeah?"

"You okay?" Spencer asks, opening the door and poking his head around. "You made Richard cry."

I snicker. "I doubt that."

"Okay, no, you didn't, but he's pissed."

"Tough shit. He deserved it."

"Not with you. Himself."

"Oh." Yeah, now I feel bad. He is so hard on himself, which is something I've come to learn since we went at each other not that long ago.

"How do you think this happened?" he asks, his innocent tone belying his curiosity.

"They are connected in ways we cannot fathom right now. Remember that he was her saviour. That is how she sees him. She fell for him first. He is supposed to be the prime alpha of this pack. I don't know, Spence. It all must add up somehow."

"Is he going to take over now he's back?"

I sigh. "I don't know. We haven't had a chance to discuss it."

"Do you want him to?"

"Not if he doesn't want it. If he does, I will step down. It's rightfully his, but if he has any doubts, then it's best if he doesn't. I hope he gets that."

"I think he probably does. He seems different. More subdued, more serious, which is saying something."

"Yeah. Guess we should get back to it."

He nods. "Cam has taken over the back. The patio is enclosed, so it will probably be okay, but just in case."

He hovers and hesitates over his next words.

"What?" I ask, eyes narrowed.

"*You* are her prime alpha, not him. He gave up that right. He doesn't get to waltz back in here and claim top dog."

I raise an eyebrow at my younger brother. "Something else bugging you there, Spence?"

His expression turns shifty. "Actually, yeah. If you drop me for him, I'll kick your arse from here to next week!" he exclaims hotly.

"Drop you? What the fuck are you talking about?" I'm bewildered about where this has come from.

"You know exactly what I mean,' he says bitterly. "Little Spenny, the third wheel to the older twins."

His whiny voice makes me snicker. "Fuck off, you utter bellend. You're not a third wheel. Never were, you just couldn't keep up."

I've riled him up good and proper and it's hilarious. He goes apoplectic and puce in the face. "Fuck. You," he spits out and emphasises that with a stuck up middle finger.

"Put that away before I shove it up your arse and make you swivel on it," I choke out, laughing so hard, my guts are aching.

"Grrr," he growls and launches himself at me, flattening me underneath him. "Tell me you won't drop me!" he snarls.

I stare into his eyes, so full of fear that it sobers me up instantly. "I won't drop you, Spence. You've been here for me through everything. But his place is also here."

He sighs and stands up, holding a hand out for me. "Yeah, I know. I just needed to hear you say it, that's all."

I ruffle his hair up, which I know he hates. He slaps my hand away and fixes his hair up with a tut.

"Bit of a needy sod, aren't you?"

"Don't be a fucking berk all your life," he mutters.

I grin and he returns it, and all's right with him again.

"Go and be with Rayne," he says. "We've got this down here."

I nod, glad he mentioned it because I'm feeling a bit needy myself. Needy for her to kiss me, wrap her tongue around mine and show me how hot she is for me.

I make my way upstairs, passing William on the way. He gives me a brief nod and carries on. I know they will take care of things down here, while I take care of Rayne. *We* take care of Rayne. Having Richard back is going to take some getting used to. I just hope he's decisive about what he wants, and lets me know soon so I know where I stand.

Chapter Forty-Five

Rayne

After William annoyingly placed me back in my nest with a fierce glare to remain where I am, I decide it's nice and cosy and I don't feel like moving anyway.

Okay, so the pain has a lot to do with that, but I'm not telling any of them that. They will keep me in here until Doomsday.

Richard appears in the doorway and looks down at me with a scared expression which breaks my heart.

"Is this because of what you did?" he asks, struggling to kneel down next to me, hurting us both.

"I guess so?" It's a question because I really don't know. Also, I don't want to talk about it, because I don't want the other alphas to know about this yet. They might get their underpants in a twist over it.

"Rayne," he whispers, his eyes imploring me to help him figure this shit out.

I lean over and pull up his t-shirt, seeing the bite mark I gave him on his chest while I was fixing up his bandage. I couldn't help it. It wasn't planned, and it definitely isn't something I want to talk about. But the impulse was a driving force, and I gave in to it. He bit me a few days ago, and now I've bitten him. We aren't mated, but we possess each other on a level that is kind of hard to deny right now. With a huff, I drop his t-shirt back down and turn over in my nest, facing away from him because I just can't right now.

"Rayne."

James's voice makes me turn my head.

"I'm okay."

"Do you want to talk about it?"

"Not really."

"Okay, I was being polite. We're talking about it. Did you bite him?"

Chewing the inside of my lip, I nod reluctantly. I'm caught out. I'm not lying to him. He asked outright. "Yes."

"Are you mated?" he asks, his voice steady, but I can see the turmoil in his eyes.

"No." I show him my neck. He must've already known that, but needed to ask so it's out there.

"You have been inextricably linked, but not in a good way, it seems. I have never heard of this prior to now, but I think maybe you need to mate as soon as possible. I'm not saying you have to jump on all of us at the same time," he adds hastily when my mouth drops open to blast him from all sides. "But you two, soon."

As silence falls, I search his eyes. I can see how difficult it is for him to say these words. He wants it as much as we all do, but he is putting his brother's best interests first. Maybe mine as well.

"I'll think about it," I murmur and look to Richard for his words.

"Hmm."

Well, that was helpful, Dick.

James sighs. "On another note, Rich, we need to have a conversation. Will you go and wait for me in my bedroom?"

Richard tears his eyes from me. The second before he does, he lets me see the longing in his gaze. I want to mewl like a kitten and curl up in my nest away from everyone, but apparently, James has other ideas.

He sits down as Richard hoists himself to his unsteady feet, making me wince with the pain he felt.

This is fucking annoying. I hope it goes away soon. His pain, obviously, but also the link I created between us. What a dumb fuck. I knew biting him was going to come back and, erm, bite me on the arse.

"Sorry," I murmur as soon as Richard is out of earshot.

He frowns at me. "Why are you apologising?"

"Because it..." I huff out a breath. "I don't know. Seemed like the right thing to do."

He snickers softly. "Rayne. You don't need to stand on ceremony here. We are enamoured with you on a level that surpasses any and all previous emotions. Being 'right' or trying to be someone forced isn't going to make us love you more. That's not possible. I told you before that you could be a rabid bitch, and we'd still want you, that's true, but it's more than that. We'd still *love* you. Knowing that you are the sweetest, kindest, bravest, most loyal omega on this earth is just icing on our cake. We adore you as you are, with no need for pretence."

Blushing, I look down, feeling all warm and fuzzy inside. "I never did answer Cam's question."

"What was that?"

"What if I found *you* all to be horrid and didn't want you."

His gentle laugh makes me look up again. "Well, do you think we're horrid?"

"Not a single one of you. You are all amazing. You've been caring and compassionate, and you haven't pressured me or tried to force your thoughts about certain things on me. You had my back with my dad, and that means more than anything. You are a decent pack of alphas, and I'd be lucky to be your mate."

"Decent?" he scoffs. "I think we're fucking brilliant."

I snort with mirth. "You are, I just didn't want to inflate that ego. Thank you for everything you've done. You are the best prime alpha a pack could have. I will be honoured to join you soon."

"The honour is all ours, Rayne," he says, taking my hand and kissing my knuckles. "You get some rest. We will take care of everything downstairs. But if you could text your dad and ask if there are any updates, I'd appreciate it."

"Will do," I say, reaching for my phone to immediately get on that.

He nods and leans forward, pushing my phone down so he can enter my personal space. I tilt my head back and enjoy the feel of his lips pressed against mine. I open up at the same he does, and sweep my tongue over his, feeling a thrill shoot down my spine. He is an amazing kisser, and I can't wait for the day that I can just kiss him for hours on end. Today isn't that day.

I pull back as a thought occurs to me. "The rut? Are you okay? Do you need me to...do anything?"

He shakes his head with a smile. "It's not as intense as a normal rut. I've deduced it's because you aren't in your heat, but it still makes me smile that it came about because you are our mate and that cannot be refuted now. We can wait until you are ready to take us again."

"Are you sure?"

"Yes. Rest your bits. They were battered last night." A wicked smile plays on his lips.

"Thank fuck," I groan in relief and flop back to the pillows. "I'm aching."

"I apologise. We got carried away."

"Don't be sorry! It was amazing."

"*You* are amazing, baby girl. Sleep now." He kisses my nose and I fall for him in a way that can only be described as love. It's warm and beautiful and needy without being obsessive. I want him to curl up with me while I sleep, but he has things to do, so I reluctantly let him go.

"Are you sure you're okay with me biting Richard?" I ask, needing to be sure so this doesn't come back in an argument further down the line.

He hesitates for a second, but it tells me a lot. "Yes, it hurts, but only because I'm eager to mate with you. I understand it completely, and I'm not going to rake you over the coals about something your instinct drove you to do. Don't worry about me or the others. We know you have a special bond with him."

I nod, taking his words at face value. I'm sure he means

them, it's just my own anxieties that are prodding at it and making me feel guilty.

"I'll come and find you when my dad messages back," I murmur and look down so I can type out a text.

"Okay." He stands up and leaves without another word.

I yawn, feeling sleepy and sore and pissed off that I'm not downstairs helping strengthen the stronghold. But I know if I get up and go downstairs, William will just pick me up and carry me straight back here. I might as well save myself the indignity of being hauled around like a sack of spuds and stay here like a good little omega.

Replacing my phone against the wall where I found it earlier, I curl up in my deliciously scented nest and close my eyes.

"Rayne?"

Cameron's voice makes me open my eyes and turn over to peer out of the wardrobe. "Hi. Everything okay?"

"That's what I'm supposed to be asking you," he says with a smile.

"I'm good."

He comes closer and sits down. "Can I ask you something?"

"Always." I take his hand and lace our fingers together. Out of all of them, I feel a kinship with the preppy puppy. He is closest to my age, so much younger than the other four and we think the same. We love a laugh and will go to any lengths to do so. Also, he appreciates a good fart comparison as much as I do.

He stares at our hands for a moment before lifting them to his mouth. He licks the back of my hand, tasting my skin before he kisses it softly and lowers it again. "What do you want for your birthday?"

His question comes out of the blue, surprising me. "Oh," I say, blinking. "Uhm, I hadn't really thought about it. You don't have to get me anything."

"It's your twenty-first!" he exclaims. "You must want something."

I shrug, feeling an overwhelming sadness suddenly drop over me.

"My parents were going to surprise me. I'm sure it was going to be extravagant and distracting."

He narrows his eyes. "You don't sound happy about it."

"I guess I always imagined having my twenty-first and then going into my last year of Uni. That never happened."

"How come?"

"I took a gap year, and that turned into three," I say, not really wanting to go into the reasons *why* my gap year became so long.

"You could always go back. What were you going to study?"

"Law, like my dad," I say, the smile forming as I think about it, despite the sadness that is still draped over me.

"Ah, yes, that makes sense, and I can see you being all lawful and in a sexy suit."

I snicker, cheering up. "Maybe one day. I have my immediate future in front of me, and it doesn't involve going to university."

"Why not?" The seriousness of his questions drives my curiosity.

"I'm here now," I say carefully. "I want to be a good omega to the pack."

"So you think going to university makes you a *bad* omega?" he asks, confused.

"Well, no, but I want to be here for you...uhm..."

"We just want you to be happy, Rayne. Take it from someone who didn't get into university. If you have the opportunity and it's something *you* want to do, then you should do it."

"But what about the pack?"

"What about us? We will come and visit you on campus and make sure that any university boys that are sniffing around you, know who you belong to."

I snicker. "Oh, I can see that, and it's not a pretty picture!"

We laugh together, but then I ask, "How come you didn't get in?"

He doesn't take offence to my question as there was none intended. "Well, I'm mostly a pretty face," he chuckles. "But I also don't do well with standardised testing. I suck at them."

"Oh. What do you do now?" I'm wildly curious. I know James and Spencer sit on the benches in Parliament, but so far Cameron and William are a bit of a mystery.

"I'm a model," he says with a sexy smirk.

I snort and clap my hand over my mouth. "Sorry, sorry. That's admirable work."

He lets out a loud guffaw. "Hey, it pays the bills!"

"I bet it does with that face," I comment and pull him closer so I can run my hands up his chest, "and this body."

"Anyway, don't change the subject," he murmurs darkly, staring into my eyes. "We will support you one hundred percent if you want to go back to your studies."

"You're sweet, but the thought makes me nervous and I'm so old now to be starting in the first year."

"What about Open University then?" he inquires seriously. "Don't make excuses when there are options. If you apply before the first week in September, you can start in October."

I want to ask him how he knows this off the top of his head, but I don't. All I can think about is the words and their meaning. I could make the pack my priority as well as studying if I do it from home. Here, in this house. I don't have to go away when the choice is staying right here.

"But what about the other alphas?"

"What about them? I know they all want what's best for you."

I chew my lip. "I'll think about it."

"Don't think too long. Registration is the first week in September. Now, back to your birthday...thoughts on gifts?"

"Surprise me," I murmur, which lights up his eyes.

"Oh, that leaves the gate wide open, princess. You might regret saying that."

"I doubt it. Something tells me, it will be perfect."

He beams at me and then gives me a quick kiss before he stands up. "I'd better go back to helping before Spence throws a shitfit."

I waggle my fingers at him and curl up again, closing my eyes and thinking about what he said.

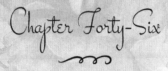

Chapter Forty-Six

Richard

James is waiting for me when I hobble out of the bathroom. The pain of this wound seems to be getting worse, probably because I'm not resting.

I take him in, sitting on the edge of his bed, leant forward, his elbows on his knees, thoughtfully staring at nothing.

"What's this about?" I ask, having a small inkling, but wanting him to say it first.

"You and this pack," he states, sitting up. "What are your intentions?"

I bite the inside of my lip before answering. "What would you like them to be?"

"Fuck off with that evasive question instead of answering bullshit. What are you planning to do now you're back?"

"I hadn't thought about it." I ignore his hiss of annoyance as I stagger to the bed, clutching my side, acutely aware that every ounce of pain I'm feeling, Rayne is too. I need to get in bed and stay as still as possible until this heals.

James gets up and grabs me under my elbow to help me back into bed. He settles me and then steps back. "You're not getting away with answering because you're playing infirm," he informs me.

"Who's playing?" I grunt as I move around to make myself more comfortable, and then freeze as the bite Rayne gave me heats up slightly. It's a reminder to keep still. I definitely caused more damage to myself last night being with her so many times. I couldn't help it though. The pain disappeared in the moment and all I could feel was happiness and love for her. But in the usual way of the universe, it's making me pay for it today.

"This is your pack, Rich. Are you taking it back now you're here?" James asks me bluntly.

He's done pussyfooting around and is demanding something of me that I can't give. "I don't know. Do you want me to?"

"Jesus Christ," he groans, dropping his head into his hands. "Stop thinking about me for just one second and answer the fucking question. Do you want to be prime alpha now you're back? Gut instinct, first reaction. Go!"

"No," I say straight away. "But if you want me to, I will do it."

"Okay, you totally ruined that. I appreciate you taking me into consideration, but I don't care one way or the other."

"Liar," I say, closing my eyes and resting my weary head on the soft, down pillow. "You care. I just don't know which way. This is *your* pack, Jay, not mine. You built it from the ground up. I wasn't even here. I don't know William and Cameron. They came after I left. What right do I have to take this pack from you and lead it?"

"It's your birthright," he says quietly.

"Ugh!" I scoff, opening my eyes and glaring at him. "You of all people don't get to throw that at me."

"Okay, you want me to ring Dad? I'm sure he'll have a lot to say when he learns you're back."

I hear the bitterness in his voice and feel the weight of the guilt that I've been trying to push away for eight years descend on me in one fell swoop. "Please don't tell him. Not yet."

"He's going to find out."

"I know. Just not yet. Please, just let me heal and fix things with Rayne first."

"Fix?" He gives me an inquisitive stare.

"This shouldn't have happened. I shouldn't have allowed her to bite me until we mated. But she was tending to the wound and her scent got to me, she was so close, her tits bursting to get free from that towel. She gave me a blow job and I fell into the feelings that flooded me. When she was done, she trailed her tongue up my chest and then..."

"I really don't need the graphic details," he interrupts sharply.

"I'm not telling you to hurt you, just to make you understand that I was drowning in emotions that were new and confusing. She grazed her teeth over me and then she bit me. There was no thought in it, just action. Instinct."

"I know."

"But it was wrong. I should've known her doing that,

when I'd already bit her and claimed her, would hurt her. I don't deserve her."

"Okay, this has spun into a massive pity party for poor Dick," he practically snarls at me. "If you're not planning on staying, then you need to tell me right now so I can figure out a way to take care of Rayne after you've gone."

"That's not what I'm saying. I want to stay. I understand why you're reluctant to trust me, but I'm also aware that we both know if Rayne wasn't here, I wouldn't be here. She is the neat little bow that will tie me to this pack again, so you win. Here I am."

"You're a fucking bastard," he hisses. "She is not a tie. You either are here one hundred per cent or you can leave, and I'll help her get over your loss. She deserves more than that."

"That's what I've been saying." Finally, he seems to get it.

He grimaces and turns away. I know he's going to make the decision for me and that's what I was hoping for. He will never accept it from me. He needs to *take* it.

Facing me again, he gives me a glare that I'm proud of. "I'm staying as the prime alpha of this pack. You will fit into our lives, not the other way around and if you *ever* hurt Rayne, I will kick your arse so badly, you will feel it for the rest of your life."

"Deal," I murmur, thankful this has been sorted. I know that I will never hurt Rayne or leave her. Maybe she will decide one day that I'm not who she thinks I am and leave me, but I'm not going anywhere. I just needed James to get angry enough with me to declare his own intentions. This isn't my pack. It never was, and never will be. I don't want it, and I'm happy to slot in wherever. Even if it means sharing a bed with his-prickly-nibs forever. Hopefully, Rayne will take pity on me and allow me to share her nest indefinitely very soon. It looked way cosier and inviting than this bed, especially with her in it.

"Fine," James states. "I will let the pack know that this has been decided, and we can all move on."

"Good idea."

He leaves with a huff, and I relax, glad to be able to shut my eyes, knowing I don't have to sleep with one eye open and can finally rest.

Chapter Forty-Seven

William

"How is she?" I ask quietly when Cameron comes back downstairs.

"She's fine. Resting," he replies.

"Good."

I turn away to head into the kitchen for a bottle of water when James storms down the stairs and declares loudly for everyone to hear, "Richard will not be taking over as prime alpha of this pack. He is staying, but not leading."

Cameron and I exchange an inadvertent look of relief. I know I had my concerns, but I wasn't aware that any of the others did. Although, I suppose Cameron is the only other one who would. Spencer and James want their brother back and that's fair enough. I'm glad that James is staying on as prime. It would throw us totally off balance if Richard wanted to take over.

"Guys!" Rayne calls from the top of the stairs, moments later. "Dad texted back. They have rounded up about fifty loose alphas so far, but Mick isn't one of them." She makes it to the bottom, her cheeks flushed and clutching her phone. "Fifty! How many can there be left?"

She is closest to me, so I reach for her and pull her into an embrace that comforts me as much as it does her. Her scent drifts around me, more pungent than it was before. Last night brought us all closer. It is a moment in time that I will cherish.

"I'm sure there's not too many left," I murmur, reassuringly. "And they will get Mick."

She screams and jumps a mile when something hits the window to the side of the front door. It is triple-glazed, so it didn't break, but I'm assuming that whoever threw the whatever it was, expected it to because there is a roar of frustration outside.

I shove Rayne behind me and catch James's gaze.

"Don't go out there!" Rayne cries as we both move forward.

"They won't," Spencer says, taking over from me in the comfort department and wrapping his arms around her.

"Give me that omega, and I won't burn this palace to the ground!" a voice snarls through the door.

"Mick," Rayne hisses.

"Take her upstairs now," I say, turning to Spencer.

"William," James says, his voice calm and quiet. "Please go with Rayne and stay with her."

I give him a filthy glare, but he steps in closer and lowers his voice. "I know you can defend her with your life if they get in and past us."

With a grimace, but fully understanding him, I stalk back to Rayne and take her hand, pulling her away from Spencer and up the stairs without a glance back.

"Wait!" she cries. "Wait! What are you going to do?"

"Ring that number your dad sent you," I say quietly, leading her into her bedroom. I shut the door and lock it. Making sure Rayne is tucked away in her nest, I haul the huge, heavy king-size bed over to the door, ramming it up against it.

I go back to her and crawl into her nest, sliding the door shut behind me.

"Are they going to get in?" she asks, her hands shaking as she tries to dial the phone.

"Nope. The house is locked up tight and clearly, the windows are strong."

By the light of her phone, I see her eyes shoot to mine. "My window is open," she whispers.

"I'll close it. Ring that number." I shove the door open and stand up, going across to the window that overlooks the street, to see several loose alphas with bats, planks of wood and several other battering instruments.

"Hello?" I hear Rayne's shaky voice as I quietly close the window and lock it. "This is Rayne Halstead. Jeremy Halstead gave me your number to ring in an emergency..." She gives me an 'am I doing this right' gesture when I slide back into the cupboard with her.

I shrug. How should I know?

"Okay," she says, nodding her head. "Yes, they're outside."

I hold my hands up to indicate I counted seven of them.

"Seven."

Silence.

"Mm-hmm."

More silence.

"Okay."

She hangs up. "Apparently that was some task force commander. He's redirecting his team this way."

I nod, appreciating the efficiency with which that all just happened.

"Please don't leave me," she whispers.

"I'm not going anywhere," I murmur, pulling her into my arms.

"Sorry you got stuck with babysitting me."

I snort. "Nowhere I'd rather be."

She looks up at me, fear in her eyes, her heart hammering in her chest. She kisses me, dropping her phone as she crawls into my lap.

"Rayne," I murmur, intending to push her away. "This isn't the best time..."

Her hand on my cock stops me from making further complaints for a moment, until my senses return. I know she is looking for a distraction, but we really need to keep our wits about us. I can't protect her with my cock in her pussy and my head swimming with sexual thoughts.

"After," I mutter, following my rejection up with a soft kiss.

She sighs but doesn't get off my lap. She snuggles into me. It's the best feeling in the world. She is so soft and warm and delicious.

"While I've got you here," she whispers in my ear. "What is it you do?"

"For work?"

I see her nod in the dim light.

"I own property. I flip houses, mostly but have several I rent out."

"Oh," she says. "That's awesome."

"It works for me. I have a team, so I don't have to go out and people."

She giggles. "People are overrated."

After more snuggling, she asks, "I'm thinking of going back to studying."

"You should, if that's what you want to do."

She tightens her hold on me. "Did you go to university?"

"Oxford."

"English Lit?"

Startled, I pull back. "How did you know?"

"No one reads Shakespeare in the middle of the night unless they're trying to bore themselves to sleep."

I snort loudly. "Ouch. Okay, missy. Hit taken. What exactly is it *you* want to do?"

"Law," she says proudly.

"Figured you say that what with your dad and all. You'd be an amazing lawyer. You have such a good heart and will fight for those who need defending."

"Thanks," she mutters, but with so much depth to that one word, I feel that she was seeking approval for something else.

"William," she says after a few moments of silence.

"Yes?"

Her breathing starts to get heavier, and she moves against me, rubbing her pussy over my cock. "Your scent is addictive. I can't keep my hands off you," she purrs.

I give up.

I only have so much willpower, and she is breaking it down with each rotation of her hips.

"Then don't," I murmur and claim her mouth in a deep kiss that stiffens my cock to the point of no return.

Chapter Forty-Eight

Rayne

With William's huge cock in my hand, I rise up eager to slip it inside me when a voice shouting my name makes me freeze and then drop his cock like a hot potato.

"Daddy?" I cry out.

William grunts and quickly shoves himself back in his pants as I leap off him and stumble out of the wardrobe headfirst, trying to adjust my yoga pants.

"Rayne? Where are you?"

"In here!" I shout out and motion to William to help me move the bed back into place, hoping that my hair doesn't look all mussed up and that William's ginormous bulge goes down before my dad bursts into the room.

Just as we position the bed back where it belongs, my dad hammers on the door. "Rayne?"

I leap forward, fixing my hair, rubbing my palms over

my nipples to try and get them to soften slightly while I glare at William to do something about his dick.

He shrugs at me, pulling his face, indicating there is nothing he *can* do about it.

"Stay over there," I whisper to him and unlock the door.

"Rayne," Dad says, bursting into the room. "Are you okay?"

"Fine, yes, fine," I babble on as he flings his arms around me. "William stayed with me."

I realise my mistake in drawing attention to the highly aroused alpha the second the words are out of my mouth.

Daddy lets me go and cuts his gaze across to William, hovering near the window on the other side of the bed.

"Hmm," he murmurs and flicks that glare back at me.

"What's going on?" I ask to distract him.

"Eli's task force has taken out the alphas that were here," he informs me, his tone going business-like. "Mick was one of them. It's only a matter of time now until the rest are brought in. For now. Many will have gone underground, and we might not see them again for some time. This isn't over, Ray-ray, but James is going to have a conversation with you all about that soon."

I nod slowly, wondering what that means.

In the absence of any comment from me, Daddy stalks over to William and extends his hand. "Thank you for not leaving her alone."

"Of course," William murmurs, taking his hand and giving it a manly shake.

It jolts something in me that needs attention. "Daddy. Richard is here. I want you two to make up."

He shoots me a death stare, but gives me a grim nod. "I'll be downstairs," he says.

Escaping my room quickly, I give William a shaky smile before I follow and knock lightly on James's bedroom door.

Pushing it open, I see Richard flat out, having slept through the entire escapade. Mind you, I was so distracted by William, and him me, we didn't hear a thing until Daddy came looking for me. I'm assuming he arrived with this Eli character and kicked some bum. Or at least took the names of the bums that Eli and his team kicked. Creeping up to Richard, knowing I should leave him but also knowing a chance like this might not come along again any time soon, I stroke his face gently.

His eyes fly open, and he reaches out to grab my hand. "Hi," he rasps, his voice hoarse from sleep.

"Daddy's here. He wants to see you."

His face goes pale. "Why?"

"It's good," I say hurriedly, realising I buried the lead there. "Can you stand?"

The withering glare he gives me, reassures me that he is doing okay. He hauls himself to his feet, his eyes on me to see if I'm feeling his pain. It's only a twinge, something I can cope with, but he lets me take his hand.

"Wait," he says, pulling away and disappearing into the bathroom.

When he returns a few moments later, he has flattened his bedhead hair with water, and I can smell minty mouthwash mingled with his pinecone scent. I giggle and take his hand again. I lead him slowly down the stairs, seeing my dad in an earnest conversation with James and Spencer. He looks up when he hears us coming. His face goes hard for a moment, but he straightens it with a monumental effort.

He strides over, meeting us at the bottom of the stairs. "Richard," he growls.

"Halstead," Richard growls back.

"Daddy," I warn, not taking any shit from either of them. Not now. Not today.

Daddy takes a second to compose himself, but then extends his hand to Richard. "No hard feelings?"

Richard takes his hand and gives it a solid shake. "Am I off the hook?"

"You saved my daughter's life. You should never have been on it in the first place. The contract you signed is null and void."

Richard nods, taking that in. "What about my crimes?"

"Mick is in custody, and that is what we set out to do." He pauses and gives Richard a meaningful look. "Your actions today were heroic, and your immunity stands."

"What?" he says, shaking his head.

I glance between the two of them and then over at James. The penny drops and I press my lips together.

"Oh," I murmur and let go of Richard to run to James, flinging my arms around him.

He catches me and lifts me off my feet, kissing the side of my neck with a soft growl. "You're amazing," I whisper.

He lets me go with a secretive smile and I hasten back to my father, who is glowering at us from across the entrance hall.

"Thank you," Richard says, his eyes on James first, but then going back to my dad's.

"Thank *you*," Daddy says quietly and to my utter shock

pulls Richard in for a manly hug, slapping him on the back as Richard, getting over his astonishment, does the same.

"Yay!" I exclaim, clapping my hands joyfully. "One big happy family."

"Not quite yet," Daddy grits out and lets Richard go. "Rayne, can I have a word please?"

I nod and follow him over to the front door.

"Are you sure about this?" he asks. "You haven't known them very long and..."

"I've never been more sure about anything in my life. They have proven themselves worthy over and over again. There is no doubt in my mind they are my heart and soul. They are my mates."

If I didn't know better, I'd say that was a tear shining in my dad's eye. But he drags me to him, giving me a crushing hug. When he pulls away, he is back to normal.

"I guess we will send you your stuff then," he says awkwardly, clearing his throat.

"If it's safe to do, can I come back and pack it up myself?"

He nods, his face breaking out into a smile. "Yes, please, do that."

I return his smile and grab his hand. "You have exposed yourself today, Daddy. Will you be okay?"

"Don't worry about me, Ray-ray. It'll take more than a few thugs to take me down."

He squeezes my hand and then with a quick wave, he leaves, heading down the steps, leaving me more worried than his words suggest, but needing to trust that he knows what he's doing.

Chapter Forty-Nine

Rayne

I close the front door and look back at the alphas.

"What did he mean when he said this isn't over, and you wanted to talk to us?" I ask James before anyone moves away.

He runs his hand through his hair and blows out a breath. "We need to move. We won't be going far, but away enough so that any last thug that went underground will know you aren't here."

"Oh. Sorry," I murmur, looking down and feeling bad that they have to give up their home because of me.

"Stop apologising, Rayne," he warns me in that tone that excites me. "It comes at a good time anyway, we need an extra bedroom, and I have just the place." He exchanges a knowing look with Richard, who groans.

"Nooooo."

"Sorry, it works for us."

"Where?" I ask, curiosity getting the better of me.

"Kensington, our childhood home. It was always going to be the plan further down the line when we had kids..." He trails off, avoiding my eyes.

"I want kids," I blurt out like an idiot. "Lots of them."

His gaze catches mine and he smiles. "Me too."

"All of us," Spencer says, but then frowns at Richard. "Well, dunno about you."

"We don't need to discuss that yet," I say hastily, letting Richard off the hook. He's been on so many lately, just give the guy a break.

He gives me a grateful smile, but answers anyway. "Yes, I want kids."

I nod and give him a soft smile and change the subject. "So, Kensington? That's posher than here."

James snickers. "Kind of. The house has been waiting for us since our parents downsized."

"Nice. So, when do we go?"

"Immediately. IPP is sending in a team to move us... probably the same ones who moved you a few years ago."

I nod, having figured that one out already. "We go in the dead of night?"

"Yep. With a heavy security team."

"Sorry."

He lets out a frustrated noise, and I zip it with the apologies.

"Oh!" I exclaim, suddenly deciding now is a good time to talk about what I want. "You're all here, so we need to have a talk."

"What about?" Williams asks suspiciously.

"I want to come off the heat suppressants. I wanted

your input on that. Do you think I should, or stay on them a bit longer...?"

Silence.

"Why are you asking us?" Spencer asks eventually. "That's your decision."

I shake my head. "No, I think it affects all of us. If I stay on them, your rut will be...erm...difficult for me and for you as well."

"Don't make this decision because of us," Cameron starts.

"I'm not. But, as I said, it affects all of us now. What do you think?"

"Come off them," Cameron states bluntly. "I want to mate with you during your heat."

The hotness level rises to scorching after that comment. My cheeks go warm, and my pussy goes even hotter.

"How long will it take once you come off them?" James asks the responsible question.

"I'm not sure because it's being suppressed *now*. If I come off them after this one, I assume a normal quarter."

"Does that work for you? For mating with us?" Richard's quiet voice catches me by surprise. I hadn't expected that from him.

"Yes," I croak out. "Does that work for all of you?"

"Whatever you want, love. We are here for you, and whatever you decide, we will be happy with."

"All of you?" I ask, aiming this at William, who has been silent and watchful as usual.

"All of us," he states. "We only want what's best for you."

I slide my gaze across to James.

He nods emphatically. "That works for me."

I appreciate his definitive answer as the prime alpha of the pack. "Okay, we are decided. If you give me an hour to have a hot bath, I can see to each of you again before we move. I know you must be eager because of the rut."

"We're okay," Richard says. "It's not like the last one. For me, anyway."

"None of us. I think we only needed you last night, and now we're okay," Spencer agrees. "Horny as fuck, but that's nothing to do with the rut." He snickers.

I giggle. "Horny fucker, are you? Good to know."

"Only around you. You bring it out in me."

"Good answer," I murmur, giving him a sultry look which he appreciates a lot. "Well, if you're declining my services, I'll go and sort my washing out and pack my bag. Which will take all of five minutes. Really need to get home so I can get all of my stuff."

"Don't worry about your stuff at your parents' house," James says.

Parents' house. Nice.

"We'll send the movers there too. Unless you want to go and pack up your room?"

I shrug. "I'm not really too bothered; they can do it."

"Are you sure?"

I nod, knowing I don't need to go back there right now. I'll have plenty of time. We all will.

"Okay," he says with a slow smile that makes my toes tingle.

Before I pounce on him, I make a quick getaway back to my room to run that bath, deciding the washing can wait. I'm fairly sure that I will be visited by one or more of them before the night is out and I want to be ready for them.

I luxuriate in the hot bubbles for about an hour and then decide if I don't get out, I'll be a wrinkled old prune.

Drying off and letting the water out, I remember that William ripped my pjs away from my body last night in a hot move that I hope he does again...when I have more than one set to hand. As it is, I have none now.

I climb into my nest, naked and flushed from the bath.

Before I can fall asleep, there is a soft knock on the door.

"Yes," I call out, wrapping myself up in the duvet for modesty's sake.

The door opens, and Spencer pokes his head around. "About your offer..." he says with a sexy smile.

"Come here," I say with a giggle, and flick back the duvet to show him I'm ready and waiting.

He steps into the room and shuts the door quietly. Stalking me, shedding his clothes as he goes, I watch him, getting pretty horny myself.

He drops to his knees and crawls into my nest, snuggling against me. "Just want to sleep with you," he says, kissing my shoulder. "Is that okay?"

I look back over my shoulder at him. "Of course."

We settle and soon he is fast asleep, his steady breathing lulling me into a deep sleep as well before we are rudely woken up by the movers.

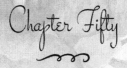

Chapter Fifty

Rayne

Three months after we moved in the dead of night to our new location, ten minutes up the road in Kensington, I'm finally being given my birthday gift. I told them repeatedly not to bother and after my parents paid my tuition in full for an Open University Bachelor of Law degree, and Daddy's expected extravagant shiny bauble of an internship in his offices after my first year, I really didn't need anything else.

But they insisted and here we are, on this freezing November night, standing in the middle of the upper hallway of the eight-bedroom, three-story townhouse. I'm blindfolded and barefoot, dressed in my comfiest, red tartan, brushed cotton pjs and fluffy dressing gown.

"Okay, come on now," I growl, getting impatient.

"Wait," Richard says, wrapping his arms around me from behind and kissing my ear. He is all healed up now from his wounds, so the link between us has dissolved to a small buzz every time he is near.

I hear a weird noise, and then Richard takes my arms and places my hands on something wooden.

"It's a small staircase," he whispers.

"I'm not going up that without sight," I snap. "Are you crazy?"

He chuckles. "I'll be right behind you."

With an unsteady foot placed on the solid step, I grip the sides of the staircase and feeling his warm body behind me, I keep going until he tells me to stop.

"James will help you up," he says.

I feel strong arms take mine and haul me onto solid flooring.

"This had better be good," I mutter.

"It will be," James murmurs. "We decided on it together and we've all had some creative input. We hope you like it."

The blindfold is removed, and I blink to adjust to the dim lighting in the loft conversion.

My mouth drops open.

Once I realised I was headed into the roof space, I figured it was an office or study where I could work on my law degree, but nope, it's more than that.

So. Much. More.

"Oh my God," I murmur, placing my hand to my mouth as tears well up. "You guys are arseholes."

Cam chuckles and takes my hand away from my face. "Do you like it?"

"I fucking love it," I purr, taking in every inch of my custom-built loft nest.

"Happy Birthday, Rayne," James says, giving me a soft kiss.

"Thank you, thank you so much." I'm so astounded by the thoughtfulness of this gift. The floor is made from one big, feather duvet type thing, hence the bare feet instruction. The walls are painted a pale pink, with a cheery yellow flower stencilled on here and there. In the corner, there is a huge, grey crushed velvet bean bag that is big enough to curl up and sleep on, with the softest blankets and pillows strewn all around it. There is a pile of textbooks next to it, so I can study while I'm nesting, and not sleeping, and a tray of food to be cracking on with.

"Seeing as you are now in your preheat, you can stay up here until you want to come back to your room down-stairs," James says. "We will wait on you hand and foot. Anything you need, just text one of us – we set up a group chat – and we will bring it to you. You don't have to move out of here, unless you want to, of course. There is a small bathroom there." He points to the walled-off section in the far corner.

"Don't worry, it has a proper floor in it," Spencer says with a smile.

I giggle and take his outstretched hand. "I'm so touched, I just don't know what to say. It's perfect."

"Good enough," William says gruffly.

Spencer leads me to the bean bag where I immediately flop down on it and purr loudly. "This is the best!"

It smells like all of their scents, which arouses me and comforts me at the same time.

"We can feel our rut getting closer," Richard says,

quietly, kneeling down next to me. "We think tomorrow might be when you go into your heat."

I nod slowly, taking in the enormity of that.

"We will leave you in peace tonight because we won't be able to keep away from you tomorrow."

I grin and lean over to cup his face and kiss him. He is all healed up now and so gorgeous, he makes my eyes water. They all are.

"I can't wait," I murmur against his lips.

"Neither can we," Cameron says softly. "Get some rest now, princess."

"Thank you. This really is the best gift ever."

"We're glad you like it," James replies.

I watch as they leave the loft nest, wishing they could stay, but I'm tired and hungry and I do need rest before my heat comes. I'm a bit nervous, but I'm sure it will be fine.

As I settle into my bean bag and pull a scented blanket up over me, my phone rings.

Frowning, I pull it out of my dressing gown pocket and answer when I see it's my dad. "Hi, Dad."

"Rayne," he says. "I know it's late, but I wanted you to know we got him."

I blink and take that in. "Andy?"

"Yes. He was found in a low-rent hotel in Lancashire."

"Has he said anything?"

"He's agreed to testify against Mick and Bryan, whom he spoke to that night he told them about you, and your connection to me."

"Good, that's good." I pause, knowing I have to try again. "Daddy..."

"No, Rayne, we've spoken about this. We have enough

to convict Mick and his crew of multiple crimes. You don't need to testify."

"But I want to! I want to make sure they go away."

"And they will. You don't need to put yourself in any unnecessary danger."

I sigh. He is as stubborn as a mule. But so am I. This isn't over. I'm just too tired and pre-heaty to argue with him about it now.

"Tell Mum, I'll call her next week and we can arrange a dinner for all of us," I say instead.

"I'll get her to call you tomorrow."

"No, next week, Daddy."

"Why, what's wrong with tomorrow?"

I roll my eyes and sigh. "I'll be occupied with my heat, okay. The pack and I will be mating, happy now?"

"Oh, err, ah, yes, okay..." he stammers and then quickly says goodbye.

Smiling and shaking my head, I drop my phone lightly on the floor and wiggle into my bean bag with a happy smile and a yawn. Things are working out perfectly. I can't wait to mate with the alphas tomorrow, and truly be theirs forever.

Chapter Fifty-One

Spencer

It's early. It's not even light out on this freezing November morning. But I can't stay away from her a second longer. Naked and chilly, I poke my head through the hole in the floor and catch sight of her asleep on the bean bag, the covers thrown off her and her dressing gown on the floor. Her heat has kicked in to make her hot and feverish.

"Rayne," I call out softly. "Can I come up?"

She grunts and gives me the finger. "No, fuck off."

My heart slams against my chest. "Oh, erm, okay, sorry..."

She sits up suddenly and grins at me. "I'm kidding, you twat. Get in here."

Relief floods me and I return her smile. "Oh, thank fuck. I was about to curl up and die in a corner somewhere."

She giggles. "Like I'd leave you to suffer."

"How do you feel?" I ask, crawling over to her, approaching her slowly, warily almost in case she suddenly *does* decide to kick me out.

"Sweaty and about to cry." Tears pool in her eyes.

I freeze. "Did I do something to upset you?"

"No, you goon. It's the heat. My emotions have gone craaaazy."

"Oh," I murmur and wonder what I'm supposed to do. Comfort her? Go away? Fuck her brains out? The last one is the only thing that I can think of, so I dive on her, gathering her to me.

I press my mouth against hers and she giggles. "Hot for me?"

"Fuck, yes."

"Then what are you waiting for?"

I glance over my shoulder, wondering if I should wait for the other men. Luckily for me, they decide to arrive, clearly having the same thoughts and feelings I was. Turning back to her when I see Rich's head appear, I smile and drop my mouth to hers again, sweeping my tongue over hers.

"How much foreplay do you require?" I murmur, "Because my cock is so fucking hard right now, I might come and knot fresh air if I'm not inside you soon."

"Oh my God!" she squeals, laughing madly and sitting up so she can remove her pj top. "That would be hilarious, but I don't need anything except your dick inside my pussy."

"You are a fucking goddess," I murmur, whipping her pj bottoms off and pushing her legs apart.

When I see the slick glistening on her engorged clit and pooling around her entrance, all other thoughts scatter to the four corners of the globe. Lowering my head to her pussy, I lick her anyway, tasting the sweet nectar she has just for me. Well, and these other four losers, but me right now. I will be the first to take her for once and it will take a natural disaster to tear me from her now.

"Spence!" she cries out, fisting her hands in my hair as she pushes her pussy closer to my face. "Fuck, yes!"

I insert a couple of fingers deep inside her, twisting and thrusting until she orgasms like the dirty princess she is.

"That's it, lovely. Show me how much you need me finger-fucking you. Show me how you can't live without it."

She writhes on the beanbag, squirming closer to my hand.

I remove it to tease her, which ignites the fire of fury in her soul.

She growls and wiggles closer to me.

Suddenly, she falls off the beanbag and lands on the floor with a burst of laughter that is infectious.

"Oww," she complains through her smile.

I snort and fall on top of her, kissing her sweet mouth. "I love you," I murmur against her lips. "Fuck, I love you."

She doesn't respond with words, but deepens the kiss, wrapping her tongue around mine in an erotic way that makes my cock twitch eagerly.

I grab it and guide it inside her slicked-up pussy with a low groan.

"Fuck, you feel amazing," I growl. "Fuck, Rayne, you are perfect."

I start to thrust rampantly, slamming my hips against hers.

She meets the thrusts head on, lifting her hips and wrapping her legs around me with a cry of elation.

"Spence!" she screams, drawing the other alphas to her in an instant.

They were holding back, giving me space to be with her, but now all bets are off. Her pheromones are bouncing around the room, her scent has ripened to a deliciously sweet, fruity perfume that makes my mouth water.

Unselfishly, only because I'm buried in her tight, wet pussy, I roll us over, so her body is accessible to the other men.

Growls of various pitch and intensity fill the room as they fall on her, their teeth scraping against her skin, their fingers nipping at her, pinching her nipples twisting, and tugging. Tongues lapping at her in a frenzy.

William's fingers find her clit and tease her until she shudders on top of me, squirting all over his hand and my chest.

"Christ on a bike," I groan, feeling the juice splat warmly on my skin. "Fuck, Rayne."

With a harsh grunt, I thrust up one more time and then stiffen when my balls tighten. I shoot my load deep inside her, feeling my knot inflate, locking us together.

"Spencer!" she moans, throwing her head back. "You feel so good. I need this. I need you. All of you."

"Use my knot to ease your heat, princess," I whisper, feeling like a god.

She whimpers, rotating her hips. It turns into a low

purr when she leans forward, her hands on my damp chest and she scrapes her sharp nails over my hot skin.

"My alpha," she murmurs, the purr still thrumming through her body. "Mine. Your cock is covered in *my* slick. It's mine, as are you."

My heart slams into my ribs when I know what she's going to do. I sit up suddenly, waiting with bated breath for her to bare her teeth. She does, opening her mouth wide before she clamps down on the side of my neck, biting me, marking me, *mating* me.

"Fuck!" I roar, my hand on the back of her head. "Rayne."

Her name turns into a growl as she draws my blood.

When she releases me, I fist my hand into her loose hair and pull her head to the side. I lick her skin, right over her jugular. She lets out a mewl and soaks my knot even more with slick. I waste no more time. I bite her roughly, my hand tightening in her hair.

She trembles in my arms as I give her the bite I've been waiting all these months for. I'm honoured that she chose me to mate with first. It doesn't mean anything, but I'm still grateful and more in love with her than I was yesterday.

I draw back, my mouth full of her blood and meet Richard's eyes. They are hooded and difficult to read.

Things have been, not tense, per se, between us since he returned, but we haven't had a chance to really talk about him leaving and how that affected me. Neither one of us wants to bring it up.

Casting my gaze briefly to James in acknowledgement of his prime status, almost as if I'm asking his permission.

When he nods emphatically, I smile at Rich and hand our omega over to him when my knot deflates.

He takes her with a grateful smile and kisses her, accepting the olive branch in the form of Rayne, the tie that has brought him back to us.

Chapter Fifty-Two

Richard

Resisting the urge to kiss my idiot younger brother for handing me our omega to mate with next, I smile at him. Things have been weird since I came back, but I think we just, without words, cleared the air between us. He felt let down by me and I get that. But he has built up a solid, great relationship with James and I'm thankful that they turned to each other when I left.

"I need to pee," Rayne says loudly, drawing my attention back to the omega in my arms.

I chuckle and release my hold on her. She stands up and stumbles over the blankets as I slap her peachy arse lightly.

"Don't be long," I order.

She sticks two fingers up at me and I know now she will deliberately take forever to come back and see to my aching cock. I deserve it. No one tells her what to do. She is a force to be reckoned with. Her strength is the *only* thing that has seen me through the return to the pack, and finding my place in it with two strangers who are wary about my every move. As if I'm about to kill James and claim prime in a hostile takeover worthy of a movie.

When we hear the shower running after the toilet flushes, I laugh out loud, and shake my head. "She's a firecracker."

"She's mine," Spencer says. "You all can fuck off now and leave me and my mate alone." His joking tone does nothing to quell the possessive growls that reverberate around the nest.

"Kidding!" he says, holding his hands up, laughing maniacally. "Aggressive, much?"

"Fuck off," I snarl, but follow it up with a smile. "We good?" I add, needing to clear the air right now with all of us before Rayne comes back.

He frowns and sits up straighter. "Yeah. I've seen that your leaving wasn't really a choice. It was a necessity. I wish you'd spoken to us about it, but what's done is done."

I nod, thankful he didn't make a bigger deal out of it. They all know my reasons for leaving now. I gave James permission to tell them. It was the only way to make them see that I wasn't trying to be a selfish cunt.

I cast my gaze over to William and Cameron. "I'm not going to ruin the dynamics of this pack. James is prime. That is not going to change. He was the one that brought you into the pack. You are his friends that he's known for ages. He is the one who knows you. But he is my brother and I belong here. I hope one day you will feel more at ease with me being here."

"We do," Cameron says quickly. "But thanks for saying that."

William grunts, which I've come to learn is his way of acknowledging words. The only one he really talks to is Rayne. But that's fine. I don't take it personally.

When we hear the shower turning off, we wait for Rayne to come back to us, which she does a few minutes later, dried but still naked.

"Making us wait is mean," I murmur, giving her a pout that makes her laugh.

"Sorry," she giggles and drops into my lap. "I was sweaty and hot."

"I don't mind sweaty and hot," I point out, giving her a soft kiss. "It turns me on."

"Well, you will have to make do with clean and cool now." She returns my kiss, twisting her tongue around mine.

I love kissing her. She makes it erotic and sexy and full of love. Before it was painful and awkward, and something I tried to avoid at all costs. Now, I could kiss her forever.

Fortunately for my cock, she has other ideas. She shuffles back and takes it in her mouth, flicking her tongue over the piercing. I smile. She can't resist it. She loves it. I dared James to get it done about ten years ago after a drunken night out when the omega he was with went on and on about the last alpha she was with had a Prince Albert.

I *never* expected him to go through with it.

When he said it made his orgasm so much more intense, I went straight down to the studio to get it done, hoping, praying it would fix what was wrong with me.

It didn't.

Until I came inside Rayne.

Then it was the best thing I've ever done.

She takes the ring between her teeth and tugs it gently, making me groan. "Fucking hell, love," I rasp, shoving my hand into her hair.

She smiles and lets it go before she sucks me deep into her mouth. She pops her mouth off and looks up at me with those stormy blue-grey eyes that made me fall for her the moment she looked at me in that car. I thought she was gorgeous and sexy, but it was her scent that made me *know* we were connected somehow. I never knew I would get so lucky as to have found a mate, and one that I adore more than anything in this world.

"I love you," I whisper.

She gives me a secretive smile and climbs into my lap. She takes my cock and shoves it inside her roughly, wanting to feel the piercing at the tip grinding against her. She clasps her hands around my neck and rides me, working her hips vigorously to bring both of us to the brink of ecstasy in as short a time as possible.

I want to beg her to bite me, but she will get to it when she's ready. Until she does, I won't force her by biting her first.

Her slick is covering my cock, thick and sweet, filling the room with the sinfully delicious aroma that is driving us all wild. William is at her back within seconds, his massive hands clamped over her bouncing tits, pinching her nipples until she cries out and floods me with slick, drenching us both. I can't hold back any longer. I grab her hips and thrust deeply, my cock jerking inside her as jet after jet of cum streams out, filling her wet pussy. My knot bulges out, causing her to gasp and skewer herself further onto it. She grips my shoulders and nuzzles my neck, grazing her teeth over my skin before she bites me, sweet and sharp.

I groan, feeling it in every cell of my body.

"Yes, Rayne. Make me yours."

I breathe in her gorgeous blueberry-muffins scent when she pulls back, her mouth covered in my blood. I tilt her head and bite down on the other side of her neck to Spence, wanting James to claim her over mine as he did previously.

She shudders, creaming me, loving me, taking me.

"Mine," I growl when she purrs deeply.

"Yours," she rasps, leaving me elated and complete.

Chapter Fifty-Three

Rayne

The softest whimper escapes Richard's lips as we sit, locked together by his knot. He is feeling all sorts of emotions right now, I'm sure. Well, we all are, but I think his are deeper than most.

Cameron edges over and kisses me, tangling his fingers in my hair. "I didn't know what love was until you walked into my life," he murmurs after a moment. "I thought I did, and I was crushed by it. But I guess young and foolish, really is a thing when it comes to affairs of the heart."

I cup his face. "I'm sorry you were hurt in the past. No one deserves that. But you can trust me with this." I place my hand over his heart and tap my hand in sync with his heartbeat. "I will treasure it, cherish it and hold it close to my own for all time."

"Christ," he murmurs, a twinkle in his eye. "Sappy, much, Hot Omega?"

I giggle, knowing he uses humour to cover up his pain. But I can see the relief in his eyes that I've given him the reassurance he does not need to be afraid of me, or of us.

He kisses me again, licking my lips and sucking on my tongue until he heats up my blood and I wiggle on Richard's knot, desperate for another rocking orgasm.

To my dismay, our time is up, and it deflates, but I'm not left disappointed for long when Cameron flattens me to the soft duvet flooring, covered in blankets, and pushes my legs apart.

"Someone around here needs to flick your clit until you come," he declares and proceeds to do exactly that, with an expertise that I thank God for.

He tugs on it and sucks it into his mouth, groaning with desire when he slips two fingers inside me.

I arch my back, inviting anyone near me to suck on my nipples, which they do. James and William take one each and concentrate to their efforts on in a spectacular fashion, which has my heat-fogged brain melting into a pool of goo.

I try to remember my name, but I come up a blank as rockets of lust shoot through my body. An orgasm erupts beautifully, gushing slick into Cam's mouth, which he appreciates with a low, possessive growl which sends goose-bumps skittering across my skin.

"Take me," I pant. "I need to feel your huge dick pounding my pussy until I beg you for mercy."

"Fuck, woman," he rasps, driving into me without a second thought.

He stretches me wide, filling me up, sliding past my slick along with Spencer's and Richard's cum.

He braces himself over me, forcing the other two

alphas to abandon their posts and gives me what I asked for: a trip to poundtown that I will never forget as long as I live.

"Fuck! Fuck!" I scream, opening my legs wider, trying to drive him deeper. "More! Harder! Faster!"

"Uhn," he grunts, using all of his incredible strength to roger me good and proper.

"Ah!" I scream, the next orgasm ripping through me, tearing my cells apart before they shoot back together.

"Ooooooh," Cam groans and shudders on top of me, his eyes closed, a look of bliss on his face. He grunts, shooting his load into me before his knot expands, relieving my heat and making it recede slightly.

I'm exhausted and my eyes close, hoping I can catch a quick nap while I'm stuck on Cam's knot. I'm sure he won't mind.

He kisses my closed eyelids and laughs softly. "Sleep away, sweet princess. You aren't going anywhere yet." He rests his forehead against mine, panting furiously.

My eyes flutter open and meet his gaze. I slide my hand up to the back of his head and tighten my fist in his hair. Tilting his head, I draw him down further and bite him, softly at first. When he falls into it, I bite harder, mating with him as I have the others.

Drawing in his fresh forest rain scent, I release him and offer him my neck. He bites down on the same side as Spencer, giving me a fresh bite that tightens my nipples and slicks my pussy.

"Mine," I purr into his ear.

"Yours," he replies, releasing me and wrapping his arms tightly around me so we can lay locked together with no interference. He has a needy side that I adore, and I want to hold him close, comforting him.

No one says a word for the longest time, until Cam's knot goes down and he lets me go to the next alpha in line.

William.

I know they're leaving James to last for the finale as it were. That suits me. But first...

I yawn in William's face, and he snickers. "Sleep now," he murmurs, stroking my hair.

"You are a prince among men," I mutter and promptly fall asleep in his big, strong arms, feeling safer than I ever have.

Chapter Fifty-Four

Rayne

Disappointingly, I wake up alone.

My fever has reached its peak and I can no longer think straight. I'm hungry, but I don't want to eat. I just want to fuck.

The feeling is strange and startling.

I've enjoyed sex in the past, but with the alphas, it's been amazing. Nothing quite like this though. It's a basic need to survive right now. If I don't get it, I will die. It's as simple as that. My stomach is rebelling with cramps that I wish would fuck right off and my pussy is throbbing with the need for a knot.

"William," I moan, looking around for him.

"Here," he says, swimming into view a moment later on the other side of me. "Sorry, I wanted to leave you to rest."

"Shut up and fuck me."

I hope he doesn't take my rudeness personally. It really

has nothing to do with him. It was the order in which we did things. I was flying high earlier. Now I'm a needy, sweaty mess with a pussy full of slick and cum that requires a knot to relieve the ache deep inside me.

Luckily for me, William is a big, strong man and he can take a few harsh words, along with picking up my body like a rag doll and positioning me on his cock without another word needing to be said.

He is a god.

As soon as he enters me, I feel the cramps dissipate and the ache recedes. Not enough to bounce on his dick like a bunny, but enough so that I can take his face in my hands and kiss him deeply, showing him with actions instead of words, how grateful I am to him and his enormous cock.

"Thank you," I mutter a few moments later when I feel capable of coherent speech.

"Thank *you*," he growls, a smile splitting his face in half as he literally uses my body to fuck his cock like a sex doll.

It's funny and I start giggling.

"Sorry, I'm not much of a participant," I pant.

"Don't be sorry," he mutters, lifting me up and down, riding me in the most delicious way imaginable. I feel the orgasm start at my toes and work its way up my body to my heart before that organ pushes all of my blood to my pussy. I clench around his cock with a soft cry, clinging to the pleasure before it flutters away.

"Rayne," he growls, pumping me harder.

I lean into him, my hands on his bulging pecs. I nuzzle his neck and then bite him quickly, clamping down while he rams me down onto his cock as far as I'll go. He comes inside me, a feral noise tearing from his throat.

I cry out when his knot inflates and slump against him, offering him my neck. He bites on the same side as Spencer and Cameron, leaving James to do the same side as Richard. I whimper as the bite hurts, but I don't want him to stop. My whole body is one big nerve-ending right now and sitting on William's knot is making it even more intense.

"Fuck, Will," I moan. "Give it to me Big Willy Style."

He snorts, his teeth still buried in my flesh for a few more seconds before he releases me.

"Oh, dammit, we missed it," Cam's voice says from behind me.

"Still stuck," I mutter, my eyes closing again.

"I wanted to see you bite him," he whispers, coming in close and stroking my hair. "It makes me hot."

"Don't think you need any help in that department," I murmur. "Where were you?"

"Making food," he says.

It's like someone plugged me in and my batteries start to recharge instantly. I sit up and look around. "Food? Gimme."

James hands me a sandwich stuffed with turkey and ham, and I bite into it, wiggling on Will's knot. The heat is receding now. It will be back with a vengeance soon, but in the meantime, I intend to enjoy the knot as well as this feast the men have made for us.

After stuffing my face with more food than I should've,

I feel too full and a bit grumpy. My heat is back in full force, and I can't seem to get comfortable.

James presses a cold, damp cloth to my forehead, murmuring soft words to me that make my fingers tingle.

"I love you," I mutter, turning my face into his lap and drawing in his gorgeous piney scent.

He stops dabbing my forehead and then leans over to kiss it, his lips hot and soft.

"You will probably never know how much I love you, baby girl," he whispers. "And why me?"

"All of you, but I wanted to tell you first. You opened up your home to me and made me feel safe and cared for. You have spent every day taking care of all of us. I wanted you to know how I feel about you."

"You are so precious. I adore you."

I smile sleepily. "Please don't take this the wrong way, but I want one of the others to fuck me again before I get to you. I want the relief of their knot before I mate with you. You deserve better than a half-hearted bite from me."

"Any bite you want to give me will fill my heart with joy," he says.

"Still, I want to do it for myself, as well."

He nods and gestures to Richard. I figured he would be the one.

I don't even have the strength to give him a wank to get him hard. He has to do it himself. I feel terrible, but I had no idea the heat would hit me so hard, so fast. I wonder if the suppressants have something to do with it. Like this is a heat times two. I hear the light slap-slap as Richard jerks off over my pussy and then I open my legs for him to slip inside me. I lie still, like a doll while he fucks me slowly, building up the slick production and increasing the anticipation so that when he does knot me, I'll feel it more intensely. He is so considerate to his twin. I hope that once James has knotted inside me, Richard will fuck my arse and I'll have both of them inside me at the same time.

I want that.

It makes my heart pound and my brain clear slightly as Richard gets closer to his orgasm. I know he won't take it personally when I don't climax, but this isn't his time. He is doing a service for his brother. Nothing more.

When he knots, I cry out, arching my back. I feel the heat dissipate slowly, clearing my mind and my senses.

As soon as Richard is able, he removes his cock from my pussy, even though he still has a bit of a knot. I grunt with the sharp pain, but I know he is giving me and James that extra few minutes before I retreat back into my heat fog.

I sit up and crawl into James's lap, smiling at him and cupping his face. I grab his cock and tease my clit with his tip, enjoying each rotation more and more as the ring presses against me firmly.

"So beautiful," he murmurs, pushing my hair over my shoulder.

With a soft moan, I slide down his length, taking him up to the hilt with one motion.

"You feel so good," he whispers. "So hot, so wet. Fuck me, my omega. Show your alpha what this pussy can do to him."

"Ah!" I cry out, gripping his shoulders and riding him hard, working my hips to give him the maximum amount of pleasure. "Good?" I pant.

"Oh, yes." His blue eyes are full of a scorching desire

that sends my blood rushing to my clit. It pulsates wildly, making me convulse on top of him.

"That's it, baby girl. Slick my cock like a good girl."

"Mmm."

"Fuck, yes," he groans, throwing his head back. "Tell me you love me."

"I love you, James St. Stevens. I want to make you my mate and be yours forever."

He gives me access to his neck. I can see his pulse beating rapidly. I clamp my mouth down and bite him purposefully, meaningfully and undeniably. His blood gushes into my mouth and I release him. He grasps a fistful of my hair and pulls my head to the side. He places his mouth over the bite that Richard gave me and applies enough pressure so his teeth sink into my flesh. I cry out with the sharp pain, but soon there is nothing but pleasure. Pleasure and love and a joint orgasm that rocks our bodies, me slicking his cock and him knotting me, the possession clear and inextricable.

"Richard," I pant. "If you are up for round of anal, now would be a good time."

"Fuck, yes," Spencer breathes out. "I want to see this."

Without words, Cam lubes up my rear hole with slick and cum that is pooling out of my tightly plugged pussy, to save Richard from having to go near his twin's cock. I snicker and push James back to the duvet, knowing that after this heat, the floor covering is going to have to come up and be thoroughly washed.

Stroking his semi back into a raging hard-on, Richard kisses me sweetly before he positions himself behind me. I lean forward and inhale deeply as he presses his tip to my rear entrance. He slides in effortlessly thanks to Cam's expert lube job and I breathe out.

"I love you, Rayne," he murmurs, making me a twin sandwich that thrills and delights their younger brother.

So much so, that he kneels next to me and presses his cock to my lips. I open up and have all three brothers inside me, knotting and fucking my holes. William and Cameron lay their hands on me, and I come again, my eyes closed in absolute, blissful perfection.

Epilogue

Three years later

James

"I'm so proud of you," I murmur to my beautiful, accomplished omega and mother of my wayward two-year-old child. "You did it."

Rayne grins up at me, her beautiful face so full of joy and excitement. "I did, didn't I?"

"You did," Richard murmurs, kissing her ear. "We knew you could. You are a super-omega."

She snorts. "Hardly. I couldn't have done it without all of you."

Her acknowledgement of all of us is sweet, but this is all her.

She has worked tirelessly over the last three years to get

her Law Degree with first class honours, while being an amazing omega to our pack and kickass mother to our daughter, Willow.

Yes, Willow.

There was no way we could refuse when her namesake came to us with the request to pass down her name to a baby girl, seeing as she only has boys, according to her. When Rayne ganged up on us, we stood no chance.

It was a done deal before we even knew about it.

But it was perfect.

Willow helped us give Rayne a gift that she loved and appreciated more than anything else we've given her, apart from her loft nest. That was when she trusted us to keep her safe and make sure her best interests were taken care of.

The rest, as they say, is history.

Join my Facebook Group: Sinfully Delicious Romance
Sign up to my newsletter: Eve Newton's News

The next book in this series of standalones for Jan 2023 is
Tying the Knot

**Happiness shattered The pain of betrayal An omega
forced to start over**

If you haven't already read Faith's story, Tied in Knots is
available now!

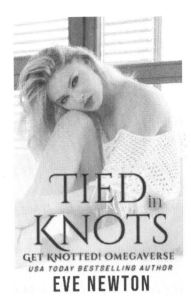

Pre Order for February 2023 - "We're just a pack, standing in front of an omega, asking her to mate with us." Corny move line, right? Effective? Meh.

Excerpt from Tied in Knots

Faith

Three Months Ago

"You're gorgeous," he pants in my ear as he pounds into me, slamming me up against the door of the dingy, dimly lit, small toilet cubicle in this dive bar in East London.

"You too," I murmur, wondering when the fun part starts for me.

"You feel so good."

"Mmm."

Sure, this beta between my legs is super cute with his brown hair and chocolate eyes, but so far, he's not doing it for me. I only accepted his offer to buy me a drink because my arsehole older brother, an alpha through and through, ditched me when some pretty omega decided he was worth going after. I'm pissed off and lonely here and I have no idea how to get back to my brother's place.

Wrapping my legs around him tighter, I plant a kiss on

his lips, twisting my tongue around his to try and bring my arousal to the surface. He is a good kisser, and it works. I gasp, going damper round his cock.

He groans and grips my hips tighter, fucking me until an orgasm ripples through my body and he comes straight afterwards with what sounds like a relieved grunt. And I mean that in the sense that he is relieved I finally came all over his cock, so he could come too.

As far as one-nighters go, this leaves a lot to be desired, but it passed some time and I feel less angry at my brother. Not that I would have confronted him about it anyway. I hate confrontation. I would rather just let it go, but hold on to the grudge until doomsday. I'm a people pleaser to my core. I hate that about myself, but I don't have a choice in the matter. It's part of my survival instinct. The rebel inside me is dying to come out, but I just can't let her. A low form of contrariness is about all I can release when the situation calls for it. I hate being told what to do, but I do it because I hate the confrontation more. I just mutter to myself about how much I dislike everything and leave it at that.

I unwrap one leg and place my dainty high heeled shoe on the floor before I steady myself enough to uncurl my other leg. Shoving my dress back down, I bend down to retrieve my knickers from the floor of the cubicle. Gingerly placing them in my tiny bag and not back on, I snap the bag shut, ready to leave.

"Can I see you again?" he asks, doing up his pants.

I shake my head, looking down.

"Why not?" he cajoles, tipping my chin up so I can look into his face.

I don't. I avert my eyes. "I'm just visiting."

He scoffs in my face, as I half-expected him to. "Sure you are. If you don't want to see me again, just say so. It wasn't that good anyway."

The rage that bubbles up inside me makes me quiver, but I don't say anything.

With a noise of disgust, he roughly lets go of my chin, and pushes past me to open the cubicle door and storm out.

"Not that good," I mutter under my breath. "You never had it so good. Prick."

I follow him out of the cubicle, hearing the door to the ladies slam shut. Glaring at myself in the mirror, I sigh. Fluffing out my light blonde hair, I then wash my hands and take a step back.

Reaching into my bag, edging the knickers out of the way, I find my birth control and take it, choking it back without water. There is no way I can go home accidentally knocked up if I fall into the one percent category of omegas who get pregnant without ever having a heat. I mean, come on…if it was going to happen to anyone, it would be me. If it did, my stepdad would kill me. He is a nasty piece of work and so much of me wishes I could stay here with my older brother, but my first heat is coming up in a few months, and there is no way I can be away from home, as horrible as it is. I have to return and double my efforts to find a nice pack to mate with like all my friends already have. I feel like the last omega spinster on the shelf, scrapping about for a pack and willing to take sloppy seconds. This would never have happened if my dad was still alive. Pete, my stepdad, doesn't give a flying fuck. He just wants to keep me around to use me as a slave.

Tears pricking my eyes, I turn to leave, shoving open the door and making my way across the noisy, crowded bar, darting around strangers so I don't touch them, grateful to see Derek, my arsehole brother, sitting at the table I'd vacated a few minutes ago with the unnamed beta.

He growls when he sees me and stands up abruptly, knocking back the chair. He grabs my arm and hauls me out of the bar and onto the wet street, the gloomy rain pouring down in the dark night. I shiver as the freezing cold December air hits my bare arms in this skimpy white dress, the rain drops adding to the icy fingers of the wind as it skitters across my skin.

"Where were you?" he asks.

"In the bathroom."

He breathes in deeply and I cringe.

His disgusted look matches that of the beta and shame fills me, but I try to push it aside. I'm an omega ready to bond and mate and have babies. There isn't anything anyone can do about that, not that I'd want them to. It's my ticket out of my family home and to a place where I will be taken care of, if not cherished.

"You're going back home tonight," Derek states. "I'll drop you off at the station."

"What about all my stuff?" I complain.

"You can get it next time you visit. Sharon is waiting in the car for me, and I don't exactly want my little sister around when I take her home."

"Oh, great," I mumble, seeing I have no choice. "Just great."

Ten minutes later, I'm on the last train home, my face pressed to the glass as I wave goodbye to the big city, my stomach tied in knots. I shed a tear to be going home where tomorrow things will be hard and humiliating and humbling.

Please let me find a pack soon. Please, please, please.

Read on: Tied in Knots

About the Author

Eve is a British novelist with a specialty for delicious romance, with strong female leads, causing her to develop a Reverse Harem Fantasy series, several years ago: The Forever Series.

She lives in the UK, with her husband and five kids, so finding the time to write is short, but definitely sweet. She currently has over fifty book in her catalogue. Eve hopes to release some new and exciting projects in the next couple of years, so stay tuned!

Also by Eve Newton

https://evenewton.com/links